CITY LIGHTS

CITY LIGHTS

A FOG CITY NOIR MYSTERY

CLAIRE M. JOHNSON

First published by Level Best Books/Historia 2025

This novel is entirely a work of fiction. The names, characters and incidents portrayed in it are the work of the author's imagination. Any resemblance to actual persons, living or dead, events or localities is entirely coincidental.

Author Photo Credit: Nancy Warner

First edition

ISBN: 979-8-89820-007-7

Cover art by Level Best Designs

This book was professionally typeset on Reedsy.
Find out more at reedsy.com

To the Chubby Bunnies. You know who you are.

Praise for City Lights

"Pairing the best of San Francisco's noir traditions with the moxie of quick-witted detective Maggie Laurent, Claire M. Johnson's second offering in the Fog City Noir series delivers in spades. Here's hoping there will be many more cases to come."—Margaret Dumas, author of the Movie Palace mystery series, *Speak Now*, *How To Succeed in Murder*, and *The Balance Thing*

"Johnson had me with the setting of *City Lights*: San Francisco after the 1929 Stock Market Crash. Spunky heroine Maggie Laurent learns to defend herself—just in time—as her latest case propels her into the dangerous world of union busting. Johnson's smooth writing, laced with noir patter, sails the plot along in this delightful continuation of the *Fog City* Noir Mystery series."—Vinnie Hansen, author of the Carol Sabala Mystery Series, *One Gun*, and *Crime Writer*.

"Claire Johnson's *City Lights* brings the labor unrest of the early 20th century to vivid life. In this rough and tumble setting Maggie Laurent is coming into her own as a smart, independent woman who is determined to live life her way. Highly recommended."—Terry Shames, Macavity award-winning author of the Samuel Craddock Series and the Jessie Madison thriller series.

Chapter One

"My son is a fool," said Constance Smith as she held up my report, shook it to emphasize her contempt, and then began reading it some more, her lips pursed in annoyance.

But not at me.

I didn't comment. Her son, Halston, had a divining rod for proposing marriage to grifters, averaging at least two proposals a year. The Moore Detective Agency had saved Mrs. Smith's bank account seven times. This was fiancée number eight. Mrs. Smith kept sighing as she leafed through my report.

Mrs. Smith reminded me of the Mother Superior of my grammar school: steely with a fierce intelligence she didn't bother to hide. Despite being dressed in the latest couture from Paris, Constance's mien and perpetual frown were Victorian in spirit. Halton, her only child, was her cross to bear in life, a thirty-year-old man who never met a gold digger he didn't fall for, even before they'd finished their Manhattans. I'd never met Mr. Smith and assumed there wasn't one.

We were sitting side-by-side on a silk-covered settee in her elegant morning room, having tea while she read my write-up on the latest floozy who'd captured the heart of her con artist-loving son. From the ranks of the monied elites, the Smiths lived in a ten-bedroom mansion in Pacific Heights, one of those gigantic Victorians with four turrets and fifteen fireplaces. Imagine owning a house so large, there were rooms dedicated to the time of day. It's not my world, but I don't let it intimidate me.

Once finished, she tossed the sheaf of papers over her shoulder onto the carpet. Someone else would pick it up. Then Mrs. Smith patted my arm and poured me more tea while muttering *sotto voce*, "An utter fool."

"Given my son's penchant for these…" she paused, the teapot held aloft, "young women, perhaps I should put you on retainer, Miss Laurent."

"Thank you, Mrs. Smith." That would help with the bills.

"Is Mr. Moore still in Chicago? I believe you said he's involved in something related to his previous employment as a Pinkerton."

Two months ago, Mrs. Smith had hired the Moore Detective Agency to get the dirt on her son's latest "fiancée," another peroxide blonde on the make with a flashy smile whom her son met in a speakeasy on Harrison Street. Nick Moore, my former boss, had left San Francisco with no plans to return this century, returning to his former employer, the Pinkerton Detective Agency. Not that I let people know he'd skipped town for good. I was doing my darndest to spread the fiction that his stint in Chicago was temporary. He'd be back soon—a relative term in my book. While Nick braved the Chicago winters trying to forget the woman he couldn't forget, I was trying to hoof it alone as a private dick while still pretending to be his secretary.

"You've done a fine job in Mr. Moore's absence," she noted.

"Thank you, Mrs. Smith." I smothered a grin with some effort.

"You wouldn't consider marrying Halston yourself, would you?"

I almost dropped my teacup. "With all due respect, Mrs. Smith, I'm not your son's type."

Halston's tastes ran to petite blue-eyed blonds with tiny waists and big hips, while I had dark brown hair and the figure of a teenage boy.

She squinted at me.

"Yes, you're too tall."

Just for starters.

And too old, I said to myself. I was twenty-four, looking at twenty-five. Halston liked them younger. I imagine it made him feel in charge. His mother probably still laid out his clothes for the morning.

She sighed. "True. At least you'd be an honest daughter-in-law. Why he eschews women of his class is beyond me. Debutante after debutante set their caps for him, but he's never given them a first glance, never mind a second. Every woman he's proposed to has nothing more than a fourth-grade education. What could be the attraction?" She threw her hands up in frustration.

It didn't take a genius to answer that question. Halston wanted to marry someone who was the antithesis of his mother. Plus, all of them had curves that would make a priest blush. But I couldn't say any of this to her.

"This one is okay," I noted.

She raised a condemning eyebrow.

"He's proposed to far worse grifters. She's the best of the bunch and might even make him happy. Or, at the very least, stop him from proposing to every blonde he meets in a speakeasy."

She didn't respond but brought her forefinger up to her chin.

I went on.

"She seems more desperate than anything else. The next con artist might be far worse, and if she convinces him to elope, then where will you be?"

"You might be right." She rang the bell for the maid. "There isn't as much money as this young woman thinks."

Last year's stock market crash had put a crimp in everyone's wallet. To Mrs. Smith, a crimp was something along the lines of fifty thousand dollars in her "wallet" of five million. For me, it was an empty wallet and two weeks until payday.

"I don't think she wants much. She seems relatively harmless as grifters go."

At the very least, she hadn't yet conned him out of a gigantic engagement ring with a diamond the size of a dime like the other women had. Shreve's, the jeweler of the monied class in San Francisco, will be crying in their champagne glasses when Halston marries. To date, all his "fiancées" had fancied diamonds weighing at least two carats. Based on my investigation, Halston's current dish hadn't sweet-talked him into so much as a stroll past Shreve's windows. And there weren't a host of chumps in her wake as she plied her con, just a lot of married men looking for a pretty mistress. My take? She wanted to be married to a benign but well-heeled man like Halston. He wouldn't beat her every other night and could keep her off bar stools as she smiled the night away while her marks bought her drinks she couldn't afford. I liked her. Her lies weren't heinous, just lies. I've discovered in the detective game that there are lies and there are *lies*.

"Expect a wedding invitation, Miss Laurent," she said and handed me a check.

As the maid led me to the front door, I realized I'd spoiled my chances of being on retainer. Still, my step was light as I tripped down her front steps to the sidewalk. Mrs. Smith's dough would keep the lights on for a while.

Chapter Two

By October, my step wasn't light, to put it mildly. Nick's disappearance at the various speakeasies and dinner houses around town told everyone that Nick had taken a powder. Permanently. When people realized he'd left town for good, the phone mostly stopped ringing. San Francisco is a big but small town. Whether he acknowledged it or not, Nick was part of the social scene. He'd been brought up in the world of easy money. Although he'd abandoned it for reasons he never told me, he had the education and confidence to go toe-to-toe with people who could afford to eat in white-tablecloth restaurants and drink at high-end speakeasies around town. His background ensured invitations to their parties if he wanted to rub elbows with high-society types. He didn't mind sharing the odd drink—booze tends to make people flap their jaws, which can be good for business—but I never got the impression he respected them all that much.

Mrs. Smith's suggestion that I marry Halston was not because I'd grace her dinner table with any aplomb. It was a sign of her desperation. I have enormous pluck, but nothing more than a high-school education. In my free time, I park myself at a table in the library and spend two hours reading the Encyclopedia Britannica. I'm still on volume "A." It's slow going, but now I know where Abyssinia is.

I'd bought a small Leica with money from the Washington job and paid the camera shop for lessons. Although eyebrows were raised when I asked what settings would be best for taking pictures in the dark and through windows, they didn't ask any questions. I've become an expert on scaling fire escapes and listening through keyholes to illicit telephone conversations. I befriended hotel detectives by handing out cigars—raiding the stash hidden in the bottom drawer of Nick's desk—accompanied by fronting for the occasional rounds of drinks so they turn a blind eye when I patrol the halls. I've purchased maid uniforms from all the major hotels and have perfected holding up a stack of towels to conceal my camera as I snap couples sneaking out of hotel rooms they have no business sneaking out of.

These small-time divorce jobs pay the office rent and the telephone, but little else. I have to scrounge up the clams to pay for my apartment every month and still pay my mother for room and board, even though I haven't stepped foot in the family home in nearly three months. She needs the money. I still have some of my stash from the Washington job last summer, but my monthly expenses were chipping away at that nest egg with no big payday in sight. Toward the end of the month, I'm down to two meals a day. I debated moving to a smaller office, but that was the third-to-last resort. The second-to-last resort would be to sell the car Catherine Washington had gifted me. The last resort would be when I was down to one meal a day. Then I'd close shop, give up the apartment, and crawl home, doing my best to ignore the chorus of "I told you so's" from my family.

Then Dickie Vance invited me to lunch.

Chapter Three

Dickie Vance is the most amazing man I've ever met. A gourmand who eats his lunch at John's Grill Monday through Friday, he's fussy, opinionated, intolerant, and holds San Francisco in the palm of his hand. The West Coast's answer to Walter Winchell, he's the gossip columnist for San Francisco's top newspaper, the *Examiner*. Nobody crosses Dickie. Beholden only to his harridan of a mother, he lives in the penthouse at the Mark Hopkins Hotel up on Nob Hill. I love him to bits because he always treats me like an equal. The only person who gives me similar consideration is Nick.

Dickie is a stickler for time, and I'm never late when meeting him. I don't care what most people think of me, but I care what Dickie thinks of me. We're partners, although not in the strict sense of the word. No one knows we collaborate now and then. I pass along any dirt I discover as possible fodder for his gossip column, and he does the same for me. For example, while investigating the wife of the butler employed by the vice-mayor, I heard a fight between the vice-mayor and his wife that was loud enough to be heard down on Market Street. She's young, rather silly, and spends her days cruising the aisles of the fancy department stores on Union Square, buying clothes they can't afford. I smelled divorce.

Dickie appreciates his gossip firsthand.

A waiter with a blindingly white apron that brushed the top of his brogues was waiting for me as I stepped through the door. With one hand behind his back and another ushering me into the dining room, he led me to Dickie's table.

I shouldn't have been startled by Dickie's penchant for outré attire, but today's outfit was truly jaw-dropping. He resembled an enormous three-hundred-pound parakeet. A bright green tailored shirt was complemented by a yellow vest and topped by a bright pink bow tie. I'm dead certain the restaurant pays his outrageous tailoring bills because he attracts customers who are dying to see what he'll be wearing that day.

"My lovely Miss Laurent." He stood up and kissed my hand. Then his eyes narrowed. "You are too thin, Margaret. Either you are not bringing in work and are, therefore, skimping on meals, or you are wasting away because your family is still pressuring you to come home. Do not lie to me. I am an excellent liar and can spot it in everyone else. Which is it?"

The waiter pulled out my chair and I sat down. While the waiter, with an unnecessary flourish, deposited a napkin on my lap, I looked down for a moment and forced my lips into a gay smile.

"A little of both, I suppose," I replied with a nonchalance that didn't fool Dickie for one second.

My estrangement from my family was ongoing. My brother, Al, had stopped speaking to me entirely, and my interaction with my mother was limited to a one-minute phone call every morning. Al was just being pig-headed. My mother? Every phone call ended with, "Maggie, please come home. I'm so worried about you." And every day I responded, "I'm doing great, Ma. Talk tomorrow. I'm off to mass."

I attended mass most mornings, but unless I was sleeping in my childhood home night after night or sitting next to her in a pew, I could have been kneeling next to Jesus himself, and it wouldn't have mollified her. It wasn't my soul she was worried about.

"The divorce trade?" he murmured.

"Not bad, but all small time," I murmured back.

"I understand you have ingratiated yourself with the hotel detectives, an excellent move. It will pay off at some point. Constance didn't call you?"

"Yes, she did. I recommended that Halston marry this one. His grifter of the month is relatively jake. Just desperate." Was it desperation I felt in the small of my back every morning when I woke up, an ugly twinge of unease that dogged me all day? "Mrs. Smith proposed that I marry Halston and save him from another disastrous marriage proposal and a hit on her bank account for a two-carat rock from Shreve's."

Dickie chuckled.

"Oh, I do love Constance. She and Mother had a falling out several years ago and haven't spoken to each other since. Pity. I must abide by Mother's wishes to maintain this enmity. Unbeknownst to mother, I sent her a congratulatory bouquet on the anniversary of her husband's death."

"Of course." I blinked. "Congratulatory?"

"Naturally. Her father pushed her into that nightmare of a marriage. Fortunately, he left her a pile of money when he departed this mortal coil. What a dreadful man, a total cad. Mother detested him. I blame him for Halston's woes."

"Mr. Smith died young?" I couldn't help but ask.

"Yes, thank goodness. He was gunned down by the husband of a woman he was having an affair with. The judge let the man off, saying it was obvious to anyone with eyes that Smith was a bounder of the first order, and he was overjoyed someone had put this man out of our misery."

Even as I smiled, I contradicted him. "You're making this up."

Accompanied by a light wave of his hand, he said, "Only some of it. I'll leave it to you to tease out the false bits. Have you heard from Nicholas?"

"Just a telegram saying he'd made it to Chicago."

Three months ago, Nick returned to working for the renowned Pinkerton Detective Agency. Nick never said anything bad about Pinkerton, but he also never said anything good. Well-known as Abraham Lincoln's security squad during the Civil War, they were also renowned as strike-breakers and recruiters of goon squads to intimidate workers. There were other Pinkertons I could call to check up on Nick, but I hadn't and wouldn't. If getting out of San Francisco didn't erase the memories of a raven-haired beauty with brilliant blue eyes and a chunk of ice for a soul, nothing would.

"Hmmm, not a wise move, in my opinion, but I imagine Nicholas felt he didn't have much choice. Now. I've brought you here today…"

All conversation stopped as our food arrived. I hadn't bothered ordering.

Dickie ate the same meal every day—grilled sole with French fries, creamed spinach, and a double slice of pecan pie with two scoops of vanilla ice cream, washed down with the secret stash of French champagne he kept in their cellar. Minus the champagne and *two* helpings of dessert, he'd assumed I'd order the same meal because it was what civilized people would eat. Fortunately, I loved fish.

"Eat up, and don't leave a scrap of food on your plate," he ordered.

Dickie took his eating extremely seriously, as in no talking while your fork was in motion. We were silent until my coffee and his *après le dîner* cognac arrived—in a coffee cup in slight deference to Prohibition—and I felt it was safe to say something.

"Why the lunch today, Dickie? I thought we were more or less limited to tea and champagne?"

He pursed his lips and seemed hesitant to speak. A first.

"Dickie?"

"I will pay you the going rate. This business is personal. I am worried about a certain cab driver friend of ours."

I'd been about to take a sip of coffee, but returned my cup to its saucer.

"The cab driver whose first name starts with an 'H' and ends in an 'N?'"

"The same." He grimaced and signaled the waiter for another cognac.

Chapter Four

Herman Peters is one of the silent millions who make up the backbone of this country. First-generation American, he lives with his parents in the Western Addition in the small enclave of Russian immigrants centered around the Holy Virgin Cathedral. Herman is one of Dickie's minions, who are all working-class stiffs relegated to anonymity by their "betters." Dickie is a master at exploiting that anonymity. His "Nob Hill Irregulars" are the maids, janitors, cooks, and gardeners of the city's elite. Herman's day job is to drive a cab for DeSoto. His second job is to feed Dickie information on the various passengers who have the misfortune to climb into his cab. If I'd had to guess, half the divorces in this town are due to Herman cataloging who enters which hotel and when. A simple man, he loves God, Dickie, and his fiancée, Vera. He'd mapped out his future. He'd marry Vera, have five children, buy a house in the Richmond District to house said five children, and drive a cab for the rest of his life.

I'd hired Herman last July to drive me around San Francisco while investigating the Washington murders. He also helped babysit Nick while Nick dried out at my mother's house. An amateur boxer like my brother, he good-naturedly admitted that Al had bested him in all of their boxing matches, and, wow, Miss Laurent, can he throw a punch. The Washington case last summer had hammered home the necessity that if I were serious about playing in the big leagues, detective-wise, I needed to know how to throw a punch. Herman and I had just started boxing lessons.

The most decent guy you'd ever meet.

"You should know, Margaret," Dickie began, "although I might pry into the lives populating San Francisco's elite, I have no interest in what you or Herman do behind closed doors."

"Well, what happens at my place isn't going to sell newspapers," I pointed out.

"That's not the point," he said with a snap in his voice.

Dickie had never chastised me before, and it made me sit up straight. He set his coffee mug down with such force that a splash of cognac jumped out onto the tablecloth.

"My peers are usually intelligent, educated people who converse with a modicum of ease. We share a unique history that binds us together. That said, I am not blind to their raging hypocrisy. I do not believe I am better than, say, a cab driver. They do not hold to the same conviction. The gates of heaven will swing wide open for the cab driver or the maid, and less wide for someone like me. I imagine it will be closed shut for the very people I had dinner with last night. Anyway, I do not judge because I see myself in something of a glasshouse. Therefore, I merely report on the various follies of my peers. Do I make myself clear?"

I nodded.

"Now, there seems to be something happening with our beloved Mr. P. I am in a quandary here because I could canvass various other cab drivers in my employ, but need I say Mr. P. is special to me? I do not want to embarrass him by making inquiries, but I believe this is serious, hence the crossing of lines I normally do not cross."

"How about I sniff around some, but not enough to raise a stink?"

"Perfect."

"Do you think it's something to do with DeSoto? Do you know John Waters?"

After I took over the agency, I'd made it a habit to read the business and sports sections of all four dailies. Nick had hobnobbed with the city's movers and shakers at the various speakeasies around town, but I couldn't waltz into a speak without a male escort. Since my brother was being a mug these days, the speakeasies were off-limits. Even if Al comes to his senses one day, no one commanding a table at one of the numerous speakeasies in town would pay me any mind. I didn't have the evening gown, the glitter on my fingers, or the fur coat slung around my shoulders to signal I was one of "them." I depended on Dickie's column to get a sense of who was who and what was what in San Francisco's high society.

Waters and his wife figured in the society columns about once a week. The owner of DeSoto Cab Company, he was gaining a reputation as a guy to watch. He'd come out of the Great War to sell surplus aircraft. When that proved to be a bust, he branched into used car sales. He was so successful that Chrysler offered him the Plymouth–DeSoto distributorship. Not only does he have rights to the dealership, but he also owns the cab company. While other cab companies went belly up, Waters not only survived but made a pile of dough in the bargain. He has an exclusive contract to sell DeSoto cars to Yellow Cab while outfitting DeSoto with Plymouths. This seems to be his *leitmotif*, competing against himself for better and greater profits. His car dealership on Van Ness Avenue is pretty swanky. A woman doesn't cross its threshold without wearing her best hat and white gloves.

"Mildly. We meet and greet at parties. Nothing more than that. New money." Dickie didn't bother to hide his scorn. "Ambitious with a capital A, he likes money and knows how to make it. He has plans to sell his fleet of cars to police and cab companies across the nation. Given his drive, I have no doubt he will succeed. It says something about him that DeSoto survived the strikes of 1921 and 1922 when many other cab companies did not. Herman considers himself blessed to be working for DeSoto, so I do not think it has to do with DeSoto per se."

"Then I bet it has something to do with his fiancée." Come to think of it, Herman hadn't mentioned Vera lately.

"That is already more information than I had before I started lunch."

"What is it about Herman that's bothering you?"

"He's lost weight. I consider myself an expert on weight." He patted his considerable stomach. "I notice when someone gains or loses weight." He gave me a pointed look.

Yes, over the last few weeks, I'd lost pounds I didn't have to spare.

"Sadly, I never see a loss when I look in the mirror. Herman is now using a different belt notch."

Some detective I was. But then Herman had a thin face that wouldn't show weight gain or loss unless it was significant, and I wasn't in the habit of taking a gander at men's belt notches. Our encounters were limited to once a week, with all our talk centered on the rudiments of boxing.

"Anything else?" I asked.

"Hard to put a finger on, but I'd say he was…sad. As you know, nothing seems to shake Herman's equilibrium, and something has."

True. I'd thrown Herman some real curveballs last summer, and nothing seemed to faze him. For something to faze him, it must be monumental.

"I'm embarrassed to say I hadn't noticed. We have a boxing lesson on Monday morning. I'll see what I can find out."

"Be discreet," warned Dickie.

"I promise."

I usually don't ask about Herman's wedding plans, because then I have to listen to at least forty minutes of the most excruciating details down to the names of his future children and the street where he wanted to buy their house. But needs must.

Like Nick always told me, *Cherchez la femme.*

Chapter Five

Herman was teaching me how to box since my brother, Al, was giving me the silent treatment these days. We'd started the lessons with simple self-defense maneuvers. If someone grabs your shoulder, go into a small crouch, spin around, and punch them hard in the ribs. If they grab you around your shoulders, spread your arms so they can't lift you up, hook an ankle around one of their legs, then turn around enough to smash the side of their face with your fist.

"Or below their stomachs, if you know what I mean," he had mumbled with a blush. He'd used his forefinger to point toward the floor. "And if someone tries to strangle you, then you bite them wherever you can and go for their eyes. You only have about eight seconds before…"

He'd paused.

"Before?"

He'd drawn a hand across his throat. "Before he crushes your windpipe, miss. Go for the eyes." His face went hard, a type of anger usually foreign to him. "Don't think twice about it. Gouge out both of his eyes. Blind him, miss."

The Biblical phrase "an eye for an eye" took on new meaning. I suppose if it were a choice between blinding someone for life and being murdered, I'd choose me every time.

Today, he picked up our boxing gear from the box in the corner of my office and handed me a pair of gloves. Now that I was looking for it, I cursed myself. Something was up with Herman. The weight loss wasn't the big red flag, although Dickie was right; Herman *had* lost weight, but what set off my alarm bells was the absence of his usual serenity. Herman was like one of those round-bottomed dolls you see at carnivals, where even the fastest, hardest thrown baseball won't topple them. The man standing before me looked and sounded like a baseball had hit him square between the eyes, repeatedly.

As I was slipping my gloves on, he said to me, his voice flat and almost mechanical, "Now, miss, tell me the first rules."

"Lead with my shoulder."

"Which shoulder, miss?"

"The left. Because it's my strongest hand."

Normally, I don't broadcast I'm left-handed, but I have to admit to a smug satisfaction that being left-handed was a boon in this case. I wasn't the only kid who'd been beaten with a ruler or slapped across the face by the nuns for using my left hand instead of my right. I was told it was a sign of the devil. Even at seven years old, I knew this was crazy. But if I didn't want to get my ears boxed, I had to write with my right hand. Outside the classroom, I did everything else with my left. Herman thought this would give me a double advantage. Not only would the creeps not expect me to kapow them with my fist—punching someone was not very ladylike—but they also wouldn't expect a punch coming from my left.

"Feet shoulder-width apart," I continued. "Go into a crouch with my knees and hips bent a little and my fist at shoulder height."

He nodded. "We worked on the jab last week, so tell me what to do first, and then show me."

His voice sounded more like a sigh than anything else.

"Look straight ahead, chin tucked under, palm faces down, make a fist, and then hit them. Right?" I curled my hand into a fist with my middle and forefinger knuckles prominent.

"Your feet, miss. What about your feet?"

I moved my feet so they faced Herman's chest. I jabbed. He easily deflected me and admonished, "Don't move your back foot. Try again."

Head, chin, turn fist, dig feet into the floor, and jab.

"Better. You're getting the hang of this.

Initially, I saw boxing as a way to defend myself. Being a woman, no one would expect a punch to the throat or the gut from me. Now that I'd had a few lessons, I liked the dance of boxing, where your feet are as important as your fist. It's a lot like tennis. Your backhand is worthless if you don't have good footwork. Being a tomboy, I'd always relished mind and body acting as one to cut through the water or swing a golf club. Boxing felt similar. The more we sparred, the closer I came to that sense of potential victory, the same self-assurance I felt when I grabbed the handle of a tennis racket or a golf club.

"Your footwork is great, miss. You Laurents are naturals."

I didn't comment. Al, who happened to be San Francisco's amateur boxing champ for three years running, was being a stinker.

"It's all that tennis. Have to be fast on your feet," I replied and swung my left arm wide as if returning a volley.

"Never played any tennis," he admitted. "Done some horseshoes out at Golden Gate Park."

Although I was used to Herman's *non-sequiturs* by now, this one had me biting the inside of my cheek to stifle a laugh. What do tennis and horseshoes have in common? Your guess is as good as mine.

"How about we work on the cross today? It's a lot like the jab, but for the cross, you're gonna pull your left shoulder back, your front foot stays flat, but your back foot turns. No, you gotta keep your body weight centered. Turn your back leg a little more. That'll give your fist some heft. That's it. Try it again."

We went a few more rounds, with me crossing and him deflecting. At the end of the last round, I surprised him and jabbed, catching him gently on the chin.

"Oh, Miss Laurent, if you hadn't pulled that punch, you'd have broken my jaw," he said with genuine admiration. "You still not talking to Mr. Al?" He refused to look at me as he slipped out of his boxing gloves.

"No. He said some pretty rotten things to me." I left it at that.

I'd had a lot of time to think about the fight Al and I had in Nick's apartment last July. The most galling thing about our whole argument was his lack of faith in me. First, he didn't think any woman should be a detective; it wasn't ladylike. Second, he was convinced I'd go under, which wasn't the worst thing in the world, but it stung that he had so little faith in my smarts and gumption. I was determined to prove him wrong. Somehow, my mother's disapproval didn't rankle as much. Her world was composed of the minutiae of life in the Avenues. Attending mass on Sunday. Laundry on Monday. Ironing on Tuesday. Baking bread on Wednesday. Bingo at the parish hall on Friday night. Catechism class on Saturday. Church on Sunday. Her life was one big circle—home and St. Ignatius—with no detours. She didn't understand my desire for more, nor did I expect her to. Her world wasn't wrong, but it wasn't what I wanted. Al's world wasn't much larger, but I expected more from him.

Even though I hoped I'd never have to box my way out of a jam, I wanted to increase my odds of staying alive if someone tried to physically overwhelm me like that snake-in-the-grass Charlie Stein had last summer. The power I felt when my glove landed on Herman's jaw only increased my confidence. I had the mental smarts to do the detective gig. All that was left was to beef up my physical game. The last few months have hammered home that you never know what may happen on a given day. Murder. Arson. Kidnapping. I suppose that was my family's point. My reaction wasn't to return to my typewriter but to take boxing lessons. All I needed was a big break to prove it to others. I had the chops for this. I didn't need to prove it to myself.

"Say, Herman," I said as I handed him my gloves. "How's the down-payment plan going?"

If Herman's greatest dream was to marry Vera, his second dream was to buy a house. He'd been driving extra shifts and working weekends to add to his kitty. The last time I heard, he was so close he'd started looking at homes.

"Oh, swell."

That sounded as if "swell" were synonymous with God-awful with a cherry on top.

"When are you guys getting married?"

He stopped putting the boxing gear away, straightened up, and stood there with his back to me. Seconds, maybe years, passed by before he said in a tight voice, striving for nonchalant and failing, "Don't think we're getting married, miss."

Ninety-nine percent of the time, I love it when Dickie is right. Now? Not so much.

I put a hand on his shoulder.

"She gave me back my ring. Said she didn't want to see me no more. Said I was too small. Not physically, you know, but that I didn't want the bigger things in life. I axed her what big thing? I'd get her the big things if she'd just tell me what they were. She said just me axing told her I couldn't get her the big things."

With a minute shudder, he wiped his face with his forearm. I'd never met Vera, but now I hated her.

"Do you want me to talk to her? Like girl to girl?"

He didn't move for a bit and then nodded.

"I just want to know what the big things are. I can get them. I'm not afraid of working hard. She works in the glove department at The White House. Tuesdays through Saturdays. We used to spend Sunday together."

That "used to" broke my heart.

"I'll talk to her."

He turned around, his face now wiped clean of any emotion.

"And miss? You're doing great at boxing. Like I said, you're a natural, but if you find yourself in a jam, all you need to do is,"—he brought his knee up—"right there. Hard. They'll go down like a sack of potatoes."

Chapter Six

I wore my best suit, hat, shoes, and gloves, and hoofed it to The White House to scope out Vera Kowalski before trying to talk to her. If she didn't love Herman anymore, then she didn't. Not that I knew anything about love, but common sense told me that if you were dumped by someone who was a nice person, it would sting more than if given the heave-ho by a raging harpy. Herman wouldn't have proposed to Vera if she weren't a good egg.

Then a mental picture of Eileen Taylor and Nick appeared out of nowhere, and I remembered how his eyes followed her around the room. He was subtle about it because Nick was a gentleman, but the desire was only banked and not out, even after he suspected she'd murdered her husband. You'd think that finding out the woman you were crazy about was a cold-blooded killer would scour the crazy right out of you. Nick had refused to be another one of her chumps and found the evidence that sent her to the gallows, but he paid for it. I didn't think his torch for her would ever go out. Just as I knew, Vera was it for Herman.

Located at the corner of Sutter and Grant, The White House didn't have that magnificent stained-glass rotunda like the City of Paris, but according to Dickie Vance, it was *the* department store in town, the swankiest of the swank. My usual interaction with The White House's wares was limited to the window displays, with my face pressed up against the glass. I squared my shoulders and smiled at the doorman as I entered the store. Soon, I was surrounded by beautiful, sophisticated women who could point and purchase merchandise I could only fantasize about buying.

When I'd left my apartment, dressed in the smart suit I'd purchased when Nick gave me some money to keep the agency afloat, I thought I looked pretty swell—until I walked through the door of The White House. Most days, fancy clothes and furs don't intimidate me. I've had enough experience being Nick Moore's secretary to know that a diamond on your finger didn't mean you were a good joe. More often than not, the bigger the rocks, the greater the condescension, the bigger the mug. Plus, I also knew I might not be book smart, but I was quick in a way often better than book smart and blessed with a savvy and intuition that rarely failed me. I had a truly enviable physical prowess. Put a golf club or a tennis racket in my hand and prepare to be beaten. People often assumed I was a tennis pro, and my golf buddies were jealous of my scores on the green.

But I'm not much of a looker. I'm tall, slim, and have features that might be striking when I'm fifty, but don't work well with my twenty-four-year-old face. With a mouth too wide, a nose too prominent, and large, dark eyes beneath a broad forehead, I lacked the delicate features of what the movies pushed as the feminine ideal. Mary Pickford and Jean Harlow were my physical antitheses.

I checked out the hats—my secret passion—while standing next to women who didn't own just one good suit, but a closet full of them, and umpteen pairs of shoes and dresses made of silk and velvet, and a mountain of hats to choose from, and fur tippets to grace their shoulders. And then there was the perfume in cut-crystal flagons with mysterious names like *Arpège*, *Shalimar*, and *L'aimant* to remind me of worlds where I'd never be welcome. Hats lined up like soldiers with veils that were little more than a whisper of fabric or festooned with the feathers of an exotic bird hammered home a hard truth to swallow: the hat I wore today would be unfashionable in a year. Maybe it already was.

Had I appeared in my usual homemade dress and hand-knit sweater, I'd have been thrown out on my keister.

Envy now warred with the knowledge I should be damn grateful for what I had. San Francisco's sidewalks were lined with men out of work. I ate three squares a day (most days) and had a roof over my head. But the reality of those sad men and my relative wealth didn't mean a whole lot of beans as the resentment began to work overtime as I walked around the store. I owned one good suit, a decent hat, and a pair of black pumps needing no excuses, but the rest of my life was shabby. There was no other word for it. Even my flat, which I'd sub-leased from Nick and I'd likened to a palace only weeks ago, now seemed threadbare in my mind's eye. That's the trouble with things you can't have. They make you resent the things you do have. Things you should be grateful for.

I took a deep breath and said a *Hail Mary* to counteract the ugly envy dogging my steps as I strolled over to the glove section. I didn't approach Vera Kowalski directly but used my compact mirror to pretend to powder my nose while studying her in its reflection. Like all the girls behind their various counters, she wore a white coat with a red cursive *WH* stitched on the pocket. Her hair was pulled back tight, which didn't do a half-bad job of hiding the recent Marcelline wave. She didn't need any make-up, but the hint of blush on her cheeks and the palest of pink on her lips upped the wow factor. I snapped my compact shut and stowed it into my handbag. Herman was out of his league with this woman. Not even the boxy white jacket covering her substantial curves or the severe hairstyle hid what a stunner she was. Gorgeous didn't quite cover it.

Vera had typical Slavic features—the full mouth, the button nose, the shiny, almost white hair with none of the brass of the inexpert dye job, and tilted eyes so blue, so bright, I could see her eye color from where I was standing, twenty feet away. God must have patted himself on the back for a job well done. Her beauty didn't make you gasp out loud, but it was potent enough.

Herman was, well, Herman. Great husband material, a hard worker, and the sort of man who'd cut off his right arm for you if you asked. I knew twenty women who'd snap Herman up in a heartbeat. Vera wasn't that woman. A small traitorous part of me sympathized with her. I'd found Herman's chatter about working for DeSoto for the next forty years, buying a new three-bedroom house in the sand dunes of the Sunset District, and filling those bedrooms with children named after Orthodox saints a little boring. It was a dream my family would have no trouble understanding.

I was the outlier.

And now the outcast.

Maybe I was jumping to conclusions, but I wondered if Vera's relationship with Herman was what she could get at the time. It was a safe future. Herman was a nice guy, maybe too nice, a bit of a pushover. I'm sure Herman told her how beautiful she was every day. But it didn't matter coming from him.

I returned to the perfume counter and as I pondered all these maybes and what-ifs, I lingered too long. A rough voice with the faintest of Irish accents said in my ear, "Beat it, sister. Now. Out the door with you."

I spun around. It was the house dick, a short man who barely came up to my shoulder. His gut hung over his belt, and he had the ruddy face of a man who'd secreted a hip flask in the inside pocket of his coat and take a nip now and then. His breath smelled of coffee, rum, and tobacco—not a winning combination—and his close-cropped hair was the snow white of a man who'd gone completely gray by the time he was forty. A retired cop, I bet. I hadn't seen him when I entered the store.

I thought fast. I began to speak in French; being bilingual comes in handy now and then. The White House was known for its international clientele. In my rambles, I'd heard several people complaining in French about the salaries of their servants while fingering a forty-dollar handbag.

"*Excusez-moi, monsieur! Je suis—*"

"Can it, Lady. I get a bonus every month if nothing's been shoplifted. You ain't ruining this month's numbers. Let's walk over here. No fuss." I followed him as he led me to a nearly invisible door near the entrance to the store. He walked with a decided limp. "I got you in my sights." He pointed a fat finger at me. "So don't come…" His voice trailed off. "Say, ain't you the dame who works for Nick Moore?"

I was saved. Time to lay on the Irish charm.

"Well, I don't know about being a dame…" I gave him my best smile to show he hadn't offended me. "But, yes, I'm Nick's secretary." I held out my hand. "Maggie Laurent. Pleased to meet you, Mister?"

"O'Grady. Seamus O'Grady. You here on business for Nick?"

I couldn't have bought a better excuse.

"He's got a new girlfriend," I confessed in a stage whisper. "He wants to buy her something nice for Christmas."

"I thought he was in Chi-town." His eyes narrowed and flattened with suspicion again.

Word that Nick had left town had even reached someone as inconsequential as Seamus O'Grady. Rats.

"Yes, he's there with the Pinkertons for a bit." If "a bit" is code for the next twenty years. When telling a lie, you need to make it as truthful as possible; a nugget of wisdom I picked up while attending Catholic school. "I'm supposed to buy something and have it shipped to him." I waved a hand. "This is all too rich for me, that's for sure."

"Me, too," he admitted. "For her birthday, I buy the missus something small. Like a pair of gloves. You should see her face when she sees the box."

I bet. Now it was time to cement my *bona fides*.

"You a retired cop? You know Detectives O'Malley and Murphy?"

He gave me one of those lop-sided grins, sort of a sideways upside-down frown.

"Sure. We play poker twice a month at Murph's place. Never see one without the other. Murph's got a sweet setup in his basement. You wouldn't know it from the look of him, but that little half-pint usually cleans up."

"He's in my parish. Nice guy." I emphasized the word "parish." Based on his accent, this man probably had a rosary in his pocket next to his flask. I didn't mention O'Malley. I knew him, of course. Murphy and O'Malley were partners.

Nick had never gotten along with O'Malley in all the years I'd worked for him. Last July, O'Malley had beaten Nick to a pulp because the sky was blue and the sun had risen in the east. O'Malley and I had several confrontations during the Washington case, and to say I hated the man was putting it mildly. The feeling was mutual. Put the two of us in a room, and it was like two cats primed for a fight. I've never figured out why Murph continued to work with O'Malley, a cop with a fist at the ready.

"Do you get a lot of shoplifters in here?"

He shook his head. "Naw. I mostly watch the help. See that little witch over at the perfume counter?" He hiked his eyes to the left, where a slender redhead was rearranging boxes of perfume for the fourth time since I'd been in the store. "She was lifting a bottle here and a bottle there. Too much for her to use, so I bet she was selling it to her friends. Weill, the owner, is a decent guy. He pays well and takes care of his employees good. She got no business doing that. I told her that if she did it again and I caught her, she'd be out the door and I'd see that she never got another job in a department store in the entire city. All us department store dicks knows each other, and I'd spread the word."

His voice held an undercurrent of righteousness I'd noticed in most of the cops I've met. Power sits very easily on the shoulders of the near-powerless. O'Grady struck me as a beat cop who never made detective because he lacked the education or the smarts. He'd put in his time, got injured, and was now a department store dick. Not that I condoned shoplifting, but I wondered if the money the saleswoman made from selling pilfered perfume was to put food on the table or help pay for the mortgage on a house one payment away from foreclosure.

I asked about the saleswoman hawking the hats and got a neutral answer. Then I whirled around to the woman I really wanted the dope on.

"What about the woman at the glove counter? Is she jake?"

His forehead ruffled into a frown.

"Vera? She used to be real friendly. With her looks, you kinda expect her to be standoffish, but she wasn't until recently. Now she's a bit snooty. Barely says good morning these days. Got rid of the cabbie she'd been seeing for years and is seeing some rich guy in a five-hundred-dollar suit who waits for her to get off her shift. Don't think she wants the other girls to know about him. Always waits for the others to file out the door before she meets him."

So Vera doesn't want the other clerks to see who she's dating. Is she afraid someone will try to poach him, or is it because he's told her to keep their relationship on the lowdown?

"Well, I won't take up any more of your time, Mr. O'Grady." I'd found out all I was going to find from him. The salacious details of Vera and Herman's break-up would be limited to the other saleswomen in the powder room when they refreshed their lipstick.

"Tell Nick, Seamus O'Grady says hi. We go back a few years. Worked on the Cavenaugh heist job together."

"Will do," I promised, and was about to walk away, but then stopped. "Mr. O'Grady, how did you know I wasn't a legitimate customer? My suit is new and my hat is the latest fashion."

He pointed at my handbag. "Dead giveaway. Doesn't match the rest of your outfit."

It wasn't like I could afford a handbag that matched the quality of my suit. More's the pity.

I wouldn't make that mistake again. Who was being arrogant and condescending now? A simple clue like a beat-up handbag told him I didn't belong. I had a lot to learn.

Chapter Seven

I had a couple of hours to kill before Vera got off work. I spent a good ten minutes goggle-eyed at the magnificent flower displays in the windows of Podesta Baldocchi on Grant. The flowers were so perfect, I inhaled deeply and imagined I could smell them through the glass. The china and crystal displays in the windows of Gump's on Post reminded me that I was willfully turning my back on tradition. So be it. My dining room table would never see a Royal Doulton plate. It wouldn't keep me up at night. I finished up at Normandy Lane in the City of Paris, the department store's homage to everything French. Entering on the O'Farrell Street side, I said *"Bonjour,"* to the wine merchant, the bookseller with magazines and books in French, the patisserie where the *macarons* were so delicate, one breath would shatter them into pieces, the butchers manning the hunks of meat and chickens on spits, and finally to the *maitre'd,* standing at the entrance to the tearoom, straight-backed with several menus in his hand.

At my *"Bonjour,"* he swept his hand indicating the tearoom, and said in an ingratiating tone, *"Mademoiselle?"*

"Merci, Monsieur, pas aujourd'hui."

When I was a kid, our family would come to Normandy Lane for special occasions, with my father picking up books in French and my mother buying a *macaron* for each of us. I have a brief memory of my father talking to the bookseller in rapid French; two expatriates conversing in the language of their childhoods. I had never asked my father if he regretted leaving France, and now I'd never know the answer.

I'd spent too much time rambling down memory lane. After checking my watch, I had to race up Grant Street if I had any hope of waylaying Vera once she got off work. I wasn't sure she'd talk to me. From what I saw of her, it was hopeless. Her job had introduced another world, one that didn't include a house in the Avenues and a cab driver for a husband. Of course, like Alice, once through the looking glass, all that lovely gloss and wealth had an equally unpleasant side to it. But if someone as level-headed as I was found herself pining for a fifty-dollar hat after spending two minutes in the store, what must it be like to be surrounded by unattainable luxury day after day?

I had one plan: offer her dinner—the Pig n' Whistle was about all my budget could afford—and try to get an answer out of her to relay to Herman that wouldn't hurt him too badly, even though I was sure that nothing I'd say would touch his heartache.

I stood on the other side of Sutter Street in front of a custom tailor's shop, pretending to be fascinated with the display of men's ties. In reality, I was watching the reflection in the glass as the employees filed out the back door of The White House. I'd waylay Vera as soon as she appeared, assuming she'd walk down Grant to Market Street and catch a streetcar to the Western Addition where she lived.

A second lesson learned today. Everyone had filed out, and I thought I'd missed her when she finally appeared. I'd been ignoring the tall, good-looking man lounging along the side of the building, pulling on a cigarette, when I should have been cataloging everything about him. He ditched the cigarette when he saw her. She squealed in delight at the sight of him, and the wattage of her smile made me want to reach for my sunglasses. Dressed in a well-cut suit, with his hat perched on his head at a gravity defying angle, he leaned over to pin a corsage on the lapel of her coat.

This guy was worthy of that smile. His features were strong—a jaw that could take a punch, a forehead broad enough to anchor his face pretty nicely, and a mouth that looked swell around the butt of a cigarette—but not so strong that he needed to grow into his features. He'd grown into them and then some. Even if he'd been dressed in a mismatched jacket and pants, a torn shirt, and barefoot, he'd still turn heads. Although his shoulders had no problem filling out his suit, he was slender with a tanned face, the warm glow from lots of afternoons on the golf course. I pegged him as being around thirty. He was tall enough that I could tail the two of them from a good distance without any problem. I watched them head down Grant toward Market Street, the pair of them so good-looking that they caught the eyes of several passersby. If this man were Herman's competition…

They chatted as they walked, he bending over slightly so he could hear her. She'd done her best to emulate the latest fashions, even though her coat was obviously handmade and not by the tailors in the basement of The White House. Her hat was of the latest fashion, *très chic*, and expensive. I'd skipped not a few lunches to buy myself a hat just like that. I imagine she'd done the same.

They crossed Market Street and headed into the Palace Hotel. I picked up my pace and saw a waiter escorting them to a table in the Palm Court. This place made John's Grill look like a dog's dinner. Held up by enormous marble pillars, the glass ceiling went on forever. Gigantic Venetian glass chandeliers glittered like a million diamonds. With all the glass and the palm trees everywhere, you felt as if you were in the conservatory of a giant's house. All in all, it was the height of posh. You'd have to be from another planet not to be wowed by all that elegance. Vera must have had kittens the first time he took her there.

This guy wasn't exactly broadcasting their relationship. They were seated behind three overgrown palms in the far corner at the very back of the room. The waiters would have to use a machete to take their dinner orders. Through the palm fronds, I saw Vera turn her face up to his, the broad smile still as broad, not realizing they were seated in the dining room's Siberia. They'd be there for a while.

I headed to the front desk and asked the Concierge where I could find the house dick.

"Casing the bar for prostitutes."

I handed him a dollar bill. "Thanks, Jimmy."

Armed with a bunch of dollar bills and cigars, I'd made a point over the last three months of introducing myself to the concierges and house dicks working in the major hotels. It hadn't resulted in any jobs yet, but it might save me from getting booted out if I got too nosy.

As I was heading toward the bar, the house dick met me halfway across the lobby. A retired Pinkerton, Charlie Rains, was known as Rainy. I doubted many people knew his first name by this point. A lanky man in his early fifties with a constant squint, his suits were nothing special, but he spent a fortune on his shoes. He and Nick had worked together in Chicago right after the Great War and were among the few Pinkertons to survive the early Capone years. Gambling, prostitution, bootlegging, narcotics trafficking, and a robust protection racket—not to mention murder for hire—kept Pinkerton in clover and coffins. Both Nick and Rainey got out and came west, partly because of the weather and partly because, as Nick said, "The longer I stayed, the more likely it was I'd get five bullets in my back."

And now Nick was back there working for Pinkerton again.

"Maggie, long time no see. How are you? Still in the game?"

I ignored the hint of a sneer in his voice. Not exactly spelling it out, but it was obvious he'd expected me to fold within two weeks of Nick's leaving town.

"Still in the game," I assured him.

"How's Nick doing?"

"Sent me a telegram last week asking me to ship him his overcoat. The nights are getting cold."

I'd kept up the fantasy that Nick and I were in constant communication, feeding the idea that he'd be back in town soon. I was only keeping the agency "warm" for him. Other than a telegram from him when he arrived, saying, "GOT HERE OKAY. STOP. NICK. STOP," I hadn't heard a peep out of him.

"Seems like a bad idea to me. You know, going back there. They've got Capone on the ropes, but there's always some other gangster waiting to take over another thug's turf. Glad I got out of there."

I nodded. There was no point in volunteering Nick didn't have much choice. He had to get out of town or he'd kill himself with booze. Chicago had been his beat in the past.

"It's only temporary. He'll be back soon. Say, do you have a line on some guy in the dining room? A looker. He's wearing a spiffy gray suit, and I'm guessing his closet has ten more like it."

"With a dame?"

"Yeah, he's making a hard sell to the broad wearing a gardenia on her lapel. The one with the blue peepers and a red hat. They're in the Palm Court, studying the dinner menu like it's tomorrow's racing sheet. If their table were any further from the entrance to the dining room, they'd be slurping up their soup in Canada."

He saluted me and came back thirty seconds later.

"Winston Barnes. Originally from New York with a hoity-toity lineage, or at least no one says different. His family's got the bucks to back up their claims that their great-great-great granddaddy signed the Declaration of Independence."

I had trouble seeing someone whose relatives openly boasted they'd rubbed elbows with Thomas Jefferson dating a woman who worked the glove counter in a department store.

"Is this the first time he walked in with her?"

He shook his head. "Been an item for two, maybe three months. They come in about once a week. Same table, the one way in the back behind all the greenery and a vase the size of the Flood Building."

That timeline jived with the beginning of Herman's decline, according to Dickie.

"In the past, he had a different bim on his arm every time he came in, but this particular tomato with the ducky chassis seems to be a keeper. Not his usual type of dame. He likes 'em lanky and brunette."

He didn't exactly leer at me, but it skirted the edges. I ignored him, but it reminded me I had less time than I'd hoped to develop my *bona fides*. The more I dug my feet into Nick's world, the more the men around me had ceased to handle me with kid gloves. Their language and expressions were coarser, even brutal at times, but they still treated me with respect. Once the near leers became actual leers, I'd have to walk away from the agency. The detective world was small. Most of them were either former cops or

Pinkertons. Once they knew for sure that Nick wasn't coming back, I had only a small window of time to prove myself. I half suspected the ghost of Nick Moore was keeping them in line for now. If I could establish my cred and earn their respect, then I wouldn't need Nick's protection.

Rainy went on. "His previous bims were society types. She ain't high class."

"How do you know she isn't a society type?"

"For one thing, she's too polite to the staff. Those other women? All la-di-da airs, as if butter wouldn't melt in their mouths. Plus, she's not wearing any fur. Society ladies sure like them furs. Got any info on her?"

I filed that one away. Handbags and furs. If I were serious about swanning into places I didn't belong, I'd need to upgrade my handbag and somehow corral a fur tippet at the very least. At this point, the only fur I could drape around my neck was if I went to Golden Gate Park and hunted down a stray fox.

"She works at one of the high-end department stores."

The less he knew about Vera, the better, but I had to throw him a small bone. He needed to keep tabs on everyone who walked in the door. I didn't want to be a hotel dick, but it might bring in some dough until I was more established. There were several women-only hotels and rooming houses in the city. Until now, I'd avoided that type of work because it seemed nothing more than stopping men from stealing up staircases and fire escapes to "visit" women in their rooms. If it helped to establish my name, or, more importantly, put money in my bank account, I'd have to reconsider. I doubted the big hotels would hire me for a day shift, but maybe they'd consider me covering graveyard.

"So, Barnes. I haven't seen any pictures of his mug in the society pages. When did he arrive from New York?" I'd practically memorized the society pages for the last ten years and hadn't seen the name Winston Barnes or his photograph in Dickie's *Examiner* column. Some dessert with Dickie Vance was in order.

"Six months ago. He's keeping a low profile. Supposed to have a fiancée back east, which doesn't jive with the action that table's seen lately. The staff here likes him. He's polite—no stuck-up Brahmin—and generous with tips.

His father bought Red Cab right before the crash and put Junior in charge."

"Kinda young, don't you think?"

He shrugged as if the machinations of wealthy fathers were beyond his understanding.

"He puts in his eight hours, but the word on the street is Pop isn't happy with his performance."

"What's wrong with him? Hophead? Boozer?"

The Washington job had soured me on dealing with the lazy sons of wealthy men, and did I want to get involved in a case with another booze hound whose favorite two words were Jim and Beam?

"Nah. Just interested in playing golf and not too keen on anything else. I hear he keeps the caddies in the jack. The cab companies that survived the strikes eight years ago are now looking to break the contract. Red Cab is at the forefront of the union-busting effort. With a quarter of the workforce sleeping in Golden Gate Park, you've got a load of guys willing to work for almost free. The union is bringing in organizers from the dock strikes up north. Things are heating up. I'd stay away from him if I were you."

I thanked him and made a mental note to send him a box of Cuban cigars.

It's when the warnings start that a case truly begins.

Chapter Eight

The next day, I called a few Pinkerton operatives I knew in New York to get info on the Barnes family. The dirt was minimal, so Pinkerton didn't have a lot on them. They mostly kept their noses clean, married other blue bloods, and voted a straight Republican ticket.

I spent the day in the morgue of the *Examiner*. Once down a steep staircase into the basement of the newspaper, I walked past a dirty elevator and a wall crisscrossed with a spider web of rusting water pipes until I reached a pair of metal doors. Like the last time I was there, a sea of gray file cabinets in long rows—like they planted file cabinet seeds—filled the room. Sitting in a haze of cigarette smoke, six men sat at a long table, clipping articles and photographs, and placing them in manila folders, while another two men typed the information in the folders on cards. I'd been here before when I was looking up info on the Washington family. Then I'd lied and said I was a student down at Stanford writing a thesis on debutantes. That lie seemed solid, and I decided to work it some more.

"Hey, young lady, you back again?" The head clipper recognized me. He still had the pointed face of a mole with a long nose, beady eyes, and a faint mustache easily mistaken for whiskers.

"Can't stay away. Too much of a party going on in here."

He brought his brows together in confusion; he didn't get the joke. I imagine working here had sapped all the humor right out of him.

"Whatcha working on this time?"

"The Barnes family. They bought Red Cab six months ago, and I'm writing an article on East Coast elites and how they are extending their business dealings to the West Coast."

As he flipped through a gigantic book and began writing numbers down on a sheet of paper, he said, "That's some pretty dry stuff you're working on."

"Tell me about it."

"You know the drill. Follow me."

As we walked through the file cabinet forest, I had the same feeling I did last time I was here: I'd be sacrificed to the mole god, and these file cabinets were merely for show. When we reached the right file cabinet, he opened it with a small key and handed me a stack of envelopes.

"Thanks, you're a pal. Is it like last time? These envelopes are filed by subject or by a person or business name. I leave the envelopes on the table up front when I'm done?"

"You got it, sister."

Rainy had been on the money about Winston Barnes. His ancestors were signers of the Declaration of Independence, and, typical of their class, they owned banks, headed shipping companies, and invested in railroad companies—all in all, significant contributors to the industrialization of the United States as reflected in their bank accounts. In this century, they collect art and sit on the boards of the educational institutions their forefathers had founded. Their wives are philanthropic marvels, hosting fundraisers for museums and symphonies. Their sons attend Ivy League colleges where they study history and the classics and probably speak Latin in their spare time. Their servants hoist American flags up the flagpoles prominently displayed in front of their summer mansions in places like Newport, while they spend their June and July sailing yachts in contests called regattas.

In addition, they built scores of tenements, cramming immigrant families in the meanest of apartments with only one window. Cholera, typhus, and tuberculosis raced through these buildings like wildfire. The luckier tenants had a water spigot in the hallway as opposed to the backyard. The residents used outhouses and chamber pots. In 1901, New York passed new laws mandating that tenements must have a window in every room, plus bathroom facilities and running water in each apartment. Imagine the gnashing of teeth when they were required by law to treat their tenants like human beings as opposed to cattle, going from earning obscene profits to earning only semi-obscene profits. It must have been hard.

Having conquered the East Coast, the West was now in their sights, with young Winston Barnes as the first foot soldier and Red Cab as the initial foray into the financial fabric of San Francisco. Good luck with that. This city was built on the gold men panned from the streams and chiseled out of rock. The current crop of the city's financial mugs had no intention of giving Barnes a place at an already crowded table. They were scrappy, ambitious, and ruthless men who didn't give a hoot about who your great-great-grandfather smoked cigars with. And from what I'd read about John Waters, the owner of DeSoto, Barnes should sell his stake in Red Cab like yesterday because Waters' middle name should be "ruthless." I didn't have a good handle on Winston Barnes, but a guy who studied history at Harvard didn't strike me as cutthroat material.

I should have called Nick, but I didn't. I sent a telegram instead.

WINSTON BARNES. STOP. RED CAB. STOP. ANY INFO? STOP. MAGGIE

Nick had been boozing it up night and day when Barnes had arrived in town, and since Barnes was a person and not a bottle of hooch, I doubted he'd made any impression. In the pre-Eileen Taylor days, anyone even remotely noteworthy would have had Nick compiling a mental dossier on them the second they stepped off the train. You never know what might happen when money and power unite. A lot of the time, bad things happen.

Although Nick would have had all the dope on the cab strikes, I held off calling him. I knew I might have to at some point, but the longer I didn't have to pull him back into his memories here, the more likely he'd put his past behind him. I didn't know then how some memories live in your bones and you carry them wherever you go. Like hauling around a suitcase filled with rocks, all you can do is shift this burden from one hand to the other, but you can't let go. These memories haunt you when the night is dark and all the noise of life finally ceases for the day. That's when they appear, and there doesn't seem to be a damn thing you can do about it.

I didn't have high hopes of getting much out of Vera about Winston Barnes, but at the very least, she deserved to know he was two-timing her. Driving a yellow roadster convertible into a neighborhood like Vera's would ensure that doors would stay shut and the welcome mat pulled off the porch the second my foot hit the first step. Instead, I boarded a streetcar and spent the time it took to reach the Western Addition going over what I wanted to say to her. By the time I stepped off the platform, I knew there wasn't any way to sugarcoat the facts.

I was going to destroy all her dreams.

Chapter Nine

Vera's house was just one of a row of one-room-wide shotgun flats. If you stand at the front door of the living room, you can fire a shot through the house and back door and not hit anything. It was located in a grid of blocks all inhabited by Russian and Polish immigrants, the specter of an enormous Orthodox church casting its protective shadow over its congregation. The fronts of these homes were built right up to the sidewalk, but the backyards were deep and devoted to vegetables and chickens.

I arrived at twilight. Children were playing stickball in the street, their chatter a blend of Polish, Russian, and English. Within five minutes, it would be too dark to play, but it'd take their mothers calling their names to bring them inside. I'd been that child, grabbing every tiny ray of sunlight before finally giving up and trudging up the front steps of my house, with my cheeks flushed from the game even as I shivered from the snap of the increasingly chilly October nights.

There wasn't a doorbell. I knocked as loudly as I could. A stout woman, a couple of decades past sixty, with a coil of braids around her head, opened the door. She had the cold, stoic eyes of the elderly. The smell of boiled cabbage hit me in the face.

"May I speak to Vera, please?"

She motioned for me to come in, but I pointed to the stoop and smiled. With a shrug, she closed the door. I waited for Vera to appear.

The Vera who stepped over the threshold wasn't the sophisticated woman who dined at the Palm Court with her rich boyfriend. She wore a faded housecoat and must have just washed her hair because it was wrapped up in a turban. Even in the rapidly fading daylight, her face scrubbed clean of makeup, she was so beautiful that for a second I wondered if I was completely off-base about Barnes.

I stood up.

"Hi Vera, you don't know me, but I'm a friend of Herman's. Maggie Laurent." I held out my hand.

Her eyes narrowed, and she ignored my outstretched hand.

"Aren't you that detective's secretary?"

There was no point in lying about it. I gave it to her straight.

"Yep. Can I talk to you for a minute?"

"If it's about Herman, I've told him we're through. Over and over again. So please go."

She wasn't being mean about it, but she had reached the point where her frustration now outweighed her compassion for him.

"This isn't about Herman. Well, it's sort of about him but not really. It's about Winston Barnes."

Her shoulders were stiff, unforgiving, but she closed the front door behind her and sat down, her butt poised on the edge of a step to stand up if she didn't like what I was going to say. She was going to hate what I had to say. I sat down next to her.

"You're done with Herman. I get that. He didn't ask me to talk to you, but I told him I'd try to find out why you broke your engagement. He doesn't—"

"I've told him over and over again. He's a nice guy. But he's not…"

She paused, and I filled in the rest of her sentence.

"Winston Barnes."

"No, he's not. Hey, wait a minute. How do you know about Win?" Her eyes narrowed again into a harsh squint, like she had slivers of glass in both eyes.

I was losing her. Initially, I thought I'd spin some yarn about seeing her at the Palm Court, but my instinct told me to be straight with her. Sometimes you need to tell the truth.

"I went to The White House and tried to grab you after work to talk about

Herman, and I saw him waiting for you at the employee entrance. How did you and Mr. Barnes meet?"

She hesitated before replying. I suspect because she didn't want their first encounter to sound like a cheap pick-up, but she coughed it up. "He came up to my counter and asked me about buying a pair of gloves for his sister."

As a pick-up line, not too creative, as a lie, it worked fine. How would Vera Kowalski know that Barnes didn't have a sister?

"He's very handsome," I noted.

"Yes, but that's not what wowed me. He was polite and treated me like I was, you know, important. Not some shopgirl he could order around. I get that a lot."

"I bet," I commiserated. "What do you guys talk about? I know he runs a cab company."

"Oh, we talk about the cab company a lot. He told me his father is mad at him and doesn't feel Win is doing a good job. I gave him some pointers. Herman talked about his job all the time." She rolled her eyes and didn't bother to hide how boring she found him. "When he asked me out for dinner, I broke it off with Herman that night."

"That was decent of you." I wasn't being snide. Even before Barnes entered the picture, Herman's dream of a house in the Sunset filled with five kids wasn't happening. Not with Vera anyway. It was just a matter of time before she returned his ring. "Do you two talk about the future?"

"Well, we talk about his job a lot. The cab company—"

"And DeSoto?"

She raised her chin in defiance. "Yes. So what? If we got married, it would be important to me that he be successful. Anyway, why would I want to marry Herman when I could—"

"You could," I said in a voice near a whisper. "But you can't, because Mr. Barnes is engaged."

She stared at me, and then there was that defiant thrust of her chin again.

"I don't believe you," she replied in a flat voice, but began to ball the fabric of her tatty housecoat with tight fists.

Barnes was squiring her around to get information on DeSoto Cab, the only real rival to Red Cab. And she knew it even if she denied it to me. Those balled-up fists told me that. Herman wouldn't be privy to the financial end of the cabbie business, but he'd know the operational nuts and bolts: the size of the fleet, how many cabbies worked days, how many worked nights, the most lucrative runs, the cost of maintenance of the cabs, and if there were any sweetheart deals with the shipping companies and the hotels. He'd blab to Vera about all of it because he trusted her and believed she was as dedicated to DeSoto Cab as he was. Because it was their future.

But how did Barnes connect Herman to DeSoto and then Vera?

If it were my job, I'd shadow DeSoto cabbies, looking for a way in. With Vera's looks, she'd stand out like a cow patty on a wedding veil. What if she met Herman at his cab stand one day after work? It would be easy to follow her back to her house, then tail her the next morning to see where she worked, thus connecting her to The White House with barely any effort whatsoever.

I didn't say anything.

"I'm going to ask you to leave now. How dare you come here and spread lies about Win?" She stood up. I had about five seconds to make my case or, at the very least, to stop Barnes from making a total chump out of her.

"It's not a lie, Vera. He's engaged to a woman named Abigail Summers. The *New York Times* announced their engagement last June. Full-page spread. They're getting married in May. Just ask him."

Her shoulders slumped, and her face crumpled in on itself.

"I'm not here because of Herman. I know it's over between you two. I'm sad for him, but I get why you might want more in a husband. Believe me. But Winston Barnes isn't that guy."

Then the street lamp went on, bathing the porch in weak light, and her cheeks were wet with tears from the quiet kind of crying when you don't even know you're crying.

"I'm so sorry."

She pushed me out of her way and ran inside. As I made my way down the front steps, I heard her sobbing through the closed door. No one likes being played for a sap.

Chapter Ten

I walked back to my office. Probably not a great idea at that time of night, but maybe I was looking for a confrontation. I didn't find it. I took the stairs to my office two at a time, double-checking that the transoms over the doors to the other businesses were dark. Then I went into the inner office, locked the door, pulled on my boxing gloves, and tore into the wall near the door, pretending that the shadow from the coat rack was a person. I feinted and jabbed at the throat. I broke an imaginary jaw. I kneed a pretend groin and on their alleged free-fall to the floor, I did a haymaker that would have left them deaf for life. I took my rage out on the wall about how few choices we have in this life. Vera had looks, and I had brains, but it wasn't enough. Nothing was enough. How could someone like me have the audacity to think I could be a detective? I smiled at the skepticism, and the constant refrains of, "When is Nick coming back?" and "You're still in the game?" even though I broke the Washington case wide open, with no help from anyone but Dickie.

I didn't break the plaster, but I pounded out my anger at handsome men with fat wallets spinning yarns and raising the hopes of young women who had big dreams and were smart enough to know that if someone like Winston Barnes didn't come along, they'd be selling gloves for the rest of their life or changing diapers non-stop for the next ten years. Barnes had opened a door for Vera, with a path out of the shotgun flat and its cabbage and homemade clothes. I didn't think Vera could close it very easily. Because of Nick's brief love affair with bourbon, I foolishly thought a door had opened up for me as well, a way to ditch the typewriter. Like Vera, I didn't want to turn around and go back through that metaphorical door.

But the reality? I'd go under by Christmas if some business didn't come my way. That door was slowly shutting in my face. My typewriter sat there on my old desk, waiting. Common sense told me to ignore it, so I did, but more than anything, I wanted to throw it through the window to the street below so I wouldn't have a lifeline.

I stopped pounding the wall when I couldn't raise my arms anymore. Slumping down to the floor, I fell asleep in less than two minutes, my hands in the prayer position, my boxing gloves cushioning my head.

I woke up at dawn, with both hips bruised from sleeping on the floor and my hands still swollen from my temper tantrum the night before. I tried to flex my hands. They hurt like hell. A couple of years ago, Nick had the super put a sink in his office because he liked to shave in the late afternoon before heading out to dinner. I blessed him for his vanity. I soaked my hands in cold water for a couple of minutes to reduce the swelling and then immersed them in hot water to ease my muscles. After thirty minutes of alternating cold and hot water, I could make a fist without too much of a grimace.

I needed a shower and some breakfast. As I started to walk out of the office, I saw a telegram on the floor. They must have delivered it yesterday and shoved it under the door. I was so mad when I returned to the office last night, I'd walked right over it. I ripped it open. It was from Nick. He'd replied to my telegram.

BARNES SHIPPING HARD BOYS TO WEST COAST. STOP. BE CARE-FUL. STOP. SEE TERRY RICHARDS AT CALL BULLETIN. STOP. ASK ABOUT IWW. STOP. DOCK STRIKES. STOP. NICK

He didn't tell me to go home or to give up this stupid idea of branching out on my own. He just wanted me to be careful. Nick, you wonderful son of a gun. I put the telegram in my pocket as a private talisman to keep going.

I called my mother for our usual sixty-second conversation.

I told my typewriter to go to hell on my way out the door.

Chapter Eleven

After a hot shower and enough bacon and eggs for two people, I felt human again. I returned to the office and phoned the *Call Bulletin*. Terry Richards wasn't in his office, but I left a message with his answering service to call me. I poured over the four dailies like I did every day, hoping for a possible lead on a job. Halfway through the *Examiner*, Richards called back.

A female voice said, "Hey, I got a message that a 'Maggie Laurent' wanted to talk to me."

"That's me, but I need to speak to Terrence Richards."

"You got her, and it's Theresa or Terry."

Way to start on the wrong foot, Maggie.

"Do you have time to meet sometime today for a cup of coffee?" I coughed twice. "Or just coffee. It's on me."

"About?"

"Dock strikes up north, the cab strikes in 1921 and 1922, and what's the IWW?"

She laughed. "You got ten years, lady?"

"I hope an hour or two of your time will be enough. Meet you at the Buena Vista in an hour?"

I wanted to meet her away from Market Street and my office. I didn't want anyone I knew to see us. That's why I suggested meeting at the Buena Vista, about a gazillion blocks across town. Any farther and we'd be having our cup of joe in the Bay.

"On Hyde at the corner?"

"Yep."

"I'll be wearing a navy jacket."

I was lucky with the cable car and arrived early, but Terry Richards was already seated and working on a cup of coffee. She was anywhere between thirty and fifty, with a face dominated by large brown eyes and a passive expression that revealed nothing. Bright red lipstick was her single ode to femininity. A heavyset woman, her cropped black hair matched a generally utilitarian sense of dress: a fairly shapeless jacket, trousers topped with a white button-down shirt, and mannish brogues with black socks. The navy of her jacket and trousers didn't match, but I doubted she cared. Dressing with a healthy nod to San Francisco's foggy and cold mornings, she'd never press her face to the glass of The White House and salivate at the latest fashions from Paris.

We shook hands, and I asked if she wanted something to eat. One thing I've learned so far in the detective business: you always operate with a *quid pro quo* in your back pocket. Info wasn't free. I didn't have much quid or a lot of quo these days, but I worked with what I had.

"Naw, I'm good. So where'd you get my name?"

"Nick Moore told me you might steer me in the right direction."

Her face softened a tiny bit. "Nice guy. How's he doing?"

"Okay." I paused. "Chicago's a rough town."

She chuckled, but not with mirth. "Tell me about it. I grew up there."

I signaled a waitress to bring me a coffee, and we chatted about the weather until my coffee arrived.

Then we got down to business.

"I covered the Taylor trial for the *Call*. Watched Nick disintegrate with every passing day. She would have walked but for his testimony."

"Yeah."

I still have nightmares about the scene at the prison when they hanged her. Nick was a hard man, but not even he could ignore her murdering her husband for fifty thousand smacks. Nick did his duty in testifying against her, but he hated himself for it.

"Were you there for the drop?"

I nodded.

"Bitch."

We brought our coffee cups together in a morbid toast.

"Can I ask you about the cab strikes in 1921 and 1922?"

"You can ask. Not sure where you're going with this."

"I've heard through the grapevine that the Barnes family, who bought Red Cab, is trying to muscle into DeSoto's territory."

She narrowed her eyes. It wasn't a nice narrow.

"Where'd you hear this?"

"Oh, around." I waved a hand. I didn't want to drag Rainy into this unless I had to, so I kept it vague and then played the "Vance" card, the only card I had to win her trust. "I can't see John Waters just rolling over. Dickie Vance says John Waters is ambitious with a capital 'A.'"

Terry sat back and studied me. Gauging how much to say, how much to hold back. "You friends with Dickie?"

The thing about Dickie is there's no middle ground. You're either his friend or his foe, and he doesn't care who knows it. If this woman didn't like him—given he was writing for a rival newspaper—I might as well throw a few coins on the table, say thank you, and leave. I'd get no more out of her. If need be, I'd return to the *Examiner's* morgue and read up on the strikes. Hearst was no friend of labor. Any articles coming from his newspaper would be biased, but I might not have a choice. No way was I going to sell Dickie out.

"He's been wonderful to me. Before and after Nick left," I stressed. I wasn't going to sell out Dickie Vance for anything.

My voice must have sounded defensive because she said, "Relax, Maggie. He's jake with me. My favorite bowtie is the bright red one with Scottie dogs on it."

"Mine is the bright green one with toucans."

We both smiled, and her face changed from the passive indifference with which she'd greeted me to a guarded but warmer gaze. Indifference was the default. I'd passed the first hurdle. How many more hurdles did I have to jump before she trusted me?

"You know Dickie…?" I left the sentence wide open. For all I knew, she was one of the Nob Hill Irregulars.

"Oh, he gives me a scoop now and then when it's something they can't print in the *Examiner* because it will cause Hearst's knickers to bunch up. What were your feelings about Eileen Taylor getting the noose?"

Was this another test?

"My sympathies were with the doctor she plugged. I'd never met evil before in my life, and I hope I never will again."

"Oh, to be that innocent," she murmured. "Okay, I'll take a chance on you. I don't know which way this is going to play. Barnes and Waters might join forces rather than take each other on, using their joint muscle to roll back the gains of 1921 and 1922 and oust any remaining rivals. Waters is a pretty ruthless son-of-a-bitch, I'll grant you, but I've done some digging into his business ventures, and trust me, he's making plenty of money. I don't think he needs to join forces with Barnes or wants to. Waters is solid financially. Barnes?" She tilted her hand back and forth. "He bought Red Cab at the height of the market. It stands to reason he's hurting if not underwater. How many beggars did you pass on your way here? There's been a glut of labor since the crash. The desperation is so thick, I can pluck it out of the air."

"That'll work in Barnes' favor. Plenty of hungry men are willing to cross a picket line these days. I've been doing some research into the cab industry. Not a nice story."

"No. The taxi cab industry's history with strikes goes back twenty years. It's a brutal way to make a living. Eventually, drivers didn't have to pay for their gas, and the payment-by-commission system gave way to actual wages. In 1915, the Teamsters-affiliated union elbowed its way in. That's when things started to pop."

"Pop?"

"No one fucks with the Teamsters."

I tried to hide it, but I blinked a couple of times at the language. I'd never heard a woman swear like that. Except for Eileen Taylor.

"They organized a strike in 1918, which meant increased wages and reduced the workday from ten to nine hours a day. The Teamsters were just getting going. Another strike in 1919 called for an eight-hour day and increased wages. There was another strike in 1921 and a nine-month strike in 1922 when the cab companies tried to reduce wages. Now, drivers earn four dollars a day plus commission."

Eight years ago, I was in high school and my father had just died. If I wanted to go somewhere, I hopped on my bicycle. I tried to remember if we ever talked about these strikes as a family, and I drew a blank. Life in the Avenues went on while all these guys were out of work. Nine months without a wage is a long time. I bet lots of kids went to bed hungry at night.

"I'm guessing the cab companies are salivating right now."

She pointed her finger at me. "Got it in one. Waters is a smart so-and-so, and it's a toss-up if he decides to collude with Barnes or fight him. Or wait it out. He's a hard man to read."

I needed to meet this Waters fellow, but damn if I knew how. We didn't exactly run in the same social circles.

"Nick said something about the IWW and dock strikes. He said you'd know the scoop."

This time, there wasn't a pause.

"I've always found Nick to be stand-up, and if he's telling you to contact me, then there's a reason."

Terry signaled the waitress for more coffee. Once the waitress heated up our cups, Terry reached into her jacket pocket and palmed a small flask in her hand. She doctored up her coffee with a healthy splash and looked pointedly at me to see if I wanted a small snort. I shook my head. Was there anyone in this town who didn't drink? The flask disappeared.

After the first sip, she muttered, "Much better. If you don't have cab drivers to pick up passengers from the ships, and you don't have stevedores to unload the cargo, then the ships stay put and can't pick up cargo and passengers at other ports."

"Okay, makes sense, but what does it have to do with DeSoto and Red Cab busting the cabbie's union?"

"Labor is labor, whether you're a dock worker or a cab driver. Barnes and Waters breaking the back of the Teamsters makes organizing the dock workers much harder. The cabbies are the canary in the coal mine. How much do you know about the blue book system?"

I created a zero with my thumb and forefinger.

"The shipping companies have created an open shop system. The unions want a closed shop."

This is another reason why life in the Avenues, with me bouncing between church and home, now seemed stifling and rarified. I had no idea what she was talking about.

"I don't understand the difference."

"The shipping companies claim to have their own union looking out for their members. Notice the contempt in my voice. In reality, it's the opposite. If you want to work on their docks, the company issues you a blue book. No blue book, no work. This makes it easy to blackball workers who agitate for better working conditions and keep the real unions out. In 1916, both Seattle and San Pedro went out on strike. San Pedro used city cops to break up the strike. San Pedro went out again in 1923. Brutal retaliation. Even the Klan got involved."

"If the Teamsters affiliate runs the cabbie union, are they separate from the IWW? And what is the IWW?"

"They're separate. The International Workers of the World is better known as the Wobblies, with some saying 'loose' and some saying 'intimate' ties to the Communist Labor Party. The Teamsters are keeping their distance from the Wobblies—even though their goals are similar—because the IWW is too closely aligned with the CLP. Plus, with the Criminal Syndicalism Act and the conviction of Charlotte Anita Whitney… Anyhow, the Teamsters can see which way the wind is blowing. It's going to get ugly and how."

"What do you know about the Pinkertons?"

"What do *you* know about them?" The flask came out again, and she took a direct sip from it. Her eyes never left my face.

"Not much," I admitted. "Nick didn't like working for them, but never told me why. I've heard it's a pretty lousy organization, but he's back with them in Chicago." She'd done some mighty spilling of beans and deserved the same back. "He needed to leave. The Taylor case did a number on him."

"I heard," she said.

Nick wasn't coming back. I might as well give up the ghost. Half the town—or at least the half that mattered—had figured out that Nick had decided to go east before he killed his liver. He was so good, Pinkerton took him back, no questions asked.

"I'm sorry to hear that," she said. "He's a stand-up guy, and I can't say that about many in this burg. I hope he only stays until he's back on his feet." She took a deep breath and took another deep drink from her flask. "Heard of the Homestead Strike in Pittsburgh? Carnegie Steel?"

I shook my head.

"In 1892, Pinkerton agents from New York and Chicago were called in by the owner, the august Henry Clay Frick, to protect the mill and act as strikebreakers. Sixteen men were killed and twenty-three others were wounded. My grandfather was one of the men killed. If a Pinkerton were on fire, I'd add a match to the flames, notwithstanding Nick and Rainy. Thanks for the coffee. That's all I'm going to say because we could get arrested for just having this conversation. If you get some dirt on Red Cab, give me a call. I'd appreciate it. See you around."

Chapter Twelve

I took the cable car back to the Powell Street turnaround and walked to Harvey Cohen's office on Montgomery Street. A short, balding man whose yarmulke was always askew, he was one of the few Jews to be admitted to Harvard Law under their rigid quota system. Harvey was considered one of the pre-eminent attorneys in the city. When I'd phoned him to tell him Nick was leaving for Chicago and my plan to keep the agency afloat, his advice had been as follows: "Do not cross swords with the mayor. He will crush you. You can joust with the District Attorney now and then. Don't make it a habit. Nick had a lot of pull in this town that you don't have. You will have to build up your reputation, which will take time. Until then, walk softly, no sticks. I'm here if you need me."

In the past, he'd always treated me as one of his multitude of daughters, and that hadn't changed since Nick left. Whenever I visited his office, he would shout to Miss Wodinsky, his secretary, "Is it my bubbeleh? Send her in!"

His outer office was a model of order. Not even the pencils would have the nerve to dull themselves under the stern eye of Miss Wodinsky, a woman with a bone-crushing handshake and an affinity for severe black suits.

In contrast, Harvey's office was an utter pig pen. Piles of folders, books, and boxes covered the floor. The top of his desk was equally messy, with stacks of miscellany so high you couldn't even see the top of his head unless you were sitting right in front of him. Balanced on top of these piles were plates of cookies, the occasional stale sandwich, and a teapot from which he poured me a cup of tea that was tepid at best. I thanked him and drank it anyway. I doubt he'd even noticed it had grown cold.

"Now, my lovely Margaron, what brings you to my inner sanctum on this resplendent morning in the glorious month of Octubris?"

This is how he talked. Whenever I consulted with him, I kept a mental list of words I needed to look up in the dictionary.

"The Criminal Syndicalism Act and the conviction of Charlotte Anita Whitney."

His normal jovial mien vanished. He leaned over to the intercom and flicked the switch. "No calls and no visitors, Miss Wodinsky." Then he leaned back to consider me, narrowed his eyes, and folded his arms to rest them on his considerable stomach. "Nu, what are you getting into?"

All the flowery language had vanished.

"Herman Peters is a cabbie with DeSoto and works for Dickie—"

"I know who Herman Peters is. Go on."

Just how far did Dickie's network of spies extend?

"Herman's girl kicked him to the curb because Winston Barnes, whose father recently bought Red Cab, has been laying it on with a trowel. Dickie is worried about Herman and asked me to get the scoop. I think Barnes is plying her for information on DeSoto. Word on the street is that Pop Barnes isn't thrilled with Junior's performance. I received a telegram from Nick this morning. Barnes, Sr., is sending out some muscle to break the cabbie union."

Based on his frown, he didn't like what he was hearing.

"Terry Richards from the *Call* thinks Waters and Barnes might join forces to push out the smaller companies and then take on the unions to reverse the gains from the 1922 strike. She gave me a brief rundown on the Wobblies and the Teamsters, brought up Whitney and the Criminal Syndicalism Act, and then shut me down so fast I barely had a chance to swallow the rest of my coffee."

He got up from his chair with a sigh and began perusing the bookshelves that lined the room. Fat leather-bound books had been double-stacked and, in some cases, triple-stacked, with thinner volumes shoved into whatever space was available. I counted eight coffee cups resting on the tops of various volumes and a stale cookie here and there. Miss Wodinsky must come in once a week to collect the coffee cups and the errant cookie; otherwise, the office would be crawling with rats.

I contemplated taking a tiny nap as I was sure it would take him at least half a day to find whatever he was looking for, but within twenty seconds, he'd pulled out a thick volume embossed in gold letters. Within another twenty seconds, he'd found what he was looking for. He read for a minute or two and then slammed the book shut with a Yiddish expletive needing no translation. He sat down, clasped his hands in front of him, closed his eyes, and began to recite:

"Quote: In 1927, the U.S. Supreme Court held that the State of California, in the exercise of its police powers, may punish those who abuse their rights to freedom of speech by, quote, 'utterances inimical to the public welfare, tending to incite crime, disturb the public peace, or endanger the foundations of organized government and threaten its overthrow' unquote." He opened his eyes. "Miss Whitney's affiliation with the Communist Labor Party was seen as a 'clear and present danger.' Her case validated the Criminal Syndicalism Act of California, which I suspect will have far-reaching and deleterious effects on our First Amendment rights, the freedom of speech." He shrugged. How a shrug could be sarcastic, I'll never know, but there was contempt in every muscle. "But what do I know?"

"What does all this mean?"

"Because of her political views and activities within the CLP, Miss Whitney was denied equal protection under the Fourteenth Amendment."

"So, let me get this straight. If I believe that neither the Republican nor the Democratic Party represents my values, and I form a third party—have meetings, distribute flyers, request a space on the general election ballot, and recruit voters—I might be arrested as a syndicalist if I were labeled a clear and present danger?"

"Such a smart little cookie." He beamed at me in approbation. "Yes."

I thought for a second and then added, "Am I a clear and present danger only because I'm challenging the status quo?"

"A matter for the California Supreme Court to decide should you have the funds to pursue it. Miss Whitney is from a wealthy family. After numerous legal maneuvers, her case reached the U.S. Supreme Court, which ruled against her. Her defense was simple. She was involved in the CLP but did not advocate violence. She still lost, even with wealth and relatives who included lawyers, judges, and, I believe, even a state senator or two. Many others convicted of the same crime were deported or given lengthy prison sentences. I caution you, bubbeleh, to avoid any interaction with the Wobblies, who are assumed to be an arm of the CLP. Whether that's true or not, I do not know. My personal opinion is that Whitney was largely convicted for her association with the CLP. She had contributed a small amount of money to them but was not a member. Although Oakland's District Attorney, Earl Warren, denies it, she was tried for her association with them and her reform activities."

"Which were?"

"Fighting for a more equitable political and economic system."

I gripped my teacup with such force that in another second, I might have broken it. After placing it back on his desk, I looked at him. "As a woman, I've only been able to vote since 1919."

"Exactly." With a plump hand, he patted mine. "Be careful, bubbeleh. Be very careful."

Chapter Thirteen

I went home, too discouraged to go back into the office. I felt stupid, a rube. I didn't like having to ask questions because I didn't know the answers. I didn't even know the right questions to ask. My small childhood in the Avenues had kept me fed and warm, and, boy, was I grateful my father hadn't been a cabbie. But men were scraping out a living by driving cabs, unloading ships, or working in steel mills and getting their teeth kicked in or killed because they wanted to work an eight-hour day. I was ignorant of all of this, even though I lived only a few miles away. Unions. Scabs. Blue Books. Strikebreakers. My barely surviving detective agency couldn't change any of this, but the knowledge that I'd never gone to bed hungry, not once in my life, made me ashamed of my emotional temper tantrum in the aisles of The White House because I couldn't afford a new hat.

I woke up on Thursday morning, determined to get some answers. Maybe not all the answers, but maybe a few. It was time to sweat Winston Barnes.

I called my mother early, as I planned on hitting the golf course that morning. Her disapproval crackled across the phone lines. If I ever make enough money at this gig, I'd pay for a separate phone line for my mother. Our neighbor, Roz O'Leary, sat with the phone to her ear morning, noon, and night. By five o'clock, the entire neighborhood will have heard that Mrs. Laurent's ungrateful daughter spent the day on a golf course—on a weekday, mind you!—instead of earning an honest living.

Normally, playing golf at Lincoln Park is a first-class ticket to frustration. It sits at the mouth of the Bay, and if the wind doesn't blow your ball fifteen feet from where you thought it was going to land, the sand traps have magical powers that lure your golf ball to its doom. But October means warmer days and less wind. On a morning like today, with nary a white cap, the water as blue as a robin's egg, the taste of salt on my lips, and the merest whisper of a breeze, I wish I could take the day off and whack a few balls, forgetting for a few hours about Herman, Vera, the mounting bills, and the estrangement with my family. Revel in the joy when your golf club slices through the air, and you know, even before seeing where the ball lands, that you've hit the ball just right. As much as I wanted to play on this glorious day, those bills weren't going to pay themselves.

I caddy most Saturday mornings, but I never pay much attention to the other golfers, and Winston Barnes wasn't on my radar. I'd been using all my free time trying to drum up business or figuring out where Azerbaijan was located, and I hadn't been out on the links for quite some time. It's hard to justify walking the greens when I'm not bringing in the green. Still, I was surprised I hadn't run into Barnes at some point over the last six months.

If Winston Barnes was as big a golf nut as Rainy claimed, he might be here on this amazing morning. And there he was. Stuck at the sand trap on the second hole. After two unsuccessful swipes and spraying sand everywhere, his ball didn't move so much as a millimeter. He threw his golf club down in the sand in frustration. I didn't see a caddie anywhere. Maybe he was like me. He liked to golf when he had the greens all to himself.

I stood at the edge of the sand trap and took a breath so deep my toenails jumped. If I were going to make any headway with this guy, I needed to park my anger back at the first hole. I had to restrain myself from taking a nine iron to his shins.

"You're bottoming out and starting your upswing at the ball. Bottom your swing in front of the ball."

Barnes stood there, his lips pursed, mentally wondering how to play this. *Do I rip into this irritating young woman dressed in dungarees and hauling a golf bag that's seen better days filled with irons that look like a bunch of knives and forks someone had melted down into something faintly resembling golf clubs, or do I take her advice because she sounds like she knows what she's talking about?*

When he didn't respond, I said, "Draw a line in the sand with the edge of your club about two inches from the ball. Start your swing at the top of the ball, and then when you hit the line, bottom out your swing. You'll bring up a ton of sand, but your ball will sail out of the trap."

He took my instructions to heart, and the ball landed three feet from the hole.

"Nice. Mind if I play with you?" I asked.

"Not at all. I'd love it. Please."

Barnes was like a lot of players I've met. He loved the game and was lousy at it. Stiff and mechanical, he couldn't feel the space between the ball, the tee, and the green. He tried to dominate his swing and didn't have a clue how to shift his weight to work in tandem with the momentum of his body.

When we'd played the last hole, he turned to me and said, "You're phenomenal. You should be on tour."

"Not until they have tournaments for women. The clubhouse and I have a deal. I caddy here, and they waive the greens fees for me. I could play this course blindfolded. Not sure how I'd do on other golf courses. Anyway, loosen up. You're fighting your swing all the time. Think of it in one long motion, not a swing and a chop. Watching you, it's almost like two movements. It should be one."

"Thanks for the advice. I'm Win Barnes." He held out his hand. I shook it.

"Maggie Laurent. Nice to meet you."

Some people have sweaty hands that make you want to slide your hand down your skirt to dry it off. Some people have damp hands so limp, it's like gripping a warm, wet fish. The only thing missing is the scales. Trying to prove who's top dog, some people grip your hand too tightly, cutting off your circulation for a second. The worst are the guys who pull a two-handed shake and hold on to you, and you have to pull your hand away from a grip so strong it's like pulling your hand out of quicksand. Barnes had a nice, firm handshake that didn't last too long and wasn't wet.

If Barnes were the bad egg I thought he was—using Vera as a snitch for dope on DeSoto—then I'd expect him to resent my advice, sneering at me playing in dungarees with my third-rate clubs. I wanted to hate this guy, and he wasn't making it easy.

"You want to grab a cup of coffee?" He moved his chin in the direction of the clubhouse.

Plonking myself down at a table and ordering my co-workers to serve me coffee would be a surefire way to lose my caddy gig.

"Thanks for the invite, but I'll take a permanent raincheck. Can't have the staff hobnobbing with the members, you know."

He blushed. "Gee, how stupid of me. You told me you were a caddy here. How about grabbing a cup somewhere else? The Cliff House is nearby." He checked his watch. "They should be open by now."

I didn't roll my eyes, but I wanted to. Only someone that privileged would think the Cliff House was just a high-rent coffee shop.

"My car's that black convertible in the lot." He pointed to a sleek roadster the length of a football field parked right next to my car.

It was identical to mine. The only difference was the color.

"Sure. Sounds fun. Let me throw my clubs in the trunk of my car."

His face was still flushed with shock when I turned around from putting my clubs away. Usually, I didn't drive to the golf course. Driving a roadster convertible while working for green fees would raise a few eyebrows with the club. I drove today because I wanted to hit the greens early in the hope of catching Barnes on the course, a hunch that had paid off. Plus, whatever impression I might have made originally, he was now unsure of me. Not a bad place to be.

Neither of us was dressed to dine at the Cliff House, but I was the only one self-conscious about it. As the waiter led us to a window table—Barnes had slipped the waiter a bill—I whispered in his ear, "We're still in our golf clothes. Is that okay?"

He gave me a look like I was speaking Chinese. "Of course it's okay. Why wouldn't it be?"

There were a million reasons, but none that would make sense to Barnes. Once we were seated, he handed me the menu the waiter had neglected to give me.

"I'm going to have some toast and eggs. I haven't had breakfast yet. Do you want something?"

A quick scan of the menu told me they didn't serve breakfast, but I didn't doubt they'd whip up two over-easy on toast for him.

"Some toast and coffee would be great. Thank you."

We sat there waiting for the coffee, both of us looking out the window at the Pacific Ocean as the waves broke with a crash against the cliff face. So beautiful, so cold. My mother says I'm half fish, but even I have the sense to stay out of it.

"I love the violence of the waves here on the West Coast. The Atlantic is so tame." He smiled. "I'm from the East Coast. New York mostly."

"While I've never been east of San Francisco." I pointed at the impossible blue of the water. "I'm warning you. That ocean is cold and unforgiving. I wouldn't try to swim in it. You need to head farther south. The beach at Santa Cruz isn't bad. Still cold, but at least you won't flirt with hypothermia. It's a little over an hour from here. Your sleek ride will probably get you there in under forty-five minutes if you drive like me. Plus, there are sharks up here."

"Oh, we have sharks on the East Coast, too. I imagine the sailing here would be amazing. Maybe I'll get a boat."

Just like that. *Maybe I'll get a boat*, like I might say, *Maybe I'll get an apple*.

"Join the St. Francis Yacht Club down on the Marina Green. I'm sure they can steer you in the right direction if you want to buy something."

"Do you sail?"

That sounded a little too eager for comfort. Like he wanted me as a sailing companion or was hoping I had a boat he might borrow.

"Nope. I had a friend who sailed. She lost her boat in a fire at the yacht club. Did you know her? Catherine Washington."

With his sharp suits and his wallet fat with bills, he was the kind of guy who'd have frequented the speakeasy owned by Catherine's brother, Philip Washington. I had to be careful what I said. Dollars to doughnuts, he runs in the same crowd as the Washingtons had. Catherine had fled on a stolen boat last July in the aftermath of the multiple murders in Phil Washington's speakeasy. They hadn't caught her yet, and I hoped they never would. I didn't think they were looking too hard. Smart and fairly ethical for a bootlegger and possible drug smuggler, Catherine hadn't been in touch since she went on the lam. Not that anyone, including the D.A., has asked.

"I heard about that. I met her brother once or twice." His brow furrowed in distaste, the usual reaction when speaking of Philip. "Wasn't he murdered by his butler?"

"Something along those lines." It wasn't remotely like that, but the public wasn't privy to the real story and never would be. "Catherine's jake. She gave me those snazzy wheels when she left town. He, on the other hand, was a bad egg."

Still, Phil Washington didn't deserve what happened to him. And like I always did when reminded of that night in the speakeasy, I began to breathe deeply, my measured in and out, trying to drown out the memory of the sounds of gunshots that went on forever and the sight of so much blood.

"Miss Laurent, are you all right?"

His voice yanked me back to the Cliff House, away from the speakeasy. My toast had arrived, and the waiter was pouring me coffee from a silver pot.

"Yes," I chirped. "Hungry, I guess."

We didn't say another word until our plates were clean.

"Do you like it here in California, Mr. Barnes?"

"Yes and no." He began to stare out at the water. "I work for my father in the family business. I hate it. I've always wanted to teach. History. But *noblesse oblige* and all that hooey. Berkeley has a pretty decent history department. Stanford, too. I'm hoping if I do a lousy job, my father will fire me, and then I can go back to school. So far, it's not lousy enough."

He turned to face me, his face bleak with the resignation of a kid who gets beat up a lot. I wondered again if his squiring Vera around was actually for real.

"Just quit," I said. "You might have some lean years, but you'd get by."

"My fiancée doesn't see herself as the wife of a professor. A millionaire, yes. A measly teacher, no. It's my duty, so I'm told, to carry on the family tradition of making lots of money. Unfortunately for everyone involved, I'm very bad at it, but I'm the only one who seems to recognize that, at least my father doesn't."

So Vera *was* a pawn, but based on this conversation, I bet he felt pretty lousy about scamming her. We sat there for a few moments in silence, watching each other.

"Seems like you're trying to please everyone but yourself, Mr. Barnes."

"It's Win." In an attempt to lighten up the tenor of this conversation, he said in a flirty tone, "Who are you trying to please, Miss Laurent?"

"It's Maggie. No one but God. Most days, I do okay. Some days, not so hot."

Like this morning. I'd have to confess lying by omission to this man. That I was stalking him, letting him buy me breakfast while trying to weasel information out of him about his fake romancing of Vera. He was equally guilty of lying, but I had enough trouble looking after my soul. I had no intention of worrying about his. I'd go to St. Patrick's later. The church frowns on lying. My act of contrition would take a couple of hours.

"What would a nice girl like you have to confess?" he said, his voice still coy.

"You have no idea." I tried to reply in an equally flirty tone, but it came out somber.

"Can I help?"

Here was someone who didn't think twice about walking into a restaurant wearing golfing cleats with grass stains on the knees of his pants and ordering eggs even though they didn't serve breakfast, so it was no surprise he thought he could solve my problems. His privilege had taught him that all problems could be solved with money or clout. When in reality, most of the world's problems had no solutions, and certainly not ones solved by a wave of a hand.

His eyes, reflecting the blue from the ocean and the sky, were almost electric, and I found myself mesmerized by the color and the earnestness I saw there. His question was so simple and said with such sincerity, his handsome face puckered in worry. Either he was completely evil, or he was a simple guy who found himself in an impossible situation, and for the life of me, I didn't know which it was.

I didn't reply but shook my head.

"Some days you can see harbor porpoises," I said, and we turned our attention back to the water.

And while we were sitting there drinking coffee and scanning the ocean for the hint of a dorsal fin, Vera Kowalski had already been dead for over three hours.

Chapter Fourteen

I didn't hear about Vera's death until Dickie Vance called me at two a.m.

"Margaret, get dressed and come to the Mark. Now. Make haste. Wear a disguise. Do you have a hatbox?"

I struggled to reply. Sleep was still holding me tight.

"Margaret Laurent, wake up!" he commanded.

"I'm awake," I slurred. "Yes, I have a hatbox."

"Excellent. Go to the front desk. Tell them you are from Liguria Bakery and delivering the cake I ordered. Remember, wear a disguise."

He hung up.

At one point during the Washington case, I pretended to be a teenage boy, borrowing some clothes from Nick. No one had blinked an eye. It was either a commentary on my acting skills or my lack of a figure. I'm a lousy actress.

Nick had pressed a wad of bills into my hand just before he left town, and with some of that money, I'd bought a full complement of men's clothes: trousers, a pea coat, a white button-down shirt, a fedora, a newsboy cap, brogues, and even a tie. With my face scrubbed clean, my coat buttoned up to the top, and my newsboy cap pulled down over my brow, I passed. I grabbed a hatbox and drove the roadster to the Mark Hopkins Hotel at the top of Nob Hill, flooring it and blaring my horn through every red light. I made it in four minutes flat. I parked on a side street to avoid waking the valet sleeping in his guard box.

Dickie's culinary yens in the wee hours of the morning must be well known to the hotel staff. The front desk didn't even blink when I said I was delivering a cake to Mr. Vance. I had a moment's trepidation when I walked by the hotel dick, a guy I knew well. He was sitting at a desk, having a smoke to keep himself awake. I held the hatbox up near my face and ducked my head as I went by; he didn't give me a passing glance. Neither did the bellhop, struggling to stifle a yawn as I headed toward the elevator. A delivery boy doesn't rate a bellhop's attention. Fine by me. On my way up to Dickie's penthouse, I debated sending an anonymous note to the manager telling him that the security at the hotel left something to be desired until I realized that I might need to come back in disguise again. No note.

Dickie was standing on the threshold of the door to his suite, informally dressed. For him, this meant he'd shed his jacket and was not wearing his signature bow tie. He didn't recognize me at first. His face fell as he'd anticipated seeing me step out of the elevator at this time of night. When I pushed back the news cap so he could see my face, he smiled.

"Once again, you have proven how devious you can be. I approve. Now come in."

I'd never been in Dickie's penthouse, even though I'd known him for years. I felt like writing a letter to H. G. Wells. I'd walked into the Victorian era and didn't even need a time machine. Acres of mahogany furniture filled the room. Numerous free-standing Tiffany lamps stood at the arms of the chairs and sofas. Every item of furniture was upholstered in red or gold brocade. Enormous armoires overwhelmed, iced with curlicues and carvings, and so tall their finials touched the ceiling. Two sofas longer than my roadster faced a huge circular table holding photographs in silver frames. Ornately carved bookcases lined the walls and were filled with gewgaws of every description: crystal vases, glass figurines, silver candelabras, pitchers of Venetian glass with matching glasses, and china tea sets. Lining the walls where there weren't bookcases or armoires hung portraits of long-dead ancestors, some in Confederate uniforms. Porcelain-faced dolls with rouged cheeks and lips, ringlets, frilly lace dresses, and tiny black patent leather shoes covered every chair, every sofa seat. My mouth didn't drop open, but it was a struggle.

"Let's keep our voices down. Mother is in bed."

Dickie's mother was stone-cold deaf. In my opinion, nothing short of a gigantic explosion wiping out Union Square would wake her up, so I didn't understand this need for caution, but I nodded to keep up the fiction she wasn't as deaf as a post. Which she was.

"When I decided to leave Charleston and move to San Francisco, Mother followed me. She emptied a twenty-five-room house into this suite. Let's sit near the window. It's not as crowded, and Mother doesn't like it when I move the girls."

The girls? I pursed my lips to silence the laughter filling my cheeks.

"It's very, um, red. And gold." I didn't mention the dolls.

"I find it bordering on Victorian bordello territory, but it makes her happy. Mine is not to reason why. Most of this was loot she inherited from her mother, a vile woman whose name never passes our lips, and what she didn't inherit were wedding presents. And we know how *that* marriage turned out."

I didn't know anything about Dickie's father other than he insisted Dickie join the Marines, which is where he met Nick, and that Dickie had fantasized about killing his father, but had settled for maiming him instead if given the chance. Not that he *had* maimed his father, I'm sure. Sort of.

"Enough family gossip. Herman phoned me from Duggan's Funeral Parlor on Market less than an hour ago. Vera Kowalski was killed this morning on her way to work, I mean, yesterday morning. Monday. A car ran her over on Market at Third. She was standing on the corner waiting to cross the street, which was crowded with people. The police believe someone accidentally began pushing the others forward into traffic. A car turned the corner, and she fell into his path."

Stunned doesn't begin to cover it. I gaped at him. It was several seconds before I said, "How's Herman doing?"

"As well as can be expected, which means he's nearly catatonic with grief."

"Did the driver stop?"

"Oh, yes. A Red Cab driver. The police aren't holding him. They're convinced it was an accident. The driver is quite distraught."

"Not so distraught that he won't cash in on killing her." It was out of my mouth before I could censor myself.

"You *have* been busy. There is more to this story. Speak." He sat back in his chair and waited.

I went through the sad conversation with Herman about Vera dumping him, how I saw Winston Barnes wining and dining Vera at the Sheraton Palace, and my uncomfortable evening with her when I spelled out that Barnes was coming on to her to learn what he could about DeSoto's business practices.

"She didn't want to believe me, but soon realized that most of their conversations centered on the DeSoto cab company and not on her. When I told her about Barnes' fiancée in New York, it sealed the deal."

"Hmmm, this sounds rather nefarious. Why do you think she was murdered?"

"Word on the street is that Barnes, Sr., is determined to break the union deals negotiated in 1921 and 1922. It's unclear whether Waters and Barnes are collaborating, but if Waters were smart, he'd stand back and let Barnes do all the dirty work."

"Waters is quite intelligent," Dickie noted, and then stood up and began rummaging around in one of the various armoires. "Victory," he said, holding up a box and returning to his seat. "These help me think. Would you like one?"

It was a box of *macarons* from Normandy Lane.

I shook my head. He ate four in quick succession. My teeth ached just watching him.

"Do you think Barnes is acting solo at the moment?"

"Yeah, I do. But the son isn't getting the job done fast enough. Earlier this week I sent Nick a telegram asking for info on Barnes, Sr. He replied saying that Pinkerton was sending out some hard boys to move things along. His very words."

His gaze sharpened.

"And I should be careful."

"Except for Nicholas, I do not have a high opinion of Pinkerton men. This is much bigger than either of us thought."

"I know they have a reputation as strikebreakers, but would they go so far as to murder Vera?"

His silence answered my question.

I shivered a little. If Nick had heard through the Pinkerton grapevine that the organization was sending some hard boys to San Francisco on Barnes' behalf…. And with Pinkerton's ugly history of busting unions…. No wonder Nick warned me. An organization that would throw a bomb into a crowd of protesters, as they did in the Haymarket riots, wouldn't hesitate to push a woman under a speeding car. Child's play. Oh, Nick.

"What if Waters is still on the fence, refusing to play union-busting ball right now, but not exactly saying no? Maybe he wants to see how successful Barnes' initial push is before committing."

"It's possible," Dickie agreed and reached for another *macaron*. "Personally, I think John Waters is more interested in selling fleets of cars than union-busting. Waters is just as ethical as Barnes, which is to say, he's not at all. But he *is* more intelligent."

This would make points with the mayor, who would do anything to avoid a major strike during an election year, which is as good a reason as any for keeping everything status quo. Waters lived here, and you didn't want Smiling Tim Stephens as an enemy. Being from the East Coast, Barnes Sr. wouldn't give a hoot about Smiling Tim's push for the governor's seat.

"Makes sense. I think Barnes is playing both sides of the fence. Say, Waters decides he isn't going to join forces with him on the union-busting ploy, then Barnes will try to muscle out DeSoto as the premier cab company in San Francisco by getting whatever inside dope he can from people like Vera. Does that play?" I asked.

"Yes. It is what I would do. I wish I did not have scruples. I would make an excellent criminal." He popped another *macaron* into his mouth.

"What if Vera confronted Win Barnes about using her to get the dope on DeSoto? Barnes goes running to his father in a panic. What if the father already has his muscle in place? Pop's all set to start his bid to kill the union *and* undermine DeSoto, and he doesn't want some shop girl mucking up his plans by running to someone like Terry Richards with her story. One guy drives the cab, and another guy pushes her into traffic. The pusher in the crowd melts away in the hubbub."

"And the son?"

I thought for a minute.

"I was playing golf with Barnes when it happened, so I know he wasn't the pusher. Maybe his father played it this way on purpose. Knew Junior was going to be on the links and put his plan in motion to absolve his son of any involvement in Vera's death. I'd swear on a stack of Bibles he didn't know it was going to happen."

"Dear, dear, dear," muttered Dickie, and ate another four *macarons* in quick succession. "This is getting…how shall I say it? Dangerous." His brow furrowed. "I think a phone call to Nicholas is in order. But first. I wish to pay for Vera's funeral and her burial. Per Herman, she will lie at home for three days—in an open casket no less—and then there will be a funeral mass on Sunday at the Orthodox Church and then the burial at Colma."

"Three days? In this heat?" It was around seventy degrees when I left my apartment twenty minutes ago. At two a.m.

"When in Rome… I know; it is horrible to contemplate. They will be raiding every ice merchant within a hundred miles to line her casket with blocks of ice. Unfortunately, I cannot attend for obvious reasons. My relationship with Herman must be kept secret. I would appreciate it if you would attend in my stead."

"Of course. I would have attended anyway."

"I will give you money to pay for her funeral and burial. Please contact Duggan's." From a pocket in his pants, he pulled out a wad of bills as thick as my wrist and handed it to me. "Then call Podesta Baldocchi. Lots of flowers. Money is no object. Have them charge my account. You may tell Herman I am paying for the funeral, but you must impress upon him that he cannot divulge this information to anyone else. I trust he will keep this a secret."

I took the bills and stashed them in the inner pocket of my coat. Dickie shook his head at me. I looked down. I had a breast the shape of a wad of bills. I then shoved it under the brim of my news cap and pushed it back a bit from my forehead. He nodded his approval.

"I'll bring back what I don't spend," I assured him.

He waved a hand.

"Dickie, I'll bring back what I don't spend," I insisted. "I'll tell Podesta to fill the church with so many flowers that they'll have to drive to Nevada to buy more vases. It feels like false pretenses. I'll appear far more generous than I am," I protested.

"If you had the money, would you pay for her funeral?" he demanded.

"Yes."

"Then there's no need to discuss this further." He reached for another *macaron*. The box was empty. "My, they are all gone. How does that happen? Now run along and get some sleep. You must talk to Duggan first thing in the morning. Are you going to avoid Barnes? The son, of course."

"No," I said with some belligerence.

"I didn't think so, but I felt compelled to ask. Be careful."

Chapter Fifteen

When I got home from the Mark, I raised the blinds so the sun would wake me up. The horror of Vera being murdered, worrying about Nick back with Pinkerton, and the vision of all those dolls watching me as I walked out the door of Dickie's penthouse meant it took me forever to get back to sleep. I dropped off at what I figured was about six a.m. and woke up around eight, with the sheets tangled around my sweaty throat and the sun beating down on me. The apartment was already warm. Most of the year, the fog gallops in through the mouth of the bay and wraps the mornings and late afternoons in a heavy damp like a gray overcoat. In September and October, the winds die down, and the fog rests off the coastline as if an invisible chain were holding it back.

This was the sort of day when not even the chill of the water could stop children from skipping school to swim at Ocean Beach. There's always one kid who gets dragged out to sea because the undertow at that beach is a killer. Where the bellhops keep easing a finger beneath the collar of their scratchy uniforms, and keep a handkerchief in the palm of their other hand to wipe the sweat from their brows as they stand in attention in front of the hotels. Where you can hear the whoosh of windows being raised as your neighbors hunt for a stray breeze to cool down their apartments because the Victorians lining the city blocks were built to keep the heat in and the clammy air out.

Coming out of the incessant gloom of summer, San Franciscans welcome the sunny skies of September. Everyone's got a smile on their face. By the end of October, men hand out black eyes to their wives with abandonment, mothers smack their children just for the hell of it, and the only people with smiles on their faces are the ice merchants. By noon, the tar on the roadways is already sticky and clinging to the bottom of your shoes. This brutal heat had lasted longer than usual.

I called my mother and took a quick shower. I put on my black suit for appropriateness's sake, even though I'd be sweating before I put the key in the ignition of the roadster. It was going to be another scorcher. While driving to Duggan's Funeral Parlor, I went through a red light as I was obsessing about those *macarons* from last night. I should have accepted a couple. It would have tided me over until I could get breakfast. With the metabolism of a hummingbird, my body protests when I skip meals.

The caretakers for the dead never sleep. Despite being early, Duggan's Funeral Parlor was open and ready to do the business of death. The low hum of a muted bell attached to the door announced my entrance. The word "parlor" was the right word. Although not nearly as crowded, it competed with Mrs. Vance's living room for the best collection of Victoriana west of the Rockies. Minus the gewgaws and armoires, most of the space was devoted to sofas with curved backs—obviously for the families in mourning—and spindly little chairs next to spindly end tables heavy with Tiffany lamps and ashtrays. Even though the sun was hammering the lace curtains, the lamps were lit, giving the room a dull glow I'd describe as appropriately somber. An older woman was sitting behind a huge rolltop desk and punching numbers into an adding machine. She took her time standing up, finishing one more column of numbers before crossing the room to greet me.

There is something about me that rubs women of a certain age wrong. Generally, they are older, usually unmarried, and always have long gray hair they torture into severe buns at the top of their heads, which must take multitudes of pins to keep in place. Their mouths rest in a constant frown. They always wear dresses with lots of tiny black jet buttons, high collars that brush their ear lobes, and skirts so long, their knees never see the light of day. I'm convinced they suffer from daily migraines, which only makes them crankier. This immediate dislike isn't based on me being a detective. In school, the nuns either hated me or loved me. There wasn't a lot of space between rascal and rebel, as far as they were concerned. This prejudice dogged me as a kid and has followed me into adulthood. I asked my mother about it once, and she said it was because I didn't walk like a lady. Whatever walking like a "lady" meant. I was a lady, and I walked how I walked.

This woman was no different. Tight bun? Yep. Black dress with a zillion buttons? Check. Pronounced frown? Oh, yeah. By the time she reached me, her disapproval was so manifest, I could have shaken hands with it.

"Hi," I said in a brisk tone. "I'm Margaret Laurent."

"Welcome, Miss Laurent. How may I help you?"

This was said in a languid, lugubrious monotone meant to soothe and convey boatloads of sympathy for my dearly departed, but what her face said was, "State your business and leave." I don't know how someone can still frown and talk, but she managed.

"I'm responsible for the expenses of Vera Kowalski's funeral and burial. I want it top drawer all the way. Please tell me the costs." I'd be grateful to spend some of this cash. It took some muscle to shove the wad of bills into my purse.

"This has already been arranged, Miss Laurent. Thank you for your concern," she replied in a voice so cold, I half expected to see icicles erupt from the ceiling, and she turned away.

That threw me for a loop. Would Herman have spent his life savings on giving Vera a funeral worthy of a queen? He might have—he was so soft-hearted—but Herman had talked to Dickie early this morning and hadn't mentioned paying for the funeral; otherwise, Dickie wouldn't have thrown all that cash my way. Had Dickie changed his mind and phoned the funeral parlor? I needed to find out. And I needed to get out of this suit. It was only nine a.m., and I felt like a frog in a pot of warming water.

"Excuse me. Would you mind letting me know who's paying for her funeral?"

"Yes, I would mind. That is private information," she replied over her shoulder. For good measure, she added, "Good day, Miss Laurent." She returned to her desk, sat down, and began hitting the keys on her adding machine again.

"Excuse me." This time I didn't bother being polite.

She looked up but kept her right hand poised over the keys.

"Do you know when the funeral mass is going to be?"

"She was returned to her home yesterday for three days of mourning. On Sunday, a mass will be performed with immediate burial after the mass."

She returned to her adding machine. I guess death is good for business.

The first thing I did when I left the funeral parlor was to get breakfast. Now that I wasn't living at home, my eating habits had taken a nose dive. I kept promising myself to get a hot plate and make oatmeal every morning, but oatmeal versus bacon and eggs wasn't a contest oatmeal was going to win. I bought my four dailies and walked into the first greasy spoon I found. After parking myself in a booth, I gave the waitress my order with a double helping of toast—sourdough—with orders to keep the coffee coming.

There was nothing in the newspapers about Vera's death, which surprised me. The *Examiner* relished stories like this. Their stock in trade was murders, bank heists, and tragic deaths. Vera's death—"Beautiful Young Woman Killed on Market Street, Onlookers Scream in Horror"—was front-page stuff. Had someone put the kibosh on this story? Terry Richards might know.

I did learn that ninety-eight men were killed in an explosion at the Maybach Mine in Germany. Pilot Jessie Miller broke the previous west–to–east transcontinental flight record from Los Angeles to New York in twenty-one hours and forty-seven minutes. In a speech in the hall of the Palazzo Venezia, Benito Mussolini proclaimed the joys of Fascism and defended Italy's rearmament program, saying that since everyone else was doing it, Italy was joining the crowd. King George V opened the seventh parliament of his reign. The German steelworker strike was settled with the workers agreeing to a three-percent wage reduction. New York began a program putting unemployed people on the city streets to sell surplus apples. I wondered what would happen when the apples ran out. But nothing about Vera and nothing remotely worth following up on as a potential lead for another job, unless King George wanted his trousers pressed. I was an ace with an iron.

I checked my watch. It was too early to waylay Dickie at John's Grill. I headed home, stripped off my wool suit with a groan of relief, and changed into my dungarees. On a hunch, I drove to the golf course. Because if Dickie wasn't paying for the funeral, then there was only one person I knew who had those kinds of simoleons.

There he was, facing the ocean, sitting cross-legged near the edge of the cliff. The wind had blown away any lingering fog and the Farallon Islands were visible and stark against the waves. I called to him from afar, not wanting to startle him.

"Mr. Barnes!"

A slight jerk of the head told me he'd heard me. When I got up to him, I saw him sitting *on* the edge. He hadn't changed since yesterday. His suit needed a good press, his tie was nowhere to be seen, and his shirt was wrinkled and stained with liquor as he had gulped something down so fast, he didn't care if half of it spilled down his shirtfront. I knelt down to grab his hand.

"Mr. Barnes, you need to get away from the edge. These cliffs aren't stable."

I had no idea if they were stable or not, but when he turned to look at me, his face didn't register anything but complete detachment from his surroundings. Cliff? What cliff? Unstable? What does that mean? He could have been facing a fireball about to engulf him in flames, and his lack of affect would have been the same. He was somewhere mentally he shouldn't be. Despite the liquor stains carpeting the front of his shirt, I didn't think he was drunk. Nick had given me a crash course in how a rummy behaved. Despite the faint whiffs of bourbon off him, whatever was going on with Win Barnes wasn't due to hooch.

"Come on. Let's find someplace to sit. I'm afraid of heights."

Which was a lie, but he didn't know that.

He let me pull him up and was clutching my hand so hard I'd have trouble flexing it the next day. I led him to a nearby bench and pulled him down to sit next to me. He obeyed, but only reluctantly, much like a kid who does what his mother says but puts up a small fight. His eyes were glued to the horizon, focused and clear. No, he definitely wasn't drunk.

I've never been known for my tact, so I said it right out.

"Were you thinking of jumping?"

He didn't answer right away.

"I had this notion of walking out to those islands." He pointed to the Farallon Islands, twenty-five miles away. In the ocean.

No slurring whatsoever. He didn't say "I had this crazy idea…" or "This may be nuts…" Nope. He was giving serious thought to walking off the cliff like there was a handy-dandy bridge right in front of him. Except there wasn't. This was a sure admission of contemplating suicide if ever I heard it.

"What are those islands out there?"

"The Farallons. The sailors call them the Devil's Teeth Islands and avoid them because of the dangerous shoals. It used to be an outpost for seals until the seal traders slaughtered all of them. It's mostly a home for sea birds now. Some fools sail out there to harvest the rocks for their eggs. Unsurprisingly, those sailors have short lifespans."

"I could sail there without a problem. I'm a pretty good sailor."

I didn't like the sound of his voice. Detached didn't quite cover it. He was speaking in the first person, but as if he were speaking of someone else. Someone he knew in the past. I gripped his hand tighter, terrified he'd let go of my hand and just walk off the cliff. He wasn't here on this planet, or didn't want to be.

"Mr. Barnes. Look at me." I snapped my fingers twice.

He didn't turn his head. I took hold of his chin and brought his face around to face me. The stubble spouting over his cheeks and chin told me he hadn't shaved since yesterday. His whiskers were rough against my fingers. His eyes were still focused on the Farallons.

"Mr. Barnes. Win. Look at me," I ordered again. He obeyed, albeit reluctantly.

I didn't like what I saw, or what I didn't see was more to the point. No life, his eyes dull. He was so divorced from the here and now, it felt like my fingers were touching a statue, an empty shell. Totally out of my depth, I kept on talking, hoping to bring him back from wherever he was. It wasn't a good place.

"Did you get any sleep last night?"

He shook his head.

"How about you come home with me and get some shut-eye?" I needed to get him away from the edge of the cliff. "Come on, let's go," I urged and stood up, pulling him up to standing.

He was docile by this point and followed me to the parking lot. We held hands the whole way. He got in the passenger seat when I opened the door. I didn't see his car, so he must have walked here from where he lived. Maybe he'd been sitting there all night. He should eat, but it was more important that he get some sleep. I was hoping some z's would drag him back from whatever desperate dreamworld he'd escaped to.

He was silent the entire drive. Once we exited the car, he groped for my hand again. My apartment was so hot, the wallpaper was sweating, but he didn't say anything.

"Let me take your coat," I said, and helped him out of his jacket. "Lie down. I'll get your shoes." He wasn't reacting so much as obeying. It was like talking to a ghost. He lay down facing me, curled up in a tight fetal position. I took off his shoes. He wasn't wearing socks, which I found strange, but I guess if you have lots of money, you can wear or not wear whatever you like.

The only thing he said to me was, "Will you hold my hand?"

"Yes. Now close your eyes."

I closed the blinds against the heat, dragged my easy chair to the edge of the bed, sat down, and propped up my feet on the edge of the mattress. With his left hand cupping his chin, he closed his eyes and held out his other hand. I threaded our fingers together. He fell asleep in less than a minute. I followed him three minutes later. My last thought before I dropped off was, *Eternal rest grant unto her, O Lord, and let perpetual light shine upon her.*

Chapter Sixteen

I woke up three hours later in my bed. Alone. No Barnes. I vaguely remembered being guided onto the mattress, hushed by a soft voice when I protested, and then sighing in gratitude when my head hit my pillow. Despite the open window, the air in my apartment was as hot as an iron, stuffy, heavy, and smelled like charred onions. Mrs. Verbin had burnt her husband's lunch again.

What should I do next? I had no idea where he lived or how to contact anyone connected with him. The man was on the verge of doing something very stupid, or he didn't care if he did something stupid. Dickie would know what to do.

All that coffee had been a mistake. Dizzy from dehydration, I stumbled to the sink and gulped down two glasses of tepid water. It didn't cool me down one iota. I stuck my head under the kitchen tap. Five minutes later, I was toweling my hair dry and felt human again. I put back on the dreaded wool suit and hightailed it to John's Grill in more of a run than a walk, hoping to catch Dickie before he caught a cab back up to the Mark. When did he write? His lunches lasted for at least two hours. I caught him just as he left the restaurant and was about to hop into a cab. He probably had a cab on order every day at 2:00 p.m., Monday through Friday.

"Mr. Vance!" I yelled.

He turned. I don't know what was showing on my face, but he leaned his head into the open door of the cab and said something to the cabbie, who nodded, got out to shut the open door, got back in his cab, and pulled away from the curb. Dickie walked toward me, and, as always on the rare times

I saw him in motion, I privately marveled at how graceful he was. I bet he was a great dancer.

"I take it this is not a 'fancy meeting you here' surprise?"

"No. I need to talk to you. Privately. How about we sit on a bench in Union Square?"

That should be anonymous enough. The restaurant closed down its lunch service at two. Without the background noise of the other patrons, anything Dickie and I said to each other would be overheard by the waiters.

He frowned.

"Is it important? I loathe walking and avoid it at all costs."

I gave him a look.

"Well, if needs must. Now, what dire thing has happened in the twelve hours between two a.m. and two p.m.? Speak. I will be unable to ask questions until we sit down, as I will be fighting back a heart attack."

I wasn't sure he was joking.

At a meander akin to a toddler learning to walk, we made our way up Powell Street. I told him about my encounter at Duggan's Funeral Parlor and how someone else was fronting the bill for Vera's funeral. Had Dickie changed his mind and called Duggan's? If not, I surmised Vera's benefactor might be Winston Barnes. On a hunch, I drove to Lincoln Park. There he was, screwy as all get out and not making a lick of sense. Terrified he was going to take a flying leap off the cliff, I took him back to my place.

Dickie made for the first unoccupied bench we saw and plopped down, panting like a racehorse who'd just won the Preakness, his face a nasty red with rivulets of sweat running down the sides of his face. He held up his hand in a gesture to be silent and pulled out a handkerchief to mop down the sweat. I sat there mute, while sweating and watching the pigeons peck their way across the square.

When he'd stopped panting, he turned to me and said, "Never ask me to do anything that foolish ever again."

There was no shade in Union Square. Normally, this wasn't an issue ten months out of the year. Today we were in full sun at the height of the afternoon, with both of us wearing wool suits. Dickie had stopped sweating, but his face was still the color of a tomato.

"I didn't call Duggan's, although I might put a call into them later this afternoon to arrange my own funeral after that death march."

"Dickie, it was two blocks!"

"Up. Hill. I loathe walking, but I detest hills. Please note."

"Noted with bells on. I'm sorry. So, if you aren't paying for Vera's funeral, then it must be Barnes because he was booby-hatch nuts with guilt. Seriously, Dickie, I thought he was going to dive off that cliff."

"Interesting. It is a possibility to consider. What is your assessment of Mr. Winston Barnes?"

"A nice guy who has a mug for a father. His upbringing doesn't give him options unless those options have him making tons of moola. He told me he wanted to be a teacher, but his father said nerts to that idea and sent him to San Francisco to run Red Cab. I did some research on the Barnes family. Mayflower types. Builders of railroads, owners of banks, and slum lords. This generation's millions are courtesy of the tenements they built by the hundreds. I'm not surprised Barnes had a wingding when he heard of Vera's death. If he knew his father was sending out 'help,' then it's nothing more than a hop, skip, and a jump to conclude that Vera's death was deliberate, even if his father hadn't spelled it out."

"Did he say anything about Vera's death?"

I shook my head. "I'm telling you he was flat-out crazy. He said he was considering walking to the Farallons."

"On water?"

"I guess so. He was a little fuzzy on that point. Can you make a couple of calls to see if he got home okay?"

By this point, the color of Dickie's cheeks, normally the color of a piece of paper, had reverted to its usual deathly white. He eased off his hat, wiped the top of his brow, and studied his hat, stained with sweat.

"I shall send one of my minions to check up on him. A fake telegram usually does the trick." He sighed. "Another hat ruined. Have I told you how much I dislike the sun? I like my stars twinkly and very distant, not hot and near. By the way, I phoned our friend in Chicago this morning, but he's out of town until next week. I left a message for him to call me straight away."

I waited for him to tell me to back off. To go back to my typewriter. I braced myself.

"I want you to keep the money. No arguments. First, I owe you funds for your discovering what lies at the heart of Herman's malaise. Although I said at the beginning of our collaboration that I could not finance you, I believe you would be wasted either as a secretary or a housewife. You are smart and fearless, and it would be a shame for you to fail just because you did not last the year it will take to build your reputation."

My hand went to Nick's telegram in my pocket.

"I'll pay you back," I insisted.

"A topic for another time. Now, what are your next steps?"

"I thought I'd pay my respects to Vera at her house."

"Hence the suit. And catalog who is there?"

"It's a long shot, but whoever shoved her off the curb might decide to pop by and pay their respects. Also, I want to see if Vera told her family about her relationship with Barnes. Herman didn't know, which tells me she didn't tell anyone, but I want to make sure. Barnes might as well have 'Episcopalian' tattooed on his forehead. Her people wouldn't approve of their marriage, no matter how rich he was. So I think she kept her lips zipped about him until she had a ring, and it was *a fait accompli*."

He stood up and kissed me on the top of my forehead.

"Be careful," he warned. Again.

I watched him cross the street to the front of the St. Francis Hotel. His cab was waiting for him to drive him the four blocks up Powell to his suite at the Mark Hopkins Hotel.

Chapter Seventeen

Vera's body lay in a silk-lined coffin on top of the family's dining room table. The mirrors had been covered in black cloth, and the walls were adorned with icons of Jesus and Mary, and Mary and Joseph holding baby Jesus, the gold leaf on the paintings shining in the soft light. Candles lit up what I imagined was a perpetually dark room; this house faced north with few windows. Every surface in the small living and dining rooms was covered in vases filled with masses of white mums, dahlias, and hydrangeas. Between the heat, the heavy scent of the candles, and the overpowering aroma of the flowers, I wondered how long I could stand there in vigil without passing out. No sign of Barnes, I didn't expect him. I doubted he even knew where she lived. She'd have been too embarrassed to tell him. No matter how beautiful she was, it couldn't compete with the smell of cabbage, the chickens squawking in the yards, the shotgun shacks, and the sheer grinding poverty of her neighborhood.

Vera had been dressed in virginal white, a sad replacement for the wedding dress that was her destiny. Her face showed no trauma, and it was devoid of the garish undertaker's paint of the dead. As yet, her beauty remained. She was still and forever young. People filed past her and kissed her forehead while laying a white flower in the coffin. Black-clad mourners huddled in groups against the backdrop of the white flowers. Old people stood quiet, stoic, resolute, and with an air of resignation as if to remind everyone, it's not only the old who die. Young women hugged each other, crying quietly as they tried to comfort one another. Some of them resembled Vera and were obviously related, others were friends. I recognized several of her co-workers.

Seeing these young women mourn their sister, cousin, or friend reminded me that I hadn't been out with my friends in ages. Since I'd started working for Nick, my day has been filled with bank robbers, confidence men, and women on the make. My world was foreign to them, the stuff of movies. Not real. They wouldn't know what to make of someone like Dickie Vance, and if I'd told them that Eileen Taylor was evil, they'd think I was exaggerating because there's always confession and redemption. This gap between us gradually widened as our lives kept diverging, with me talking about bootleggers while they talked about their boyfriends becoming bankers, lawyers, or doctors. I wasn't interested in filling my hope chest with embroidered hand towels or window shopping for wedding sets. Nor did I care if Mickey Handley liked me, and I didn't think Liam Flannagan was cute. He looked like a potato with hair. Wedding talk bored me. Most of them were now married, and some even had children. And when I reached out to them, they couldn't get babysitters, or they were on dates with their fiancés, or…or…or…I couldn't help but wonder if it were me lying in that casket, whether my friends would be crying together in grief or trying to hide the confusion on their faces because they didn't know the woman lying in her coffin.

Vera was surrounded by people who loved her but didn't understand her. Would she have bucked all this tradition and turned her back on her faith for Winston Barnes? Dollars to donuts, the icons, the relative poverty, and the old faith with its rigid precepts wouldn't fly with Park Avenue. I might be Catholic while Vera was Orthodox, but we shared a world, both nurturing but stifling, rich with tradition but hidebound, and close-knit but claustrophobic.

I spied Herman standing against a wall, talking with the only person who looked out of place, a tall man on the other side of thirty with auburn hair. Herman's face had lost that perpetual serenity and gentleness usually characterizing him. I doubted it would ever return. Had Vera lived, he would have worked his fingers to the bone to win her back, which was hopeless as she'd abandoned more than just Herman himself, but he didn't know that.

Now, he didn't even have a snowball's chance in hell.

I walked up to him and put a hand on his shoulder. "Herman, I'm so sorry," He replied in the standard platitude I was finding increasingly irritating. "She's in a better and holy place, miss."

I nodded because that's what one does. Privately, I reject that notion. To this day, I resented my father's death when I was barely a teenager. I have yet to hear a justification that made sense to me. His death meant Al had to take up a paper route to put food on the table. My mother needed my salary as a secretary to keep our home from foreclosure. *We must accept God's will* isn't good enough for me, but I keep it to myself.

"Miss Laurent, this is Tom Morgan."

I held out my hand.

"Pleased to meet you, Mr. Morgan."

"My friends call me Tommy."

He didn't grab my hand so much as slide his palm across mine and match our fingers one to one before curling them around the width of my hand.

"Have we met before?" we said simultaneously and laughed together.

The lilt of his voice told me he was Irish, from the south like my mother. His accent—although similar—was nasally and sharp.

"You're from Limerick."

"Good catch. What would an American girl like you know about me being from Limerick?" He flashed a grin at me. It was one of those crooked smiles you see on children but rarely on adults. And he had dimples. And deep green eyes and a pale complexion that wasn't too pale. And high, nice cheekbones. And a bit of a pointed chin so that when he smiled, he looked a little impish.

I returned his smile with one equally flirty.

"My mother's Irish. My friends call me Maggie."

"Maggie it is."

I realized we were still holding hands. I pulled away, reluctantly. We eyed each other. Something was happening. He broke eye contact first and turned to Herman.

"I'm really sorry about Vera, Herman. Will light a candle for her, sure. See you soon. Nice to meet you, Maggie." He tipped his hat at me and walked toward the front door with the physical grace of a natural athlete. His hand was on the doorknob when he turned around and looked right at me, his gaze thoughtful and, I thought, surprised. He put his hat on, well back on his head so I could see his face, and then he winked at me before slipping out the door.

The word "wait" was on my lips, but he was gone. Who was this man? I turned to Herman.

"Mr. Morgan, is he a cabbie, too?"

Herman shook his head. "Just a friend. Thanks for coming, miss."

"Mr. Vance sends his regrets and told me to tell you how sorry he is about Vera," I said in a low voice.

"That's nice. Did you have a chance to talk with her?"

"Yes, I did," I admitted. "But she told me she didn't think you two would be happy together."

Which was sort of true. There didn't seem to be any point in telling him about Winston Barnes. Talk about rubbing salt into wounds.

"She was wrong," he said with a vehemence I'd never heard from him.

During this whole exchange, Herman's eyes had never left Vera's coffin. Even when introducing me to Tommy Morgan, he kept his gaze fixed on her. He had the ring she'd returned to him on a length of string around his neck and was fingering it as if it were a rosary.

Although desperate to escape so much sorrow and the now-revolting smell of the flowers as the heat in the rooms increased, I needed to do three more things before I could leave. I said goodbye to Herman and told him I hoped to see him soon. He nodded but didn't commit to any day or date, which I took as a bad sign. Then, I made my way to where Vera's co-workers were huddled together, clutching their handkerchiefs.

"Hi, I'm a friend of Herman's. Are you friends of the family?" I lied, knowing full well that the three of them were Vera's co-workers at The White House.

The stealer of perfume started crying, and it was the brunette selling handbags who spoke up.

"All of us worked with Vera at The White House. She sold gloves." Vera had already been relegated to the past tense. She gestured with her handkerchief. "Susan here sells scarves, I sell handbags, and Nancy sells perfume. I'm Anne. Nice to meet you."

I stuck out my hand. "Maggie. Nice to meet you, too. This is so horrible."

They all nodded, and the tears began again.

"Vera was the nicest person," Anne said around her tears.

"That's what Herman says. He's pretty busted up right now. I can't figure out why she gave him back her ring. Do you know? Did she meet someone else?"

A silent semaphore went among the three women, how much to say and how to say it so Vera didn't come across as common or cheap.

Nancy spoke first. "We were all shocked when she appeared at work one day with no ring on her finger. She was pretty mum about it, but we were pretty sure there was someone else."

"Any idea who the new guy was?"

All three of them shook their heads.

"We never met him. He must have been from money. She'd come into work wearing the most beautiful gardenias." Anne signed in envy. "So maybe not such a surprise she ended it with Herman. It's just… We like him a lot. Herman's a good egg, the nicest guy. Why wouldn't she want to marry him?"

"He's a sweetheart," I agreed.

Susan said, "I remember the day she came to work and showed us all the ring. She was bursting with happiness."

"When did they become engaged?"

Like I didn't know. In every other conversation we had, Herman had never failed to remind me when they got engaged. He'd practically carved the date on my arm.

"About two years ago?" Susan looked at her co-workers for confirmation.

"And then…I don't know," said Nancy. "In the last few months, she'd snap at you if you even mentioned Herman's name. She wasn't mean or anything," she backpedaled. "Just that it was over, and she was sad about it, but that was that."

I certainly didn't blame her for ending the engagement. You can't marry someone out of pity. I shook their hands again, but this time in a goodbye, and repeated the condolences I'd said several times that morning.

All three were roughly my age, dressed in their Sunday best. Like me, they'd spent a small fortune on their hats but carried cheap purses. I grew up with these types of women. Good Christian women, hard-working, some nicer than others, some plain, some good-looking, some with the tendency to become doormats to their husbands, and some who'd insult their husbands in public and humiliate them in private. All so different but relatively content with the cards life had dealt them. I wondered what made Vera different, made her see very quickly that Barnes was her ticket to a sophisticated world where she wasn't behind the counter but in front of it, which made her sound mercenary. Everything I'd heard about her from Herman belied that, but he wasn't exactly unbiased. She believed she had the right to climb out from behind her counter, her metaphorical cage. All she needed was the opportunity, and along came Win Barnes.

I had no problem in singling out Vera's parents among the mourners. Their faces, slack with shock and disbelief, stared at their daughter lying in her coffin. She couldn't be dead. She wasn't going to be buried in two days. They were so dazed, they weren't even crying. That would come later. I remember when my father died. I didn't cry for six months, and then I couldn't stop crying for another six months. I repeated my condolences one more time and fled the house. In the cab ride back to my apartment, I used the buttons on my suit jacket to say a rosary in her honor. The rituals of Vera's faith might be different from mine, but prayers are universal. Like grief.

Chapter Eighteen

s soon as I reached my apartment, I called the D.A.'s office. It was almost closing time, and I hoped he was still there. Matt Doyle's secretary told me he had only five minutes to spare. Could I make it down to City Hall within the next twenty minutes? Typical power play on his part. Aside from the mayor, I bet he pulled this nonsense on everyone. I gave serious thought to arriving well after the twenty-minute deadline, but now was not the time to be petty. Vera's death demanded I ignore his machinations. This was bigger than my ego, and I hoped it would be bigger than his.

Doyle and I had clashed repeatedly as the Washington case unfolded, but we came to an uneasy truce once the bodies began to stack up. We respected each other, but I wouldn't say we trusted each other and tended to lock horns every time we met. I was always telling him things he didn't want to know, and he wasn't telling me things I wanted to know. I didn't expect this meeting to go any differently. Still, I needed to raise a red flag at a minimum.

Doyle's secretary greeted me with a big smile before picking up the telephone and announcing my presence. A bleached blonde who favored very red lipstick and tight skirts, Stella King was Doyle's official gatekeeper. Doyle's predecessor had a penchant for bleached blondes, and Stella was a holdover from the previous administration. Doyle had kept her, so she must be competent, but she never struck me as particularly bright. She fluttered her hand before returning the phone to the receiver, so there was no way to miss the rock on her right hand. I guess she figured that dislodging the current Mrs. Doyle and becoming Mrs. Doyle II was hopeless, so she hooked some other sap.

"Congratulations, Stella." I pointed in the direction of her hand.

She simpered, said the usual stuff when someone gets engaged, held out her hand so I could admire her ring, smiled some more, and then said, "He'll see you now."

I went in.

At the sight of me, he stood up and indicated with his hand for me to sit down. He pulled out his cigarette case and lit one up.

"Hello, Maggie. How are you?" he asked, eyeing me with concern, but he was smiling. It wouldn't be too long before I wiped that grin off his face.

"Peachy. You don't look so hot, Doyle."

Most people would peg Matthew Doyle as handsome in that brown-eyed, black-haired Irish sort of way. In his late thirties or early forties, he didn't need any pointers on how to wear a suit. Politically astute and exceptionally well-connected—as in related by marriage to the current mayor—he was smart and knew it. And if you weren't sure of how smart he was, he'd papered the walls of his office with a bunch of impressive degrees he'd received from various educational institutions. Today, brackets of exhaustion framed his mouth, and his eyes were a little bloodshot. I didn't think it was from cigarette smoke.

"New baby. Kid came out screaming and hasn't stopped for a solid week."

"Congratulations. Boy or girl?"

"Boy." Exhausted or not, he couldn't hide the pride in his voice. What is it about men and their sons? I didn't get it. Kids are kids. "What brings you in today? You know, every time you come into this office, someone is about to be murdered or has been murdered. Which is it?"

He was joking.

"Murdered."

I was not.

He didn't roll his eyes, but he wasn't exactly on the edge of his seat.

"Who and when?" he asked and yawned.

"Vera Kowalski, yesterday, at the corner of Market and Third. Someone pushed her off the curb and, conveniently, a cab ran over her. She was dead by the time they reached San Francisco General. She was on her way to work at The White House."

He rolled his eyes.

"Jeez, Maggie, it happens four times a month at that corner." He looked at his watch.

"Okay, in the three minutes I have left, I'll spell it out for you. First, Vera used to be engaged to a guy who's a cabbie for DeSoto."

"One of Vance's boys?"

My spine stiffened. I made a mental note to tell Dickie that City Hall had the dope on his relationship with various cabbies.

"No," I lied. "I have no idea what you mean." I enjoyed lying to Doyle, as I bet he enjoyed lying to me. "Second, she drops the fiancé and starts dating a guy named Winston Barnes, who was giving her the fast pitch."

He sat up.

"Yeah, figured you knew him. No one else is in on the news, but the house dick at the Palace Hotel verified that Barnes has been squiring her around for the last few months. I saw them, Doyle, with my own eyes, the pair of them looking pretty cozy. So far, everything's hunky-dory except Barnes is being cagey about being seen with her. The house dick told me Barnes always booked their table in outer Siberia. They practically needed guide dogs to find their way. I'm certain she hadn't told her family she had a new beau. Barnes wouldn't cut the mustard with them. How am I doing on time?"

"Cut the sarcasm. Win Barnes is a hell of a nice guy, and his family essentially prints money. Why wouldn't her family approve?"

"The Barnes family earns its money on the back of the zillions of tenements they own, but I digress. Her family lives in the Western Addition. Orthodox is too mild a word for it. How would your family react if you brought home a fabulously wealthy woman, but she was Jewish?"

"I get your point." He rolled his hand. "Go on."

He was interested now. His cigarette would singe his fingers in a moment.

"I don't know if Barnes is interested in her or not. What he *is* interested in is DeSoto. In between piling on the charm with a shovel, he grilled her about DeSoto's business practices. Her boyfriend had bent her ear for a couple of years about how DeSoto operated. You know, shop talk."

He shook his hand as the cigarette burned his thumb and forefinger. He threw it into the ashtray and lit another.

"Maggie, you can't come in here and start accusing—"

"Listen, you Irish lug. The Barnes family buys Red Cab. His father sends Win out west to run the company. Pop wants to bust the union gains from 1921 and 1922, but he also wants to join forces with DeSoto and wipe out the competition. I hear Waters is more interested in selling cars than busting unions. He's not yet buying what Barnes is selling but is sitting on the sidelines watching things unfold for now."

Moving forward on his seat, his backside on the edge, he began to take harsh, brief pulls off the cigarette. I had him.

"Smiling Tim's campaign for the governor's seat come this November won't appreciate a massive cabbie strike any time between now and November. Barnes, Sr., lives on the East Coast and doesn't give a fig about Smiling Tim's prospects for Sacramento. If Barnes can destroy the unions while also putting a serious dent in DeSoto's dominance of the cabbie trade in town, it's a win-win for Barnes. He hires Pinkertons to scope out the competition, and they see this run-of-the-mill cabbie engaged to a woman who makes Louise Brooks look homely."

At the word "Pinkertons," his lips thinned. It was the only tell I saw, but it told me enough.

"Barnes, Sr., instructs his son to sweet-talk Vera, but I'm guessing this strategy isn't working fast enough. Even the kids hawking the newspapers down on Market Street know Red Cab is hemorrhaging money, partly because Pops bought the company for top dollar before the stock market crash, and partly because Win is lousy at his job. You with me, Doyle?"

He nodded. This was ringing bells and not ones he wanted to hear.

"How do you know he sent out the Pinkertons? Did Moore contact you?"

I ignored the question about Nick.

"Pinkertons are involved. Tell me different," I said.

His lips got thinner.

"This next part is just a hunch. Vera discovers that Win Barnes is only sweet-talking her for information on DeSoto. She confronts him and threatens to, oh, I don't know, set up a meeting with Waters? Go to the newspapers? Either scenario is not going to play well with Barnes, Sr. Win calls his pop in a panic. I'm guessing Pinkerton has already salted local labor unions with undercover snitches, and one of them got his marching orders. Pop Barnes didn't care how Vera was silenced; he just wanted it done and fast before she blabbed to the newspapers."

"This is all specula—"

"The day after her confrontation with Win Barnes, someone pushes her off the street corner into an oncoming—"

"Aren't you jumping to conclusions here? There wasn't anything in the newspapers about it."

He didn't say it like I was jumping to conclusions, but I guess he had to put up some fuss for form's sake. I rolled my eyes so hard my eyebrows complained.

"The *Examiner* adores stories like this. Someone put the muzzle on this story. It might even have come down from Hearst himself. Normally, they'd have had ten reporters at her house, photographing her in a coffin, beautiful in her white dress, surrounded by flowers, interviewing her family and friends. A Red Cab ran her down, Doyle. Use your noggin! All this is connected. I might be wrong on the tiny stuff, but on the big picture?" I spread my hands out. Pinkertons aren't exactly Boy Scouts, Doyle. Shoving a twenty-two-year-old woman under a moving vehicle would be all in a day's work for them."

He dropped the cigarette into his ashtray and cursed. Rubbing the burn mark with his thumb, he said, "How do you know Win Barnes wasn't courting her for real?"

"Well, I imagine his fiancée back in New York might have something to say about it," I said dryly. "Big wedding slated for this June. Vera didn't take my news very well."

"You spilled the beans?"

Mary, Mother of God, give me patience.

"No, I didn't *spill* the beans, as you so eloquently put it. I told a young woman being courted by a man currently engaged to another woman that she was being played. I didn't have to spell out the grift, but she was a smart cookie and figured it out pretty quick."

Doyle got up from his desk and went over to his window to look out on Van Ness.

"Any proof?" he said out of the side of his mouth.

"Not yet," I replied.

I had no intention of telling him about Barnes trying to hop, skip, and jump to the Farallons just yet. If Doyle knew the family, he might tell them I'd saved their son from taking a stroll off a cliff into the Pacific Ocean. Better not have anyone around bearing witness to Barnes' breakdown over Vera's death. I might find myself shoved under a cab.

He whipped around. "Stay out of this one, Maggie. Do you hear me?"

I stood up and made my way to the office door. I turned around. "I just spent the last two hours at a vigil for Vera. You know me well enough to know I'm not going to let this slide. If you let thugs like the Pinkertons start murdering innocent people in this town, you and the mayor might as well resign. You're ceding control to them. Don't be a fool. Look for the cabbie who ran her down. Bet he's on vacation right now. Or in a ditch with a bullet in the back of his head."

Shaking with anger, I could barely wrap my hand around the doorknob. I slammed it shut, hoping it would wake him up.

Chapter Nineteen

I returned to the office to check the answering service and to see if I had any mail. No one wanted to hire me, but numerous car dealerships were offering deals galore for yours truly. The lack of work and my confrontation with Doyle left me as cranky as a bag of weasels, and instead of raiding my meager larder, I had dinner at the Pig n' Whistle and spent money I shouldn't have.

A decent night's sleep didn't erase the cranky. I felt the distance from my family the most on the weekends. Aside from my daily one-minute phone call with my mother, no one in my family had contacted me since Nick had left town, not even a distant cousin. I was *persona non grata*. The nuns had castigated me as willful, ungrateful, obstinate, and headstrong as they dragged me by the ear along the hallways while lecturing me on how *bad* children went to hell, and if I didn't mend my ways, I'd spend eternity in agony from hell's fire. No doubt, all my relatives repeated those same epithets while socializing after mass, standing close enough to my mother so she'd hear them gossiping about me.

I'd stopped going to the church where I'd been a parishioner all my life and now attended Notre Dame des Victoires on Bush Street. The mass at Notre Dame was said in Latin, but the priests were French. The voice of one particular priest reminded me of my father's. As I listened to the rise and fall of the elegant Latin, I wondered if he'd be disappointed in me, too. I honestly didn't know. With the hindsight of an adult, I could see he was a fairly average man. He believed in God, was dedicated to his patients, had a bit of a temper he was ashamed of, was adept at any sport he took up, and adored my mother. I'd inherited my height, looks, and physical acumen from him, plus a distinctly Gallic way of looking at life through a slightly sardonic lens.

He'd left his small town in France for the lights and sounds of a city whose Barbary Coast district was more notorious than even the most dissolute alleys of Marseilles. Did he ever regret emigrating so far away? I remembered the grimace on his face as he'd read the weekly letters from his mother begging him to return home. Would he have shunned me, too? My heart said no. But with no one to hand me a hymnal or nudge me along the aisle to get the best seats, this was cold comfort on yet another hot morning while I stood, knelt, and crossed myself as I'd done for twenty-odd years. But alone. As I filed out the door of the small church, I couldn't help but ask myself if it was worth it.

After mass, I drove back home, changed, and took the streetcar to the golf course to caddy for the morning. I was assigned a surgeon who was one of the worst golfers I'd ever met. Fortunately, he was a good sport about it. This guy liked walking around the course, laughing with his fellow doctors about his abysmal shots, and winking at me now and then to let me know he knew it was just a game. The morning went by quickly. The surgeon gave me a decent tip, and I had money weighing down my pocket for the first time in what felt like ages.

Walking toward Geary to catch the streetcar home, I heard a car pull up next to me and call my name.

"Hey, Maggie, you want a lift home?" It was Ted Stevens, another caddie.

"You bet," I said and hopped in. That would save me some jack.

Ted drove a sleek Riley convertible you don't see too much of on the streets of San Francisco. Fresh off the boat from England, you could hear the car yawning in boredom as it took our hills without so much as a whimper. Ted should have been wearing an Ascot, and I a hat with a brim the size of Mars.

Ted wrote novels when he wasn't carting golf bags over the links. None of these books had a plot—he'd written about five of them—and characters killed off in chapter three would appear again in chapter twenty. Strange, stream-of-consciousness stuff leaped from what he had for breakfast that morning to ruminations on the Knights Templar, all on the same page, hopping from one disconnected thought to another. He knew they were unreadable, but he didn't care. He liked to write.

By his appearance—his arms as skinny as wire coat hangers, his posture appalling, and balding although not even forty—you'd never know he was an ace golfer. Supported by a trust fund, he didn't need to work for the peanuts we earned as caddies. I asked him once why he bothered, and he replied, "Caddying gets me out of the house. Mother's been on an incense kick lately and it's killing my sinuses." He lived in a huge Victorian in Cow Hollow with his parents, who were pillars in San Francisco high society and followers of whatever crackpot cult grabbed their fancy.

Their current shyster of the moment was a con man named The Amazing Victor. Pronounced "Veek-Twar," he blew into town about two years ago and took the money set by storm. The file cabinet in my office had a drawer filled with information on grifters, confidence men, bunco artists, and counterfeiters. Eddie Wójcik, aka The Amazing Victor, had a prison record as long as the California coastline. After a few stints in Joliet for bank robbery, he wised up. He graduated from robbing banks to fleecing rich people. He changed his name to The Amazing Victor—as in victory over death, cornball to the max—and claimed to be a bridge between this world and the next via your bank account. Nick thought he was harmless. A fool and his money…

I'd attended one of his séances last year, and I had to pinch myself throughout the whole "show" to keep from laughing. Ted's mother had changed her name from Marjorie to Alexandra-Queen-of-the-Dark-Mist, all one word. Ted told me his father, Clarence, wasn't as dedicated to Victor's schtick as his mother, but his father was happy to play along. Anything that made his mother happy, made his father happy. Ted knew his parents were goofy, but it didn't bother him.

I didn't know what to wear to a séance, so I wore what was then my best suit. I was both woefully overdressed and underdressed simultaneously. Alexandra-the-Queen-of-the-Dark-Mist and all the guests, including the men, wore floor-length caftans in gold brocades, red velvets, and turquoise silks. Ted and I were the only people in "normal" clothes. Victor was a hoot. He had a white beard down to his waist—clearly fake—and his purple velvet caftan was embroidered with gold and silver stars of varying sizes. His hat was also purple velvet and pointed like a witch's hat. Clouds of white hair flowed over his shoulders and down his back. He held a staff covered in gold sparkles that he pounded on the floor when calling the "spirits."

Ted and I stood in the far back of the large salon near the door so I could flee the room if I started laughing uncontrollably. I had to give it to The Amazing Victor. He'd honed his grift to a tee. He kept his revelations with the spirits specific enough for me to suspect that he researched the background on his marks before he agreed to "commune" on their behalf, but vague enough so he wouldn't get caught telling whoppers. All of the spirits were happy, or they were on the verge of becoming happy. None of them were sad or had regrets. Life on the other side was wonderful, and they were universally grateful for having left this mortal coil. As a final parting, Victor always stressed how much the dead spirit loved the person requesting the séance.

I'd told Ted about Victor and his numerous stints in Joliet. He said his father was wise to the grift but didn't care. His father had a monthly "budget" on how much he would let Victor siphon off, and he enjoyed entertaining. Plus, he liked wearing caftans.

I returned his greeting. "Hey, yourself. I saw you hanging around the first hole. Didn't your guy turn up?"

"Naw. He'll make good, though. He's a nice guy."

A hinky feeling crawled up the back of my neck.

"Winston Barnes?"

"Yeah, you know him?"

"Sort of. Terrible golfer. Not as bad as the doc I just caddied for, but pretty bad."

Ted rolled his eyes. "He's the worst, I agree. A few weeks ago, I'd told Barnes about my parents and their penchant for séances and Ouija boards. He called up Mother yesterday, asking when the next séance was. He's coming to our house tonight and will make my time good then. Veek-Twar is holding one of his dog and pony shows."

Strike me down with a feather. Barnes didn't strike me as the dramatic type.

"Barnes buys that claptrap?"

"That's the weird thing. When I first told him about it, he thought it was a bunch of malarky, and we had a good laugh about it. His mother communes with the spirits, and although polite about it, Barnes made it obvious he thinks she's a screwball. I guess he changed his mind. Want to come? There'll be lots of food."

The words were out of my mouth before he could take a breath.

"What time?"

There was only one reason for Winston Barnes wanting to speak to the dead. To apologize to Vera.

Chapter Twenty

Rifling through my closet and finding it singularly lacking in caftans, I put on my best suit and arranged my best hat at a decidedly dangerous angle. I drove the roadster to Ted's house on Steiner in Cow Hollow. This area had been shaken pretty badly during the 1906 earthquake. The force of the earthquake had bent the streetcar lines like they were made of taffy. The fires hadn't reached this far, and wood-frame houses are a damn sight better at weathering earthquakes compared to brick. The neighborhood is called Cow Hollow because once upon a time, the city's dairy farms were located here. Some nights, Ted claims he can hear the lowing of phantom cows as they are being driven into phantom barns. Of course, this is the same man who believes there's a rational connection between his morning toast with marmalade and the Crusades.

Ted answered the doorbell in his usual tweeds and school tie, and I stifled a tiny sigh of relief. If he'd appeared in a caftan, I'd have fled down the stairs without uttering a word.

"You're just in time. The fun's about to begin," he whispered, rubbing his hands together in anticipation.

The spirits had been very kind to The Amazing Veek-Twar since the last time I'd seen him. He'd ditched the purple velvet and had upgraded his fake beard and wig; less like dyed horse hair and more like human hair. Now, he was resplendent in what can only be called vestments: skirts over skirts and mantles over mantles of exceptionally expensive brocades in various colors of cream, which should have clashed but didn't. His pointed witch's hat had been forsaken for a square hat resembling a bishop's miter. The robes, miter, and staffs were sheer blasphemy, but it did solidify the impression that Victor's floor show was legit, and not a load of bunkum being peddled by a former bank robber wearing a velvet caftan.

The last time I saw Victor's act, he was plying his grift solo. Since then, an assistant had been added to the original con, a woman who was barely twenty if she were a day. Dressed like a nun in a plain white habit with Ophelia-like blonde tresses down to her waist, the bored expression on her face told me she wanted to drown herself and fast. She was clutching a bunch of staffs, now in numerous colors, elaborately carved, and painted with gold leaf. This girl was clearly Victor's latest twist. Ted's mother kept glaring at her and then at Victor in a proprietary way. I'd say Alexandra-the-Queen-of-the-Dark-Mist wasn't too pleased about this latest turn of events. Clarence was either oblivious to his wife's infatuation with this con man or didn't care. The girl ignored her.

I'm glad I didn't spend the money to buy a caftan because his acolytes were now clothed in what looked like fancy togas, but not cheap togas made out of worn bedsheets, mind you. Nope. white silk all the way. The edges of these costumes were embroidered with gold thread, and the waists of the wearers were cinched tight by gold lame belts. Only half of the room wore togas. The rest of the guests didn't get the memo on the dress code. The men wore morning coats and the women were dressed in the latest gowns by Calliot and Worth. This was a recruitment drive under the guise of a fancy dress party.

Alexandra-the-Queen-of-the-Dark-Mist's toga was a sight to behold. Gold threads ran through the fabric and danced in the candlelight when she moved, giving the impression that she might ascend right there and then to the great beyond. She'd crowned her dark hair with a tiara of interlocking stars made of gold.

Ted and I stood at the back of the room. Clarence was seated in a chair near us. Whatever he was drinking was plastering a broad smile on his face.

"Your mother looks great," I whispered to Ted.

"She loves to dress up," he confessed.

The script hadn't changed much since last year. It was the same song and dance but with the addition of the assistant, who was called upon to hand him a different staff depending on the wealth of the customer asking for a "session" into the beyond. The better the clothes, the gaudier the staff. At certain points in the show, she'd stand behind Victor, purse her lips very slightly, and blow air, causing the candles near Victor to dance, signaling his "connection" with the other world. A natural actor, Victor's deep basso voice was simultaneously commanding and gentle. Even the guests not dressed in togas were soon mesmerized. His bank account would be pretty well set by Sunday night.

The Amazing Victor was only one of many so-called "spiritualists" who flooded big cities after the Great War. Nick thought they were mostly con artists in search of patsies desperate to communicate with the dead. Thousands of American soldiers were buried in cemeteries in France, England, and Belgium. I understood the appeal of someone like Victor. If you fall for his schtick, he opens a tiny door to the afterlife, giving grieving relatives the opportunity to say "I love you" one last time.

Or apologize and say how sorry they were.

I scanned the room for Win Barnes. He was standing against the opposite wall, wearing the same clothes I'd seen him in two days ago. His dress shirt still had whiskey stains down the front, and the wrinkles in his pants had wrinkles on top of wrinkles. He stood there blinking uncontrollably, his hands twitching and kneading the fabric of his pants. If possible, he looked even more disheveled than when I had seen him at Lincoln Park about to nosedive into the surf. I was about to whisper in Ted's ear that I wanted to talk to Barnes when Win interrupted Victor's schtick and shouted, "I need you to talk to Vera, Victor."

Victor must be used to strange outbursts—those unruly spirits—as he turned toward Barnes with an air of benevolence and concern. No doubt, Veek-Twar had scoped out the guest list, and if he could add Win Barnes' name to his list of marks, his bank account would be very happy.

Barnes began shouting even louder, "I need to know if she's happy and if she forgives me for hurting her."

People began to whisper to one another. This was Barnes' social set. Most of the people in this room knew him, and he was having a nervous breakdown right in front of them. I crossed the room in something less than a run but faster than a walk and took his hand. It was clammy, and when I wrapped my fingers around it, his pulse pounded against my palm. It was rapid and far too strong. Then Barnes dropped his chin onto his chest and began to shake ever so slightly. I was amazed the man was still standing.

"Please, Victor," I said in a calm voice. "What do the spirits say about Vera?"

You don't maintain a first-class grift without being on the ball. Victor sized up the situation immediately and segued his usual spiel about how happy Vera was, how she forgave Barnes, and to please let her go. Victor didn't know she was being buried in the morning, but it didn't matter.

Barnes gave a little sob and fell against me. Ted rushed over to help me keep him upright. Ted's mother came up to me and said in a harsh whisper that was very unspiritual, "Get him out of here, Ted. Upstairs. The maids' room near the back of the attic. Now," she hissed.

We were ruining the show.

With Clarence's help, we managed to get Barnes up two flights of stairs. Barnes was snoring before his head even hit the pillow. After removing his shoes and covering him with a spare blanket, I turned to Ted's father.

"Thank you, Mr. Stevens," I said. "An acquittance of his just died, and he's taking it hard."

"I'll speak to him in the morning about laying off the whiskey," slurred Mr. Stevens.

I blinked as bourbon fumes from *his* breath singed my eyelashes. If only it were that simple.

Clarence returned to the party, and Ted and I sat with Win for a bit, making sure he was well asleep. After about forty-five minutes, Ted whispered, "I'll keep an eye on him. If you don't mind, will you bring me a plate of food?"

The floor show had finished by the time I made it downstairs. I began to load two plates piled high with food for Ted and myself when I felt a tap on my shoulder. It was the Amazing Victor.

"I hope your friend is well?" he said in a deep basso voice that I'd bet my last dime was manufactured.

"Thank you. He's asleep. You were very gracious and kind, and I appreciate it."

He bowed and said, "Many people have trouble with the death of their loved ones."

"Yes. I still miss my father these many years later."

How could I be so foolish? That simple admission opened the door for The Amazing Victor to make his spiel about the afterlife, etc. After giving me a quick once-over of my fashionable and expensive outfit, he named a price that would give me peace of mind for good. He'd been wonderful in dealing with Barnes, and I was grateful, but I wasn't going to let him think he had me pegged as one of his marks. I fancied dollar signs where his pupils should have been.

"Thank you, but I attend church five days a week, and God assures me that my father is in heaven. I can't ask for more."

Victor's eyes narrowed and focused on the small cross that never left my neck. It had been a confirmation present from my father.

"You are Catholic?"

I nodded. "I must say, you should send a note to our bishop, letting him know the address of your tailor. Your robes are positively, well, religious in nature."

My dig bounced off of his magnificently clad shoulders without so much as making a dent. He tilted his head and smiled at me.

"Your bishop and I share a treasured role. We both seek to soothe and administer to people's troubled souls."

"While charging them a fortune?"

"I believe the Catholic Church still passes the collection basket every Sunday?"

"Yes, it's much more efficient than robbing banks."

The kindly twinkle of a grandfather vanished and was replaced by the flat eyes of the hard man on the make.

"Listen, sister. I make people happy," he snarled in a low voice with no trace of sonorous basso. "Who's to say I'm not performing a service equal to some priest? The people I help are experiencing a type of miracle. The gift of peace."

There was no point in sparring further. More debating over faith versus grift, and I'd brain him with this plate.

"Yes, Mr. Wójcik, you're right." He flinched at the mention of his real name. "Who can say? Now I must take some food up to Ted. He'll wonder what's keeping me. Thank you again for your kindness towards Mr. Barnes."

He bowed and said, "Your name?"

"Zelda-of-the-Black-Hat. Good night, Mr. Wójcik."

Chapter Twenty-One

While Ted and I ate, I asked him if he wouldn't mind staying with Barnes for the night.

"Sure, no problem," he said. "I'll bunk in the other bed and keep an eye on him. Go home, Maggie. It looks like he hasn't slept in a month of Sundays. He'll probably sleep until tomorrow afternoon. I'll take him home when he wakes up."

I asked Ted to make sure he ate something when he woke up—Barnes' trousers were hanging on his hip bones—and drove back home. A note was shoved into the door frame with my name on it. It was from Doyle, but not written on formal City Hall letterhead. Interesting.

"Stay out of this Red Cab business. Maggie. Please. MD."

He could take a hike. I crumpled it in my hand and threw it in a corner of the room. Before turning out the lights, I sponged down, pressed my best suit, and polished my shoes. Vera's funeral was in the morning.

The weather had finally broken, thank God. It was like the clouds had been cleaved in two with a knife to let the fog back in. I put on my now-hated black suit, called my mother, went to mass, and then took a cab to the Orthodox church where God would hear a host of voices praying for Vera's safe journey to heaven.

I arrived early, but even so, the church was full, and most of the mourners were standing. The few seats available were reserved for the elderly. It felt like the entire population of the Western Addition neighborhood of Russian and Polish immigrants had filled the church. I pressed myself against the back wall of the church into one of the few remaining spaces. The church was awash in white flowers.

The ritual of circling the casket and the kissing of her cheek was repeated. Herman moved toward the casket as if every cell in his body hurt. Stiff and wooden, he bent over the lifeless body of the woman he had so deeply loved. The misery on his face only hardened my resolve to find out who killed her, no matter how dangerous. He shuffled back to where he'd been standing, with two men propping him up, their arms around his shoulders and waist. Based on the faint resemblance in the planes of their cheekbones and broad foreheads, I assumed these two men were his brothers. Funny, I knew nothing about Herman's family. I didn't even know where he lived.

The service took three hours, with most of the attendees standing through all of it. The service wasn't said in Latin, so I couldn't follow it, nor did I try to mimic the rituals. Some were the same, but many weren't. I'd brought my rosary and fingered the beads with the same prayers and meditation as if I were standing surrounded by stained glass windows depicting the Stations of the Cross, as opposed to icons lining the walls. I added the eternal rest prayer immediately following the Fatima prayer. When I'd finished, I made a second vow, entirely un-Christian-like, to bring to justice Vera's killer. I would attend their hanging and ask God to send them straight to hell. No mercy.

I didn't attend the burial at Colma. I had no place there. I'd already received my fair share of questioning glances, much like my parish would question the appearance of a stranger at a funeral mass for a parishioner. The church was so packed, I couldn't see if Vera's co-workers were there, but I suspected not. We weren't part of this community where everyone knew everyone else's family down to third cousins once removed. At least it was like that in my parish. My presence probably wouldn't even register with Herman. He was with his family, and whatever small comfort they supplied would far outstrip my repeated condolences.

I nipped out the door when the service was over. Standing in front of the church was Tommy Morgan, finishing a cigarette.

"All done?"

I nodded. He hiked his thumb in the direction of Van Ness, and we began walking away just as the crowd began surging out of the doors. We didn't speak until we hit a small coffee shop with years of grime on the windows.

He paused at the front door. "Only place open on Sundays around here. You won't get a decent cuppa, but how about some coffee that will burn a hole in your stomach?"

"Just what the doctor ordered."

"Grand."

I breathed through my mouth as he led the way to a booth in the back. The smell of grease was so potent, I lost whatever soupçon of appetite I had. The tabletop looked clean enough, but that was all I could say about the place.

Once we sat down, he asked, "You hungry? Do you want something?"

Normally, I'm not too picky about my food, but I'd have to be near starving to eat here.

"Thanks, but no thanks. I just want to warm up." Although the church was packed to the rafters, I'd become chilled after standing there for hours.

The waitress poured our coffee, and I smelled the burnt-wire smell of a pot having been reheated about twenty times. No matter. It was hot. I wrapped my hands around the cup. As sometimes happens, it was colder now than it had been when I'd woken up. The fog had lifted, and the chill of late October had walked right in on its wake.

"Bit better than these killer hot days we've been having, though." He shivered. "Feels like home."

"How long have you been here?"

"Oh, a while," he replied. "I go back and forth."

"Do you still have family in Limerick?"

"No, not really. Are you good friends with Herman? Seems like an odd fit. You all posh-like," he pointed to the suit, "and Herman being, well, Herman-like."

I took a sip of the coffee and made a face.

"You weren't kidding about it burning a hole in my stomach. Do you think it'd be rude to ask for a fresh cup from a fresh pot?"

"In here? Sure you're joking. Likely they make it once a month and keep reheating what the other customers don't finish."

My eyes widened.

"Just kidding you. Say, Mary," he shouted to the waitress behind the counter, a woman with Irish written all over her. "Is coffee made out of peat bog? Could you get us something brewed in this century?"

"For you, Tommy, anything." She grinned at him and began wiping down the counter, ignoring his request.

"Love how she just hops to at your every command."

"Amazing, isn't it? Now, you and Herman."

"Oh, he and my brother spar together. He's teaching me how to box." The less said about Herman, Dickie, and our wee collaboration, the better.

He spat out a mouthful of coffee in surprise and raised his napkin just in time so he wouldn't spray me with that swill.

"You?" He didn't bother to hide his astonishment. "Why would you need to know how to box?"

"You never know. It might come in handy. Do you box?"

"Being known to throw a few punches now and then. Fair enough, I guess," he said with a shrug, deprecating and modest, but I had the distinct impression that he was better than just fair. He was built like my brother, Al, slender and graceful. What he lacked in heft, he'd make up for in speed.

"So, do you drive a cab, too? How do you know Herman?"

"No, good with a hammer and a shovel when I can't get any carpentry work. In the trades. Typical." He grinned and, yes, that was typical of many of the men I knew in the parish.

"Did you know Herman's fiancée? Vera."

"No, not really. I met her just once. Herman talked about her now and then." Like with almost every breath. Spend more than an hour with the man, and he'd bring her up in conversation at least four times. "Have you been in San Francisco long?"

"Not long. It was tragic what happened to her, just tragic," he repeated. "Guess we never know when our number is up. Poor girl."

I didn't say anything because, although it *was* tragic, I'll never believe it wasn't just some random twist of fate.

When I didn't respond in kind, he said, "He'll find someone else. Men like

Herman always find someone else. He's the marrying kind."

"Maybe." I wasn't so sure about that.

To change the mood, I said, "And you, Mr. Morgan? Are you the type of Irishman who never marries or the type who waits until he's fifty and long in the tooth?"

"You got me." He laughed and pointed to himself. "Not planning on getting married. Bit of a ne'er-do-well to be honest. No woman in her right mind would sign on with me."

"Good to know," I said with a flippancy to show I didn't care.

We both laughed, and that strange click between us happened again, the same sense of knowing each other from somewhere. That I'd know how his hand would feel in mine. How it would feel if he ran his hand along my cheekbone. He felt it, too. His eyes widened, and he said, "Are you in your right mind, Maggie?"

He wasn't joking, and he touched my hand, briefly, and then quickly put it back on the table.

I was right. His touch felt familiar and right and warm, even though his hand was cold. It was a couple of seconds before I responded, and then it was light and flirty.

"I'm not the marrying kind either. And you have no idea how in my right mind I am, Mr. Morgan," I teased.

"Good to know," he replied with equal sass. He threw a few coins on the table. "Shall we go before this coffee poisons us into an early grave?"

When he saw the look on my face, he apologized and touched my hand again. "Sorry, that was crass of me. Sometimes I speak before thinking."

I opened my mouth to say something, I hardly know what, and there it was again. That click. That spark. We stared at each other. The green in his eyes began to be eclipsed as his pupils grew. We left the coffee shop hand in hand. We walked a few blocks in silence until I pulled my hand away to hail an oncoming cab.

Neither of us said goodbye. Through the window of the cab, I watched him watching me. Then the cab turned the corner, and I sat back against the seat. I opened the window because all of a sudden an odd heat washed over me, even as I shivered from the cold.

Chapter Twenty-Two

I arrived at the office early on Monday to find a note shoved underneath the door addressed to Nick.

Janie Morris was a typist for Hardesty's, which is shorthand for one of the most prestigious law offices in the city. I'd visited Hardesty last summer pretending I needed a job, when in reality I was trying to get dirt on one of their clients. Janie's supervisor, a miserable old hag if ever I met one, would have had me dragged out of their office by my hair with a pack of snarling dogs nipping at my heels if she could have gotten away with it.

Janie Morris's note read:

Dear Mr. Moore: I need your help in discovering what is going on with my brother. All of a sudden, he's become secretive, and when I ask him what is going on, he yells at me. I am terrified he is involved in something illegal. Although he assures me he isn't doing anything wrong, he still won't tell me what he's up to. I asked some lawyers I know to recommend a detective, and they said you were the best. Can you help me? We've got a phone, but it's on a party line, and I don't want Hank to know I'm asking for your help. I work at Hardesty's and get off at six. Maybe you could meet me at the entrance? That would be best. Sincerely, Jane Morris.

Janie worked in the Flood Building. I'd walk down to meet her this afternoon at the end of her day.

Monday mornings were devoted to boxing lessons with Herman, but in his state of grief, I didn't expect him. I was studying the notes I'd made of the *Examiner*'s files on the Barnes family when I heard a knock on the office door. Tommy walked in. I put a hand to my stomach. All of a sudden, I was breathless.

"What are you doing here, Tommy?"

"What are you doing here, Miss Detective?"

I shoved my notes in the desk drawer.

"I work here. That explains me."

"Never would have figured you for a detective."

"I'm full of surprises."

"Can't wait to find out, but it might have to wait. I'm here in Herman's place. He asked me to give you your lesson this week. Still under the weather, he is. Do you mind?" he said in a low voice.

Delightful shivers ran up my spine. No one had ever talked to me in that sultry tone or if they had, I wasn't interested. I walked over to the cardboard box in the corner containing the boxing gloves, picked out a pair of gloves, and threw them at him. He caught them.

"You seem to be a man of many talents. I don't believe for one second that you're nothing more than fair to middling at boxing. Bet you're going to clean my clock."

He pulled on his gloves very slowly. "As if I'd harm a hair of your beautiful head."

I rolled my eyes.

"Cut the blarney. Flattery isn't going to get you anywhere." I pulled on my gloves and walked over to stand facing him. "Where do we start?" I raised my gloves in a boxer's stance but led with my right hand to fool him that this was my dominant hand.

I waited for him to move, to feint. But he just stood there, studying me.

"What? Is there something wrong?"

He shook his head a couple of times. "No," he said and raised his gloves. "You're so right and yet you're so wrong, Maggie."

We sparred for a few minutes, but neither of us was too serious about it. Although not conscious of it happening, suddenly I found myself with my back against the wall. He'd slowly but surely moved me backward, pinning me until I couldn't reach back to give my punches any momentum.

"Sneaky," I murmured, crossing my arms in front of me. My eyes were focused on his gloves, ready to block his arm when he tried to clip my jaw. Was he going to nail me with his left hand while I watched the right? But he moved his glove slowly up the side of my neck until it rested against my jaw. He drew it along one side of my jaw and then the other, resting it beneath my right ear.

I couldn't move. I half expected the room to erupt in thunder and lightning strikes, the energy between us so thick. I didn't understand this. We'd spoken maybe twenty sentences to each other. I'd met him twice. I had no idea who this man was. Did he drink his tea black? Did he have brothers or sisters? For all I knew, he could be married with a wife and ten children back in Ireland. This was no callow youth with fumbling hands, unsure and embarrassed. I knew nothing about him except that the smell of cigarettes clung to his clothes, and his breath on my cheeks smelled like sweet tea.

I remembered Al and I walking into Philip Washington's speakeasy and seeing his sister sitting at a table in a black wig with her mink coat slung over the back of her chair. And he'd fallen for her, just like that. Before she'd even opened her mouth, she owned him. At the time, I thought he'd lost his mind. My upbringing didn't prepare me for inexplicable attraction. Marriage was presented as a union between two people who might be smitten with each other, and who marched to the altar in lockstep with similar moral codes and goals. This heat between us felt feral and so marvelous, I relished the warmth crawling up my back. Is this sin, knowing that this might be wrong, but not caring, and, even worse, denying to yourself that it's wrong?

He brought his left glove up to my face, holding my jaw in both hands. We locked eyes, and then I did the same. He was taller than me, but it wasn't much of a stretch to lift one arm and then the other to cup his face with my gloves.

"Tommy?"

He leaned toward me and brushed his lips against my ear. "Why did you come into my life, Maggie? Why now?"

"I..." I was speechless and yet with a million questions on my lips.

"Shush. Don't speak. *Is tú, mo chuisle.*"

With my body flush against the wall, I should have felt trapped, that hard flat plane along my back with nowhere to go. I bent my body toward him, soaking up his heat, raising my head as he kissed my neck, the length of my collarbone, my chin, and then finally my mouth.

Oh. So this is what the fuss is about.

He pulled away after a bit and walked back to stand in the opposite corner of the room, watching me the whole time.

Finally, he said, "Let's go for a walk."

My face flamed with embarrassment, every molecule of shame marching up my cheeks to my hairline. "Did I do something wrong?'

He laughed and wiped his brow with his hand. "No, darling. Not at all. Trying my damn best to be a gentleman here, and with all your charms, you're making it nigh impossible. I could use a drink, but that's probably a bad idea. How about we go to Golden Gate Park? Walk around."

"Sure. My car's out front."

"You have a car?" To say he was shocked was an understatement.

"Someone gave it to me as payment for a job." I wrinkled my nose. "Sort of. It's complicated."

So desperate to keep the agency afloat, I hadn't played hooky for weeks. How wonderful it was to lock the office door and leave without a second thought. To skip down the flight of stairs of my office building and hear another's footsteps echo my own. To have someone sit beside me in the car and laugh at my jokes, the two of us flirting back and forth. I kept taking sneak peeks of Tommy's hands resting on his knees, strong-looking hands with long fingers. The sort of hands that could hold a hammer and yet were graceful enough to play the piano. Like many men with buckets of charm, he wasn't classically handsome. In some ways, that was more powerful. Truly handsome men like Win Barnes are untouchable in a way. Tommy's well-defined cheekbones and green eyes were enough. And his smile? Oh boy, his smile. I kept both hands on the wheel, but I wanted to run my finger along his jawline and thread my hands through his hair. I'd never experienced this almost savage want toward a guy where I was a little breathless around him.

We did all the tourist attractions you never do because you're a resident. We rode the carousel. We bought ice cream from a man singing Italian opera as he scooped out our ice cream from a cart. We walked around the Concourse below the de Young Museum. We had tea in the Japanese tea garden to warm up from the ice cream cones. We talked to each other until we were hoarse. He asked me about my upbringing, how my parents had met, about Al, and what I liked to do in my spare time. He asked me about the car, and I told him about the Washington job, sticking to the official version more or less, but it was obvious I was center stage in that mess.

"So, you're trying to make it as a detective? Peeking in windows and the like?"

"Sometimes," I admitted. "But it's more than that. For the last week, I've been studying up on strikes, labor unrest, the Wobblies, and the Communist Labor Party. If the stevedores go out on strike, then the cabbies will honor the picket line."

"Stay out of that business, Maggie. You could get hurt," he snapped at me. Before I could respond, he said, "Wasn't Moore a Pinkerton?"

"Yes, for several years after the war. In Chicago. He's back working for them now. Temp job."

"That's not what I hear. Word is that he's skipped town for good."

"Been checking up on me?" I was coy, but something niggled at the back of my brain.

"Just a bit curious. Asked Herman. I don't know many lady detectives, never mind those with a killer left hook." He wriggled his eyebrows and smiled. The niggle went away. "He left you in charge of the agency?"

"Not really. I worked as his secretary for several years, and then when he left for Chicago, I fell into it. More out of necessity than anything else." I didn't mention the enormous bender Nick had gone on, although it was common gossip by this point. "But I found I liked it. I'm good at it. Through our various cases, I've got contacts all across the country. Ex-Pinkertons mostly."

"You gonna investigate me?" He smiled, but it didn't reach his eyes.

"Not if you behave yourself. Or is it if you don't behave yourself?"

"Say, the fog is rolling in. Shall we call it a day? I just remembered. I've got to see a fella about a job. With any luck, he'll hire me. Plum forgot because of you. I'll be by later this week for another boxing lesson."

"Boxing or kissing?"

"Believe me, Maggie, you don't need pointers on kissing."

He grabbed me by the shoulders, dragged me close to him, and kissed me hard. It was more of a press than a kiss, like he was claiming me. Then he dropped his hands and ran across the Concourse as if on fire.

The words, "I'll drive you—" died on my lips.

Chapter Twenty-Three

I had just enough time to return to my apartment, park the car, and skedaddle over to Market Street to meet Janie as she walked out of the Flood building. Downtown San Francisco at six o'clock is a madhouse. As I walked, I kept well away from the curb and hugged the sides of the buildings as best I could. Weaving my way in and out of the men propped up against the walls of buildings with their hands outstretched for change, I tried not to think about Vera. In a crowd like this, it would be easy-peasy to push someone into oncoming traffic without anyone noticing who'd done it. People were walking fast with their eyes downcast, desperate to get home. Of course, there were no guarantees that such a hit would be fatal, but I'd bet my neck that the Red Cab driver had gunned it as he rounded the corner to make sure Vera wouldn't survive the hit. I never knew that being a detective meant compiling a list of surefire ways to kill people.

As people jostled me in a frantic bid to catch their streetcar, cross a street, or hail a cab, the thought of returning to this frantic five-days-a-week dance—go, go, go to work, then go, go, go home, made me slightly sick to my stomach. My job might mean slinking around hotel corridors or taking pictures of men kissing women who were not their wives, which is tawdry, sure, but sometimes it was bigger than that. If I compare typing up Harold Washington's will versus identifying his killer, who wins? In my book, I do.

I waited for Janie a few storefronts down. Her witch of a supervisor wouldn't free the secretaries from their desks until six on the dot. By the time Janie had covered her typewriter, hit the bathroom, and put on her coat, I figured she'd exit the building at 6:10. Bingo. She didn't even wait until she'd reached a discreet doorway before fumbling through her handbag for a cigarette. My life seemed to be populated by petite blondes. With my height, they always made me feel like a mountain troll hovering over them. Janie, a bubbly blonde who tended to talk in hyperbole, wasn't the exception to the rule. I liked her the second I met her. Sweet, kind, and far too nice to be working at Hardesty's, I'd had visions of hiring her as my secretary, visions that died very quickly as my bank account dwindled.

She was dragging on her cigarette while looking around for Nick.

"Hey, Janie, it's Maggie Laurent."

She blinked a couple of times, and then she smiled. "Maggie, how are you? I'm supposed to meet someone but—"

"Actually, you're meeting me. Let's hit the Pig n' Whistle, and I'll explain everything."

We walked fast, too fast for conversation, with me still hugging the building side of the sidewalk. Although crowded, the waitresses knew me and steered us to a booth in the back. I'd be good for a decent tip.

I insisted Janie order something off the menu as she must be starving because I sure was. She ordered the cheapest sandwich on the menu. I did the same but added two pieces of apple pie. As we ate, I gave her the lowdown.

"I was Nick Moore's secretary when I met you at Hardesty's."

She paused her chewing to give me the side eye.

"Yeah, I lied about looking for work. I was trying to get the dope on the Washington family. I knew I wouldn't get one of the top-tier guys, but I was hoping to speak to one of the lesser attorneys."

"Not a chance," she said between bites. "Only Mr. Hardesty interacts with the la-di-da clients."

"I should have known. It was obvious the second I crossed the threshold and got thrown out on my keister by that witch. You really helped us solve the case. Thanks for the info. I appreciate it."

Her eyes widened. "The case? You were involved in that case! The butler shot all of them, didn't he?"

"Yes," I lied. None of what appeared in the newspapers was true, but I'd made a pact with Doyle to keep my lips zipped.

"Mr. Moore is wonderful, isn't he?"

Here's where I had to be truthful.

"Nick wasn't working on that case." This wasn't lying so much as omitting that he'd been nice and cozy with Jim Beam at the time. "I took it over. He's working in Chicago for a little while,"—like for the next twenty years—"and I'm trying to run the agency. What's going on with your brother?"

She hesitated, twirling her spoon around in her coffee cup for so long, it must be cold by now.

"I won't charge you, Janie. I said you were a godsend during the Washington job, and I meant it. How can I help? If I don't turn anything up, I'll give you a couple of recommendations for another P.I. agency."

Who turns down free help?

"My older brother, Henry. We call him Hank. He drives for Red Cab."

That made me sit up and blink a few times. I rolled my hand for her to keep talking.

"He likes it and it pays okay. He's saving up so he can get married to Franny, his high school sweetheart. I've never heard him complain until now. The company was sold about six months ago to a Mr. Barnes out of New York, and the word among the other cabbies is that Red Cab plans on breaking their current contract."

She was on the money there. Literally.

"How does he feel about Winston Barnes?"

Maybe I'd been reading Win Barnes all wrong.

"Oh, he says Mr. Barnes is jake. Nice guy. Seems on the up and up. But then last month, two guys came out from New York. Real hard types. Mr. Barnes said they were accountants, but nobody believes him. Ben Foster didn't have his gas receipts up to date, and these guys roughed him up pretty bad."

My hunch about Barnes populating the company with Pinkertons was right.

"What's up with Hank then?"

She bit her lip so hard, it turned white, debating whether to spill or keep quiet. "You can't tell anyone."

"Cross my fingers and hope to die," I assured her.

"Hank's been sneaking out at night after our mother's gone to bed. She's a little deaf, so none the wiser, but I heard him walking down the hallway and out the front door last month. I waited for him to come home. Two hours later, he sneaks back in. I confronted him, thinking he was meeting his girlfriend, Franny. He denied it, but wouldn't tell me what he was doing. We had a horrible fight, and now he's not talking to me. He's snuck out at least three times since then. Franny's my best friend, and I asked her in a roundabout way if she was seeing Hank on the sly, and she said no. I believe her because then she got all worried he was two-timing her. I lied and said he was working extra hours at night to earn more money so they could get married sooner. He didn't want her to know about it, so she shouldn't say anything. Wanted to surprise her."

If it hadn't been the connection to Red Cab, I'd have put it down to Hank two-timing his fiancée. But now...

"How about I shadow him one night? Find out where he's going."

"You can do that?"

"Sure. No problem. He doesn't go out every night, right?"

"No, it's usually Wednesday or Saturday nights. He snuck out last Wednesday night, but so far he's stayed home. Do you think he'll sneak out again ?"

"Maybe. Today's Monday. How about I come to your place on Wednesday night? Where do you live?"

"At 11th and Mission," she replied. "Two houses in on 11th. We're the duplex with the pots of geraniums on the porch."

The Mission District in San Francisco is anchored at one end by the adobe Mission San Francisco de Asis and the recently built Mission Dolores Basilica. Janie lived at the far end of the district, on the edge between the Mission District and the South of Market. The newspapers kept the fatality count from the 1906 earthquake fuzzy, but it was common knowledge that most deaths occurred in the South of Market area. The influx of population after the Gold Rush—mostly working-class immigrants, Germans, Italians, and lots of Irish—had entrepreneurs draining the swampier areas of the city to build housing. You can tell where the water mains broke during the earthquake because the South of Market was one of the worst-hit areas of the city. What the squishy soil didn't destroy, the fire finished off.

Whatever Barnes, Sr., and the Pinkertons had in mind for Red Cab, I'd do everything in my power to thwart them. *Bastards,* I said under my breath as I walked back to my apartment, with no intention of confessing the sin of blasphemy.

Chapter Twenty-Four

The next morning, I went to early morning mass and only followed the liturgy by dint of rote. I hadn't slept well, my sheets rough against my legs, and my pillow too lumpy. I was too hot, too cold, too sleepy, not sleepy enough. I longed to see Tommy again, and I didn't want to. I felt helpless around him and didn't like feeling off-balance, unsure. Yet, I relived that afternoon over and over again. Wiping my face with his handkerchief as ice cream dribbled down my chin. The feel of his hand in mine. Warm, sure, strong. This was bigger than anything I'd experienced in my small life. I'd been kissed before by boys who didn't know where to put their hands. The kisses felt fine if a little awkward, sometimes too wet, sometimes too dry. Kissing Tommy made me feel desperate, like I was starving and afraid I'd never eat again. Is this the essence of sin? When you didn't care where it would lead?

I filled the car with gas and drove down Highway One with the top down, fast enough that the wind burned against my cheeks. The Pacific Ocean lay to my right, gray and angry as it crashed against the cliffs. Once past Half Moon Bay, I floored her, risking a speeding ticket and trying to drive away from myself and my thoughts about Tommy Morgan. I deliberately took those curves too fast, forcing my mind to concentrate on the road and my hands on the wheel, refusing to give my brain any space to Vera, Tommy, or my family. All that mattered was the road. When I hit Cambria five hours later, I was okay again. It was dark by the time I got home. I didn't even bother to undress. Even taking my shoes off was an effort. Crawling under the covers, I fell asleep five seconds after my head hit the pillow.

On Wednesday morning, I returned to the office to check my messages—there were none. I hit the library and read about Acapulco, acceleration, and advertising. I knocked off for lunch and then returned to my apartment for a nap. I needed some shuteye if I was going to tail Janie's brother tonight.

I woke up, fuzzy-headed and groggy. I struggled for a good fifteen minutes to keep my eyes open. My dinner consisted of an apple, a pear, and a handful of crackers. It didn't fill the hole, but a cup of black tea strong enough to stand a spoon upright helped.

I unearthed my "surveillance" clothes from the back of the closet: pea coat, trousers, sweater, scarf to cover my face, a newsboy cap, and a pair of rubber-soled tennis shoes I'd dyed black. The pants hung on my hips, and I had to move up the notch on my belt or they'd be pooling around my ankles. I needed to eat more. I patted my pockets to make sure I had my tools of the trade: a small flashlight, matches, pocket knife, and a cheap cigarette case filled with cigarettes. People aren't super suspicious if you're smoking a cigarette while standing somewhere you shouldn't be standing. I'd perfected the art of smoking and not inhaling. I still thought cigarettes were nasty, but it gave me a good cover.

By the time I'd finished eating and dressing, it was eight o'clock. I had some time to kill before I had to beat it over to Janie's house in the Mission and decided to head over to the office. Who knows? Between the hours of two and eight, a potential job might have called the answering service or sent a letter, requesting my services. With my newsboy cap pulled down, my scarf wrapped around my mouth and ears, and my eyes concentrated on the pavement, I didn't make eye contact with anyone. With my recent weight loss, I looked more than ever like a teenage boy, but there was always the chance I'd run into someone I knew. The rest of the offices were dark. No one was getting their teeth drilled tonight.

The answering service relayed several messages, all of them trying to sell me something I didn't need or want. Not even a hint of a job. After banging my head on my desk in frustration, I opened the file drawer named "Scam Artists" and pulled the file with the name "Wójcik, Eddie" on the tab.

Eddie's file wasn't very thick, but thick enough. Sure, the people who stuffed his pockets with dough had it to lose, but my encounter with him and the dropping of his mask made me wonder how "harmless" he was. Whenever someone like him would blow into town, Nick would send out an S.O.S. across the country to his fellow detectives. Most private dicks had been Pinkertons previously, so Nick knew them personally. It was in everyone's interest to keep tabs on these jokers. Grifters gravitate to big cities because that's where the money is.

Eddie was a smart bank robber. In other words, he got out of the bank-robbing business and started to target women with money, mostly widows. Eddie had a string of wives in four states. I assumed he hadn't bothered to divorce any of them, so at the very least, he was a first-class bigamist. Once he'd spent their money, he hightailed it out of town. At some point, the light bulb went on. If he were soaking the women, why not soak the men, too?

He wasn't the first con artist to ride the wave of spiritualism, but he'd capitalized on the craze and created his Amazing Victor persona. I could get him nailed on bigamy charges, but I held off reporting him to the D.A. I'd be shocked if Doyle didn't have ten file cabinets full of dope on men and women like Eddie Wójcik running their scams.

If there was one thing I've learned from working with Nick, there's something of a sliding scale when it comes to crime. Had Eddie been bilking your average family out of their eating money, Nick would have turned him over to the D.A. in a red-hot minute. A guy scamming rich people looking for kicks? He wouldn't waste his time. San Franciscans didn't pay much mind to Puritan ethics. The city had been built on the riches gleaned from the streams and mountains of the Sierra foothills, and miners weren't exactly the church-going sort. Sure, we had our bluebloods who had their pews at Grace Cathedral, but they weren't particularly sanctimonious. It was one of the salient reasons why Prohibition never took hold here. Victor was skating the edge a bit because people did care about financial crimes—bank and stock swindles were a big no—but he gave a good show. At some point, I expected him to rent a theater and fully legitimize his con. I'd pay to see it.

San Francisco didn't have old money like New York, Philly, or Boston, but at the end of the day, new money in a bank account is the same as old money.

I didn't know where Ted's family got their money, but I suspected it was on the older side based on what family gossip Ted had let fly. Probably Philly. If it were Philly, then it stood to reason the family was awash in Revolutionary War heroes with a healthy amount of clams in the bank—not Vanderbilt or Rockefeller-esque clams—but enough for Clarence Stevens to fund his silly wife's hobby of flirting with con men. Stevens wasn't a fool. Like Nick, he thought Eddie was harmless yet entertaining.

I typed up an update on Eddie Wójcik's current scam with four carbons to send to our contacts in New York, Philly, New Orleans, and Chicago for their files. Eddie could run, but he couldn't hide. By the time I'd typed, stamped, and posted my letters, the fog had rolled in, which made it harder to tail someone but easier to stay hidden.

The lights in the houses go out early in Mission. The men who worked swing shift had already left home, and the ones who worked in the daytime were in bed. I parked myself in the shadow between two houses across the street from Janie's house. She'd described her brother as short and stocky with a slight limp, a holdover from a broken leg.

Shortly after the clock at the Ferry Building chimed ten, Hank Morris slipped out the front door and began to make his way down 11th Street until it ended and Bryant began. Jeepers, the fog was thick tonight. The foghorns were going crazy, and it was a struggle to keep up with him. Fortunately, Hank was a chain smoker, or I'd have lost him. The farther we got away from Mission Street, the fewer the street lamps. I kept my eyes on the faint glow of a match now and then, and the sight of him under the odd street lamp.

This type of fog could get you killed. Visibility was down to twenty feet, and people still drove as if they could see for two hundred feet. The outlines of houses floated in and out of the mist, and except for the occasional porch light, it was like a sea of dark, house-like shapes threatening to gobble you up. I kept my eyes trained on Hank Morris and his cigarette, while my ears stayed alert for the sound of an oncoming car. I'd be lying if I didn't think of Vera when stepping off every curb.

Despite his bum leg, Hank walked fast. He turned left on 17th, left on

Folsom, and then stopped in front of a large one-story building on the corner of Folsom and 21st. A faded sign painted on the side of the building advertised it as "Holz Sheet Metal and Engineering." Holz had gone out of business. A crude hand-written notice saying "For Rent" was taped up against one window. There were only a couple of houses on this block of Folsom. It was mostly composed of empty lots, garages, gas stations, and places like this, blue-collar businesses struggling to survive. Cars were parked on both sides of the street. In this part of town at this time of night, the entire block should have been deserted of cars.

Hank knocked on the door in a complicated rat-tat-tat, which must have been a secret signal because the door swung open just a hair to let him in. The windows facing the street level had been painted over, and I didn't see any light coming from the windows under the roof line. They'd been painted over, too. There'd been a tiny sliver of light before Hank had slipped into the building, but whether I could find a window that hadn't been painted over was another matter. Whatever Hank's business, he wasn't cheating on Franny.

I crossed the street, walked for half a block, and looked up, hoping my hunch was right. Bingo. A faint glow lit the roof from a couple of skylights that hadn't been painted over. I'd never be able to replicate the tattoo on the door to be let in. If I could climb up to the roof, I might be able to hear and, even better, see what was going on.

I scoped out the alleyways on both sides of the building. One side was a bust. Although it had a garbage can, it lacked a fire escape. The building next to the sheet metal shop was a deserted-looking, weathered two-story wooden structure with a noticeable tilt; it had probably been a barn once upon a time. Luckily for me, it had a fire escape along one wall and a garbage can I could stand on. I gauged the distance between the two buildings as no more than three feet. I stood on the garbage can and was tall enough to reach the bottom of the ladder. I hoped to God the ladder was locked so that it didn't descend when I pulled on the lowest rung. The screech of that rusty pile of junk as it hit the ground would wake up people sleeping three states away. I grabbed it, waited, and pulled slightly, ready to jump down and run out of there should I need to, but it didn't budge. It had been locked. I guess they figured it would only be a broken ankle if you had to jump from there to the ground. You could crawl away from the fire.

I scaled the ladder, thinking I'd jump between the two buildings. Easy. One side of my brain issued a loud warning: if I missed, I'd be looking at two broken ankles. At a minimum. The other side of my brain made a silent raspberry as it reminded me I had long legs. I looked along the roof line for a pole I could grab onto and steady myself when I reached the other side. Nothing doing except a tall smoke stack on the edge of the roof. Needs must. I pushed off the ladder with my left foot, reached for the smokestack, and threw my arms around it. I barely made it. Maybe it was more like four feet as opposed to three. The smokestack rocked a little but held tight. I waited a few minutes to see if anyone had heard me hit the roof and decided to investigate. Nothing.

Fortunately, the roof seemed sturdy enough and didn't have much of a pitch. I eased my way toward the closest skylight. I'd been right. It hadn't been painted over, and a few panes were broken. I could hear just fine. The room was filled with men, all working class by the looks of them, some still wearing their driver's caps designating them as Red Cab or DeSoto employees, and lots of men with the tanned faces and lean looks of men who were down to one meal a day if that. The room was buzzing with chat, which explains why no one heard me jumping onto the roof. Then a man came out of a back room and climbed onto a wooden box to raise himself above the crowd. The room went silent. He began to deliver a fiery speech on the inalienable rights of workers and why they should join the IWW.

Tommy Morgan.

Chapter Twenty-Five

All of the machinery and equipment had been moved out. There must have been over a hundred men in the room, standing cheek to jowl, their faces rapt in response to Tommy's speech. The Amazing Victor could have learned some pointers from him. His voice wasn't loud, but he had a knack for working the crowd, stoking their anger, riling them up, and then defusing the situation with a funny joke. Heads nodded in support when he targeted the wealthy at the expense of the working class and laughed at his jokes. But every time he fed the rage, it was greater than the bar set before. He spoke to them in the simple language of a man who needed a job or wanted to keep the job he had. Tommy spoke of the injustice of men like Barnes, who lived in the lap of luxury but didn't give a good goddamn for the men who worked for him, didn't care about whether their kids had three meals a day, or whether they had a roof over their heads. These men were powerful, and he stressed you had to match power with power. The IWW was only as powerful as the people who worked on its behalf. Who could and would demand a decent paycheck and fight the demand they return to working twelve-hour days. He closed his speech with a line that would resonate with me for weeks: "The Rockefellers aren't standing in bread lines, now are they?"

Like The Amazing Victor, he knew you had to woo your crowd first, hook them, and then demand the money later. In Tommy's case, it was membership in the IWW.

"Sure, we'll meet again this Saturday night, right here at eleven o'clock. Use the special knock. Bring a friend, but make sure they aren't a snitch or working undercover for the Garda. Don't leave all at once. Only five at a time, count to a hundred, then five more can leave."

He could be a carpenter. I'm sure he picked up a hammer at some point, but I couldn't shake the feeling he'd lied to me. I remember what Harvey had said about people getting deported if they violated the Criminal Syndicalism Act. Was he lying to me about his political activities because he was afraid of being deported? Still, he'd lied to me.

The men filed out slowly. When the last of the crowd was gone, he pulled out a flask and took a deep drink. The grin on his face told me he was right pleased with himself. While sipping his whiskey, he waited a good fifteen minutes before leaving and locking the door behind him. I waited for another fifteen more, said a prayer to the Virgin Mary that the ladder wouldn't rip out of the wall, and leaped from the top of the building to grab the first rung that came into my hand. It held. I moved slowly, a rung at a time, listening to see if anyone heard me. When my foot hit the garbage can, I let out a big sigh. The street was now empty of cars. For caution's sake, I lit a cigarette and walked back to my apartment.

Despite being exhausted, I couldn't sit still and paced for another hour until Mr. Verbin pounded his ceiling with a broom handle and shouted at me to go to bed. I lay on top of my bedspread in my clothes, still wearing my shoes. I wasn't even sure of what I felt. Admiration, trepidation, and surprise? Yes. But other emotions I couldn't name gnawed at my bones, this soup of sensations jumbled together in my head. My chest hurt, and my pulse beat out a rapid thump thump thump of, "Tommy, Tommy, Tommy."

Around four a.m., I made a brief plan. First, I'd tell Janie what her brother was up to. It was up to her to confront him. These were dangerous times. Photographs of the labor strike in San Pedro with the cops wielding billy clubs and using saps on the strikers kept playing over and over in my head. Strikers had been killed in San Pedro. Of course, Hank might tell her to jump in a lake because he might feel he didn't have a choice. Barnes was already making cuts in the workforce. Yes, the union would fight them, and the cuts were probably illegal, but in the meantime, they'd push these men to the limit and then paint them as violent communists, lawless men who were threatening the fabric of this great country. I could see the headlines now: "Strikers Believe in the Hammer and the Sickle, Not the American Flag."

I fell asleep around four-thirty, no closer to answers than at 12:30, 1:30, or 3:30 p.m. My mother called at eight. We had strained conversation number seventy-five, where I assured her I was fine. She assured me she was fine and begged me to return home, like she did every morning. I said I'd be late for mass, like I did every morning, and we hung up. I ate breakfast at my favorite greasy spoon. When the waitress saw my face, she plopped a spare pot of coffee on the tabletop and said, "Have at it, sweetie."

On my way to the office, I picked up my four dailies like I did every day. As I opened the front page and saw the headline staring me in the face, my phone began to ring. On autopilot, I picked up and said, "Hello?" in a voice so unlike mine that I half wondered who was using my phone.

It was Dickie Vance.

"Meet me at John's Grill for breakfast. I assume you've heard the news."

"I…I…" It was hard to speak. I swallowed a couple of times. "I just bought a paper and saw." After a pause, I said, "I've already had breakfast."

"Have another."

"Are they open for breakfast?"

"They are for me. How many dailies did you buy this morning?"

"Four."

"Excellent. Bring all four. Please make haste, my dear."

I tucked the newspapers under my arm, locked the door to the office, and took the elevator to the street level, something I don't think I've done the entire time I've worked for Nick. I don't remember walking to John's Grill, and was shocked to find myself at the entrance to the restaurant. Dickie had a waiter waiting for me to open the door. He led me to Dickie's table, who was sitting in his usual bench seat. He had a bottle of cognac in his hand and was doctoring his cognac with a thimbleful of coffee from the pot on the table. I've never seen him do anything so inelegant.

The waiter gestured to the coffee pot. I nodded. He poured me a cup and then left.

"I ordered for you. I trust you like kippers. I wrote the article for the

Examiner. Do you have a copy of the *Call*? Let me read it."

Even in my shock, it struck me that Dickie was wasted as a society gossip hound. His article on Winston Barnes was top-notch. He laid out the discovery of Winston Barnes' body late yesterday afternoon by some fishermen hunting for seabird eggs. Barnes had washed up on the rocks of one of the Farallon Islands, dressed in the same clothes he'd worn to a party at the Stevens' house four days earlier. His time of death was inconclusive due to the water. Although originally from the East Coast, he'd moved to San Francisco six months ago to head Red Cab. He was well-liked, erudite, and will be greatly missed by his family. Services would be private and held in New York at a later date. There was a large photo of him next to a much smaller picture of his father. The family resemblance, although strong, couldn't hide the pensive look on Win's face—as if he hated having his photograph taken—versus the hard stare of his father, who seemed to relish the lens on him.

The other newspapers reported a similar story, although not half so well written.

I lay the *Examiner* down on the table.

"Do you know what happened at Clarence and Marjorie's party? You are friends with Ted."

It was said as a statement, not a question. I'd never told him about Ted, but I was too tired and shocked to pepper him with questions. Perhaps it was better if I didn't know.

"I detest that type of event, so I did not attend and pleaded a headache. Anyway, Mother is convinced Marjorie is stark-raving mad. I am beginning to agree with her. That fraud Victor is just one of a long line of scam artists she's promoted over the years. One must wonder about Clarence as well."

"I get the impression he's amused by it. Also, she goes by Alexandra-the-Queen-of-the-Dark-Mist now."

"Heavens to Betsy, she is a veritable fruitcake. Mother will love hearing that. The guests I interviewed were cagey, not wanting to speak ill of the dead. I hope to all the gods in heaven you attended that silly affair."

"Yes, I was there. Ted invited me. Remember when I told you about waylaying Barnes at the golf course and he told me he wanted to walk to the Farallons?"

Dickie nodded.

"He got his wish," I said it *sotto voce*, but Dickie heard me all right. We sighed in unison. "Barnes was the picture of sanity then compared to the wingding he had at the Stevens' place the other night. If it weren't a full-blown nervous breakdown, it was a good imitation of one. Ted's mother wasn't pleased."

"I would imagine not. Tell me down to the very last detail what you can remember."

Our food arrived. The smell of the fish nauseated me, and I pushed the plate away. Dickie said nothing but began to eat. I began to talk. When I'd finished, I held up a newspaper and shook it.

"This doesn't surprise me. He was frantic, Dickie. Hadn't slept or eaten for at least two days. I went to Doyle about Vera, but he wasn't too interested, or he did a fine job of acting uninterested. He knows… I mean, knew Barnes. They ran in the same social set, so Doyle wasn't about to sweat him about Vera's death based on my say-so. In my limited experience with the D.A.'s office, it would take an act of Congress to get him to consider Barnes as a suspect in her murder, even if I were standing next to her and he shot her. People in that world don't go around murdering people. As you know," I added with a large helping of snide. Doyle couldn't have prevented the murders of last summer, but he sure ignored a lot of red flags.

"Barnes was playing golf with you when Vera was killed, so he has an airtight alibi and couldn't have pushed her into traffic. Who did?"

I shrugged.

"I don't know, but I'm certain he knew who did, or at least who'd ordered the hit. He was being eaten alive by guilt, Dickie. If anyone was a candidate for suicide, it was Winston Barnes."

Dickie finished his last kipper and pushed his plate away. He didn't even bother with the pretense of the coffee this time. He filled his coffee cup with cognac. "Yes, I would have agreed with you except for the small matter of a bullet hole in his head when they found him."

Chapter Twenty-Six

"Surely Barnes wouldn't kill his own son," I said in a loud whisper.

"Oh, my dear. Many men see their offspring as mere pawns or puppets to move around on their chessboard of life. My father despises me. He's found his perfect son in my younger brother, an odious man for whom I have nothing but contempt. A bully as a child, he is an even greater bully as an adult. Of course, it's seen as praiseworthy in his world. He's considered a financial titan."

I stared at him.

"I see you're horrified by that little admission, but it's true. I am fortunate. My mother chose me over my father and brother. Her fortune is her own, and she walked out the door of her childhood home with some struggle, but not as much as you would think. Most women would have chosen their husbands, leaving their children to the whims of fathers like Barnes."

"Do you know Barnes, Sr.?"

He banged his coffee cup on the table with such force that I jumped.

"I don't need to. I grew up surrounded by men like this. Men who are venal, cruel, arrogant, and, in most cases, stupid. Win Barnes was a gentle, sweet man, a perfect specimen to be crushed by the likes of his father. I am not speaking ill of the dead, but his taking the job with Red Cab told me he did not have the backbone to defy his father. More's the pity. He might be alive today if he'd had."

"He told me he wanted to be a history professor. You defied your father?"

"Much to his dismay. I think he was shocked. It was the first time I'd ever stood up to him. One very grim day, when he had been screaming and yelling at me for over twenty minutes over what a worthless person he had for a son, I'd had enough. His language was excessively vulgar, and being humiliated in a similar vein was nearly a daily occurrence. I stood up and told him to go to hell. Then I walked out of the room and packed my trunk, leaving that horrible house, never to return."

"What did your mother do?"

"He screamed some more, demanding I be banished from the family, thrown out on the streets, exorcized from the family Bible, and my name never be spoken in his presence again. My mother might look like she's this sweet, southern belle, but she's quite steely in her own way."

These were the last words I would have used to describe Dickie's mother, but I didn't interrupt him.

"She told him that I was her son, and if he were going to make her choose between the two of them, she would choose me. She'd never liked my brother as it was obvious he was on track to become a carbon copy of my father; nevertheless, she always treated him with respect. She appeared in my room as I was filling up my trunk and said, 'Where do you want to live?' I replied, 'As far away from that man as possible.' 'Will San Francisco suit?' That was fifteen years ago, and I've never regretted leaving for a single minute. She misses the South, I'm sure, but she has never displayed any regret."

He couldn't miss the tears in my eyes.

"Your mother and Al will come around. I assure you."

"They didn't choose me. No one chose me. They pushed me away, all because—" I threw up my hands. "All because I want something different. It's not like I'm robbing banks, for heaven's sake. I go to mass nearly every day. I say my prayers. It's just... I don't want the life my mother is living, and neither of them can understand that."

He reached over to pat my hand with one of his very plump hands.

"Nick and I chose you, Margaret. At some point, you will have to accept that you're an 'other,' someone who can see beyond the narrow confines of what society has deemed acceptable. It's a hard road to walk."

"I respect their choices. Why can't they respect mine?" I demanded.

"Because they do not understand. You have to accept they might not ever understand. This road might be lonely, Margaret, but you will find like minds."

"I've found one." I smiled at him, even if it was a weak smile.

"Yes, you have. But I stress, it can be lonely. Do you think I don't know what people say about me, my clothes, my outré ways of speaking, and even my weight, all for their amusement and scorn? That I'm a fairy, a pansy, and a queen. I might be all of those things, or I might not be any of them. My point, my dearest Margaret, is that I refuse to make excuses for who I am. You stand in a trench for weeks on end, day after day, with men around you getting chopped up by Gatling gun fire, and life's choices become very simple. I live on my terms. I trust you will never find yourself facing a bunch of Jerrys trying to mow you down with a Gatling gun, but at some point, you will have a similar moment when it all becomes clear." He paused. "At least I hope you do. I've never been happier than I am now."

He snapped his fingers, and a waiter came running with a fresh pot of coffee.

"Gino, can you please make up a plate of scrambled eggs for Miss Laurent? The kippers weren't to her liking."

I looked down at my hands, which were twisting my handkerchief into knots.

"You think they will come around?"

"I can't guarantee it, but I hope so. If not, then you will have some difficult choices to make."

After warming my hands on my coffee cup for a couple of minutes, I said, "I don't think Barnes' father had him killed. Based on his state of mind at the Stevens' toga party, I think it was suicide."

"I trust your judgment, but some people—I include myself among them—will blame the father nonetheless. He essentially pulled the trigger when he placed Winston in an impossible position."

"I suppose so," I agreed. "Would your father feel responsible if that had been you?"

"No, and I doubt Winston's father will feel any guilt. My father would have handed the man who sold me the gun a cigar and put him on his Christmas card list."

"I wanted to ask you. Did word come down to embargo the Vera Kowalski story? I gave Doyle a heads-up, and he yawned in my face. Literally. He's a lousy actor. This story is being squashed. Four dailies in this town and not one paper printed a single syllable about her death."

Dickie's hand hovered over his coffee cup, still.

"What did Mr. Doyle say?"

"People were killed at the corner all the time, and I was making a mountain out of a molehill like I always do."

"I cannot say yes or no. It is not under my purview, but it is certainly the type of story that normally would have been front-page news, assuming no one had assassinated the King of England that day. *The Examiner* normally drools at the thought of a headline along the lines of 'Beautiful Young Woman Cut Down in the Flower of Her Youth,' to be followed by an editorial on the lack of traffic police on downtown Market Street, Hearst's favorite screed."

"I said as much to Doyle. That's when he yawned in my face."

"I really do not know, Margaret. I am loath to ask around because why would the society columnist care about a woman who sold gloves at The White House? It would raise some eyebrows at the very least. Call Terry Richards and see if the *Call* was told not to print the story. If it extended to them as well, then… Now, here are your eggs. Eat every scrap."

Chapter Twenty-Seven

I usually caddied on Saturday mornings. Soon enough, the weather would be too cold and wet for most golfers, and business would dry up—although there were always those golfers who'd tee off in a hailstorm. Mac, the head caddy, called me on Friday at seven-thirty a.m. to ask me if I was free to caddy. My larder was bare, and a generous tip would be appreciated. I threw on some clothes and decided to drive. I arrived at the golf course in under twenty minutes. Mac pointed to a guy standing near the first hole. "He asked for you."

"Haven't seen him before. Where did he get my name?"

Mac sighed. "Just get your backside out there, Maggie. He's been waiting for a good forty-five minutes."

I walked up to him. The man was clean-shaven with a slender face but a solid body. He'd probably been dead skinny as a teenager and put on the pounds slowly, year by year, and yet told himself he was still in fighting shape when he saw himself in the mirror every morning. I doubt he could run a nine-minute mile, but if he punched your jaw, you'd feel it for weeks. Hatless and decked out in a light-yellow cashmere V-neck sweater over a formal white shirt, navy blue tie, white knickers, and yellow and white argyle socks to match, he should have looked ridiculous, but he carried it off okay.

"Hey, I'm Maggie Laurent. Nice to meet you." His eyebrows reached his hairline. If he'd asked for me, then he shouldn't have been surprised when I stuck out my hand. "You did ask for me, didn't you, or did Mac get it wrong?"

He shook my hand and said, "I didn't expect you to be so tall."

"I'm shorter on Tuesdays."

"Funny. I'm John Waters."

Now it was my turn to be surprised.

"I see my reputation as the worst golfer in the history of Lincoln Park precedes me."

"Naw, there's worse. Trust me. Are those your clubs propped up against that tree?"

"Yes."

I walked over to the bag and pulled out his driver. "Whack the hell out of it and keep it as straight as you can. If you veer at all to the right, you're going to find yourself trying to maneuver around a bunch of trees."

I hauled the bag of clubs over my shoulder.

"You got that okay?" he called to me.

I didn't roll my eyes, but I wanted to.

"I'm stronger than I look."

At the third hole, I started asking questions.

"So why did you ask for me, Mr. Waters? I don't believe I've caddied for you before." I knew I hadn't, but I didn't want to be rude.

"Dickie Vance recommended you."

I blinked a few times. "Dickie? On a golf course? Surely you're joking."

Waters laughed. "I agree. Highly unlikely. I was having dinner at the Palace last night, and he came over to my table to say hello. He said to look you up. Believed you caddied at the golf course here. He wasn't certain, as in, and I'm quoting, 'I'd sooner stick a fork in my eye than play golf. There's a ball and a club, and you hit the ball into a hole? Sounds utterly moronic. Anyway, I'm allergic to grass.'"

"That sounds like Dickie. I made him walk two blocks last week, and he'll never forgive me."

He raised an appraising eyebrow. "Caddy by day, detective by night, or is it the other way around?"

I don't know how he managed it, but he was both flirty and not just a little condescending.

"I can't afford the greens fees here, so I caddy most weekends, and they let me play golf now and then. I'd use a four iron for this hole. It's one hundred and fifty-six yards. Straight shot." I handed him the four iron.

It fell about twenty feet from the hole. Not bad, but not great.

"Do you mind?" I reached out for the club, and he handed it to me. I could play this hole with two broken arms. I grabbed a spare ball from his bag, teed up, and hit the ball. It came within a foot of the flag. I marched ahead, keeping the club, tapped the ball into the hole, and then walked back to him.

"Your turn." I held out the four iron.

"Okay, I should have known," he said, followed by a sheepish grin. "If Dickie was recommending you…"

I didn't want to play mental games with this guy. "Those are my *bona fides*. If they aren't good enough for you, then I can find you another caddy."

He held up his hands in mock surrender.

We played the next few holes in silence until I said, "I assume you've heard about Winston Barnes."

"Poor bastard. Yes, I heard. You knew him?"

The note of incredulity was hard to miss. What was a nobody like you rubbing elbows with a guy like Win Barnes?

"Not really. I caddied for him one morning. Like I'm caddying for you."

He blushed. "We're getting off on the wrong foot here. I apologize."

"I don't hold grudges, Mr. Waters. Finish the play, and while we walk to the sixth hole, I'll tell you why Dickie wanted me to talk to you."

As we walked, I gave him some tips on how to improve his swing. I figured the more I impressed him with my golf skills, the more he might respect me as a detective.

"I've read everything I could about you, Mr. Waters. Correct me if I'm wrong, but I get the impression you're more interested in selling fleets of cars than you are in running a cab company."

"More or less. DeSoto provides the seed money for me to invest in expanding my sales operations." He swung. "Damn."

His ball had bounced off a tree and into the brush.

"Hard luck. Relax. You're clutching that golf club like it's the last life vest on the Titanic."

"Thanks for the tip. The last time I looked, cars don't go on strike. I'd rather sell them, frankly. Do you think there's going to be labor trouble?"

I coughed to hide my disgust. The sidewalks were paved with men begging for spare change. Families were sleeping in their cars in front of houses they used to call home. This was just the beginning of hard times, very hard times, and only a fool wouldn't know that. But those who wear cashmere sweaters and whose only worry is that they sold only two hundred Plymouths that month, compared to three hundred the month before, seem to be able to turn a blind eye to those men and children without a home. My mother had three more payments on our mortgage. If she missed the last one, the banks would kick her out without so much as a "I'm sorry, Mrs. Laurent." I thought of the money Dickie had given me. I'd use it to pay off the mortgage even if it meant I went under. It was robbing Peter to pay Paul, but if I didn't have to contribute to our mortgage, it would help with the bills. I didn't think Dickie would mind. It would be my Christmas present to her.

"The docks are a powder keg waiting to blow, Mr. Waters. It's in your interest to keep the cabbies happy so they don't join the dock workers' strike. Barnes bought Red Cab before the stock market crash. I don't know this for certain, but I'm guessing he paid too much for it. I think he's up to his neck in debt and probably used stock as collateral for the purchase. Now his stock is worth only pennies, and he's sweating bullets. In an attempt to recoup his losses, Barnes is already making noises about rescinding the gains made in the 1921 and 1922 cabbie strikes."

His face hardened, and he began to regard me with both respect and wariness; he'd underestimated me and wouldn't be that foolish again.

"You know this for a fact?"

"Not about his financial woes, but his plan to bust the union contracts, you betcha."

"How old are you?"

"Twenty-four going on ninety-five. I hear things."

"Where does DeSoto come in? What iron should I use for this hole?"

"A four wood and then a five iron. If you join him, Barnes will have a better chance of killing the current contract. That's only part of his plan. He's hired Pinkerton ops to find out as much as they can about your operation so he can start taking over your territory. Either way, he wins. You two crush the unions, he'll reap profits. If he makes inroads into your territory, he'll reap profits. I've never met Barnes, Sr., but hiring Pinkerton ops? Watch your back."

He worried his bottom lip for a bit and then said, "He's hired Pinkerton?"

"Yep."

"My cabbies are getting their tires slashed and the gas siphoned out of their cars."

I held my hands out wide. "There you are. My take? Barnes is too desperate to wait for you to throw in with him. He's moving on to Plan B. Undermining your company. How powerful are you?"

"Fair to middling," he said, followed by a deprecating shrug I took for fake modesty.

"Barnes is East Coast. According to Dickie, you're established in this town. When was the last time you had dinner with the mayor?"

"Two weeks ago."

"You belong to the Pacific Union Club?"

He nodded.

"Invite him for cigars one afternoon and soon. Mention oh-so-casually about your cabs being vandalized. Wouldn't it be a crying shame if you had to pull your business interests out of San Francisco? He'll get the hint. Smiling Tim is fast on the uptake. At the same time, meet with the head of the Teamsters' union and ask for his help in stopping the vandalism. He'll be thrilled."

"And what if it's the Wobblies vandalizing my cabs?"

"If it *is* the Wobblies or the Communist Labor Party trying to horn in on Teamsters' turf, then nothing you do will stop the Teamsters and the IWW from duking it out, but I don't think it's them. I'd start with Smiling Tim. He has the clout to demand that Barnes pull his hired thugs out of the city. He plans on running for governor in November and doesn't want anything to rock his political boat right now. Losing a big-money guy like yourself will look bad. If the vandalism stops once he gives Pinkerton the boot, then you'll know who to blame. If not…" I shrugged.

He leaned on his golf club to study me for a second or two. "If I weren't married, I'd get down on my knees and propose to you right here and now. You play golf like an angel and are one hell of a smart cookie. What more could a man ask for?"

"Ask your wife, she might know."

He grinned. "Plus, you're nobody's fool. So, after I talk to the mayor, I sit tight and do nothing?"

"That would be my advice. I can't see Barnes holding out for much longer, especially since the market isn't bouncing back as people predicted. In six months, he'll beg you to buy Red Cab. But what do I know? I'm just a secretary."

"I need more smart people on my staff. You're hired."

"I have a job, Mr. Waters. If you ever need a detective, give me a buzz. The Moore Detective Agency is at your service."

"Do you know what happened to Win Barnes?"

"A nice guy with a not-so-nice father."

Chapter Twenty-Eight

I phoned Terry Richards when I got back to my apartment. Her answering service picked up. I left a message for her to call me. I wondered if her sources at City Hall had let anything drop about Pinkerton sending out his troops. I'd have to be careful not to put Nick on the spot. He needed that job right now, and if they knew he was feeding me dope about the goings on in San Francisco, he'd never work as a detective again. In any state. Pinkerton had a long reach. I'd barely hung up after leaving a message at Terry's answering service before she called me back.

"What's up, Maggie?"

"Do you have thirty minutes? I'd like to talk to you about Vera Kowalski, the girl killed at the corner of Market and 3rd the other day. The one run over by a cab."

"Not the type of thing I write about. Thanks for your call. I have to—"

"It's really important. Can I come to see you?"

"I threw my back out yesterday. I'm at home. I'll call you next week."

"I think her death is tied up with Red Cab and union-busting."

There was a long silence before she said, "You don't think it was acciden-tal?"

I'd only voiced my suspicions to Dickie and Doyle. If I wanted her help, I'd need to come clean. I took a big breath.

"No, I don't."

They could've heard her sigh in Oregon.

"I live on Union near Washington Square. 2511, upstairs over the liquor store, Apartment 2." She hung up and didn't sound too pleased.

Terry wasn't any more welcoming in person than she'd been on the phone. I couldn't help but notice that her back seemed fine. She motioned me to a seat whose arms had been shredded down to the stuffing. As I walked across the room, an enormous black cat who'd been sunning himself in the window jumped down and began to thread through my legs, begging for pets.

"Meet Beany. Ignore him or you'll be stuck petting him for the next six hours."

"I like cats. No worries." I sat down and gave his chin a few scratches. He had one of those deep purrs like the hum of a truck engine, and although missing one eye and half of an ear, he'd come out on top in any fight.

"Beany, you pest, come here."

He pretended to ignore her, and then, with a casual saunter, plopped down on the floor next to her and began to clean himself.

The apartment was a decent size, with a tiny kitchen, but what looked like a bedroom and a bathroom down a dark hallway. It reminded me of Harvey Cohen's law office. Bookcases were stuffed with books, and stacks of books were piled here and there around the room. Black and white photographs had been pinned to the bare walls, most of them portraits, a lot of them of Terry. Several large canvases painted in bold colors, mostly landscapes, were leaning against the wall. An easel holding a half-finished painting was propped up near the window. There was a coziness about this flat that I envied. It was a home. My place was nearly threadbare in comparison, filled with Nick's worn-out furniture. The only personal items I could claim were my clothes. I suppose it reflected my hope that Nick would return to San Francisco one day and move back in. I was a squatter and nothing more. Keeping the apartment for him. Maybe I needed to rethink this, and if it was that impersonal when Nick was living here, what did it say about him?

"So, what's up?" she asked around a freshly lit cigarette.

Before I could say anything, the door opened and a young woman with short-cropped red hair—maybe my age, maybe a little older—wearing large horn-rimmed spectacles came into the apartment with a bunch of daisies in her hand. The glasses made her blue eyes look slightly bug-eyed. Her clothes were splattered with paint, as were her hands.

Terry's face hardened, but the newcomer didn't seem to take it personally. The ease I sensed growing while petting Beany had vanished. Terry's shoulders were now tense, and she was frowning. The young woman breezed past both of us with a wave and went hunting through the cupboards in the kitchen for a vase.

"You're home early," Terry said in a flat, impersonal voice, the opposite of welcoming. "This is Lorna, my apartment mate."

"Hi, Lorna," I called to her. "I'm Maggie. Nice to meet you."

"She's a friend of Dickie Vance's."

Some sort of verbal semaphore was going on between them, but I couldn't read what it meant.

"Oh, how nice. Hey, Maggie. Imogen didn't feel well, so I thought I'd come home." She plopped the vase full of flowers next to me on an end table covered with newspapers, magazines, and jars of paintbrushes.

"Who's the photographer?" I pointed at the walls.

"I am," admitted Lorna.

"She's an assistant to Imogen Cunningham," Terry chimed in.

The name didn't register.

"Sorry, I know almost nothing about photography. Would you be insulted if I said I really liked them?" The room got a little less chilly. "What kind of camera do you use? I bought a Leica for photographing men cheating on their wives. I'm getting pretty good, but this? Wow. It's another level."

Lorna scrunched her brow. "You take photographs of people cheating on their spouses?"

"Maggie is a detective," Terry butted in. "She works for Nick Moore."

"Oh, how nice," she repeated in a voice that didn't sound as "nice" the second time around. "Anyone want some tea?"

Terry gave her the smallest shake of the head, which I interpreted as her saying, "No tea, we need to get her out of here."

"Thanks, I'm good," I said. "Based on the paint on your hands, I'd say you're the painter as well. I'm as educated about painting as I am about photography, but the canvas on the end is swell."

I pointed to a picture in vivid blues, reds, and yellows of a large fishing boat. The men were working side by side, their frowns, the resignation on their faces, the slight bulge of their muscles hinting that they did this back-breaking work day in, day out, all surrounded by tons of fish. I could practically smell them. It gave the sense that they were in a type of purgatory, their day never done.

"Told you it was good," muttered Terry.

She blushed. "Thanks, my dad works on a boat. I'm from Monterey. I'm still trying to find my way, art-wise. Landscapes sell, but I'm not sure that's what I want to paint. I'm having a show soon."

"Oh, let me know when it's happening. I'd love to come. I've never been to an art show before, and I'd—."

"So the woman who was killed?" Terry had no intention of letting this conversation continue. Lorna stared at Terry.

I managed a weak smile and ignored the rudeness.

"First, you should know, I don't have proof. I've already gone to the D.A. about it, and he yawned in response. There won't be any help in solving this case from his end."

"Surprise, surprise," she drawled. "There's no political or social advantage for him to exploit in the death of a young woman getting run over by a cab."

"I'd agree with you, except he tipped his mitts a little. I'd swear on a stack of Bibles he knows there's something hinky about it. She was the ex-fiancée of a friend of mine, who drives a DeSoto cab. She worked at The White House selling gloves. All of a sudden, she dumps him, with no explanation, but begins seeing someone else on the sly. She doesn't tell her co-workers who this guy is. In fact, she doesn't blab to anyone that she's seeing him. He's way out of her league, like big money, but she takes his interest at face value. It helps that she was an utter knockout. He was a dish, too. Handsome enough to give Douglas Fairbanks a run for his money."

"Was? Let me guess. Winston Barnes."

I raised my eyebrows as high as they could go.

"I have friends who work at the Palace Hotel. Everything you say makes sense."

"So you know that his father bought Red Cab before the crash and probably paid way more than it's worth. I'm guessing he has plans to break the union concessions granted in 1921 and 1922."

"You know this how?" Her voice was neutral, but she leaned forward. If she thought my theory was a bunch of malarky, she would have leaned back in her chair. I was learning.

"Because he's hired Pinkerton to stir things up."

She lit another cigarette but didn't say anything.

"The IWW is mobilizing cab drivers on the quiet. I don't know if that's a push to dislodge the Teamsters or in response to Barnes' plan to break the unions."

"Probably a little of both. You've been busy."

The room was getting warmer, and not because anyone had lit a fire.

"I had a little tête-a-tête with John Waters today."

"Really?" She sounded impressed. "I can't get that guy to sit down for one measly interview."

"I caddied for him. He's happy enough with his little empire. He prefers to sell cars and has no intention of joining Barnes in his schemes to bust the union."

"You believed him?"

"He can make more money by selling Plymouths, plus I get the impression that he has an understanding with Smiling Tim. Strikes are bad for business and mayors running for governor. Yeah, I believe him."

"Not sure *I* believe it, but then there's Smiling Tim to consider. You might be right," she said as she rolled another cigarette. She didn't smoke it, and I got the impression she just wanted to do something with her hands. "He has a reputation as a wolf. Not that he's hit on me," she qualified. "I'm not his type."

Lorna gave a hoot of laughter from the kitchen.

Terry laughed with her. "Enough out of the peanut gallery," she admonished over her shoulder. "He didn't make a play for you?"

"Oh, he tried," I replied. "But he wasn't offensive and backed off when I let him know I wasn't interested. Fairly charming about it. I can shrug off a heavy come-on if they don't get nasty. The most interesting part of the conversation? He admitted that DeSoto cabs are getting their tires slashed and gas is being siphoned out of the tanks."

For the first time since I entered the apartment, she sat up straight and began to sit on the edge of her chair.

"You're sure?"

"Yep, he told me himself."

"Well, well, well," she said under her breath. "Do you mind if I interview the cabbies? Waters won't give me the time of day, but the cabbies might."

"It could be the IWW trying to put a wedge between Waters and Barnes," I pointed out.

"Could be," she admitted. "There's only one way to find out. Ask a bunch of questions. How does Vera's death figure into this?"

"Win Barnes was pumping her for info about DeSoto under the guise of wining and dining her. This is largely speculation on my part, but it's the only scenario that makes sense to me. She finds out Barnes has a fiancée back in New York. Vera confronts Barnes, and he panics and tells his father. Papa Barnes puts out a hit on her, and Win Barnes commits suicide because he couldn't face that he'd essentially put a target on Vera's back. If she'd come to you with some story about Barnes trying to undermine DeSoto, would you buy it?"

"In a heartbeat," she replied. "So let me get this straight. Barnes wants to collude with Waters in busting the union, but also muscle his way in on Waters' territory?"

"That's about the size of it. I don't think it will be possible to identify Vera's killer. Pinkerton isn't going to give him up."

"No, probably not," she admitted. "Sometimes you can't have everything."

"Was the story squelched by the *Call*?"

"Yes and no. We're small fry compared to the *Examiner*. We take our lead from them. They didn't run it, so the editor didn't give it a second thought. I'm not saying the word to embargo the story didn't happen, it just didn't get down to my level. Did you ask Dickie?"

"Yeah, he said he didn't know, but admitted it was the type of story the *Examiner* would normally give a front-page spread. Vera Kowalski was movie-star gorgeous, which alone would have had the photographers stampeding to get a picture of her."

"You'll let me know if you uncover anything else?"

"Sure and likewise."

"Things are going to blow sky high. Men are losing their jobs, businesses are going to hire scabs and undermine union contracts, and the unions are going to do everything in their power to keep the concessions they've won so far and make inroads into those trades not yet unionized. That's my take. It will keep me employed, you can bet on it."

Lorna came into the room holding a tray. On it was a teapot and two cups.

I stood up. "I won't take up any more of your time. Thanks, Terry. If you have a chance, will you send me whatever you can come up with on Barnes, Sr.? I got what I could from the newspaper morgue, but you might have contacts I don't have. Anyway, nice to meet you, Lorna. I'll see myself out."

I could hear them fighting five seconds after I closed the door behind me.

Chapter Twenty-Nine

I returned to the office and had barely hung up my coat when someone knocked on the door.

Finally, please God, let it be a job, I whispered to myself and shouted, "Come in," and arranged my face so it looked professional and detective-ish.

The Amazing Victor walked in. He must have been waiting outside for me to return. There wasn't a minute between me stepping into the office and him following me inside. When out of his ridiculous costume, he was jaw-dropping handsome. The flowing white locks were nowhere to be seen. Under his fedora, his real hair wasn't gray at all, but a soft brown. With high cheekbones, a dimpled chin, and large brown eyes the color of brandy, I could now see how he'd pulled off all those marriages. His suit, expensive and stylish, had been cut and tailored to hide a portly figure. It mostly did its job.

"Hi, Eddie." If he were looking for a smidgen of enthusiasm in my voice, he'd have to hunt high and low.

"Zelda-of-the-Black-Hat, I presume."

"Good thing I have 'presumes' on sale today. What can I do for you?"

I didn't ask him to take a seat, but he sat down anyway. He gave the room a couple of once-overs and then sneered.

"Pretty cheap operation you have going on here, Miss Laurent. A nobody with a no-account office." He sneered some more. "A desk, a file cabinet, a wastepaper basket, a phone, and a typewriter. The Moore Agency doesn't inspire much confidence."

"That's the result of earning an honest dollar. We get results, minus the theatrics. Sometimes, window dressing is just window dressing. Like capes and staffs and candles."

"Honest?" He snorted twice to make his point. "Hanging in the halls of hotels and hiding behind lampposts while trying to catch some poor sucker stepping out on his wife once or twice."

My Irish began to ratchet up.

"Sometimes. Or it can be about alerting widows to con men whose sole passion is to clean out their bank accounts. Of course, your track record with marriage shows your general contempt—or is it veneration?—for the institution as long as the bride is loaded. How many wives do you have? Six at last count? Let's not forget another institution you disdain: the banks and how they have the nerve to keep their money under lock and key until you come along with a gun. I hope we understand each other, Mr. Wójcik. Thanks for stopping by. Now if—"

"Where's Moore?"

That question threw me a little.

"He's in Chicago on a special job for Pinkerton," I lied.

"I don't think so." The snide factor was on high again. "No one in town thinks he's coming back. You won't last another six months."

"I suggest you leave and—"

"You gonna turn me into the D.A.?" The melodious tones that had characterized his show at the Stevens's house were gone. It was the flat, hard voice of a guy brought up in the Bronx.

"No. Keep your grift limited to rich people like Marjorie and Clarence, and we're fine. I hear you're going to marry one of your marks, then all bets are off, and I go to Doyle. It will be up to him to bring any charges against you, but the last time I heard, pretending you have the power to speak to the dead isn't a crime. You're not holding a gun to their heads. Plus, as you so politely put it, I'm a nobody. Do you honestly think I have the juice to waltz into the D.A.'s office and lay down the law?"

"Not what I hear. Doyle likes you."

News to me.

"Nice to hear. I have to admit, Eddie, fleecing rich people is a hell of a lot better than robbing banks."

"I served my time," he snarled. "That stuff's in the past."

"Yes, you did, but not 'past' enough if you start rattling the wrong cages. For heaven's sake, Eddie, you'd have to be crazy not to know that the D.A.'s office has a file on you. If we do," I hiked a thumb at the file cabinet, "they do. They keep tabs on all of the major grifters who float into town. Keep your antics limited to the show, and the D.A. will look the other way. If you get greedy and some society guy doesn't appreciate how much dough you're shaking down his wife for, he'll pop you. I can't think of a single state except for Utah that doesn't consider bigamy a felony, so you need to keep your nose clean and not piss off Doyle because he will nail you for those marriages if you push your luck. You force Doyle into a corner, and he'll throw the book at you because he's pissed you forced him into a corner. Are we done?"

He fumbled with a cigarette.

"How do you know the Stevenses?"

"I'm friends with Ted. I saw your show last year, and I must say, you've upped your con. Pretty snazzy. Nice addition of the girl."

"My niece."

I didn't bother to hide my grin.

"Is that what they're calling it these days, Eddie?"

"Victor, if you don't mind." He took a couple of drags and eyed me. "I'm thinking of moving to Los Angeles. I understand the movie crowd is much more enlightened and not so hidebound compared to here."

"What a great idea. Aimee Semple McPherson is killing it down there. Put on your bishop's robe and miter, and within a year, you'll have the money to build a temple all your own. You could graduate from the living rooms of the rich to a real stage."

He drew himself up in his chair and threw his shoulders back as if gravely wounded by my comments.

"Are you mocking me, young woman?"

"Not at all. You've been in San Francisco for a couple of years now and have probably reached the end of what you can glean from people. Unless we experience a plague, the folks with money have run out of people you can 'commune' with. It's a limited market. Like rich widows. You don't strike me as stupid, and I'm sure you don't want to go back to the Big House. It only makes sense to sell the con for a while and then move on to fresh markets."

He stood up and made a movement like he was swirling a cape. I guess it was second nature by now.

"You should know, Miss Smart Aleck, that I have nasty friends in nasty places. That mouth of yours is going to get you in trouble one day."

"I'm quaking in my boots, Mr. Wójcik."

"I reiterate. *Very* nasty friends. I can't say it's been a pleasure. I sincerely hope we don't meet again."

"Likewise, Mr. Wójcik. Don't slam the door on your way out."

Chapter Thirty

My encounter with Victor left me cranky and out of sorts. I drove to Ocean Beach and watched the tide go out. Usually, the sound of the surf calms me down, but his crack about me being cynical bothered me. Was it true? Was this what my mother and Al were on about? Although she liked Nick, my mother had never been keen on me being his secretary, but he paid well, and we needed the money. I guess she assumed that eventually, I'd tire of working weekends and the occasional ten-hour days. Soon enough, I'd get married and recreate her happy life. But I wondered if it went deeper than that. Was it because she saw me changing in ways she didn't like and was losing respect for who I was becoming? The ocean didn't give me any answers. It never did.

By the time I parked in front of my apartment, it was dark, and I was still grouchy. The gas gauge was nearly empty, and I'd have to use some of my precious funds to fill the tank. Or skip lunch tomorrow. I trudged up the stairs, kicking the risers as I climbed to the third floor. A body slumped against my door jolted me out of my foul mood. I ran down the hallway. It was Herman.

The man weighed a ton, but adrenaline gave me inhuman strength, and I was able to haul him into my apartment, ignoring his groans. I sat him on the couch and then turned on all the lights and did a quick reconnaissance of his injuries. He'd been beaten up. A split lip, a couple of black eyes, already rising into massive shiners, and a few bruises on his jaw told me someone worked him over good. Knowing Herman, he gave as good as he got, but someone had beaten him with something because one of his wrists was sitting at an angle a wrist shouldn't be sitting at; it was swelling up before my very eyes.

"Okay, I need to get you—"

"No hospitals."

"Herman, for heaven's sake—"

"No, I'm okay."

"No, you're not! Your wrist is broken. You need to have it set."

"Not going to the hospital, miss. No!"

Then it dawned on me. Herman might not have money for hospital bills.

"You have to have your wrist set!" I screamed at him in a panic. *Deep breath, Maggie, take a deep breath.* "How about I take you to my mother's house and phone Dr. Chase? The guy who helped to dry out Nick. You don't have a compound fracture from what I can see, but it sure is broken."

He didn't say anything.

"Okay?" I pressed.

"Okay," he whispered and then passed out.

I felt for a pulse, and it was strong. I held off calling an ambulance. I called the house instead. Al answered.

"Al, it's Mags."

"If you're not coming home, we have nothing to say to you."

I bit back a nasty retort. *This is about Herman*, I said to myself.

"I need to talk to Ma. Will you give her the phone?"

Fortunately, Al handed her the phone. I half expected him to hang up on me.

"Maggie, what's going on? Are you okay?"

"I'm fine. It's Herman. I came home and found him slumped against my front door with the daylights beaten out of him. I got him inside my apartment. He's got a couple of shiners and a busted lip, and they worked his face over real good, but the real problem is that whoever attacked him, broke his wrist. I'm thinking with a tire iron." Before she could say anything, I said, "It doesn't look like a compound fracture. He just passed out, probably from the pain, but he refuses to go to the hospital. His pulse is good. I want to bring him to our house. He's agreed to let Dr. Chase set his wrist. He can stay in my old room until he's recovered."

"Do you want me to call Simon?"

Huh, Simon, is it?

"Yes, please. Can Al take a cab to my place and help me load him into my car?"

"You have a car?"

"Yes, I do. I'll explain later. Let me speak to Al."

He came on the line.

"What do you want?"

When we were kids, we got along great. When we didn't, all hell would break loose. We'd pummel each other until our parents separated us. This was one of those times when I wanted to break every bone in his body, the irony not lost on me.

"I want you to get a cab, right now, and come over to my apartment. Herman's been beaten up something bad. Whoever attacked him meant business and broke one of his wrists. I think he was worked over with a tire iron. He won't go to the hospital but has agreed to let Doc Chase treat him. I need your help loading him into the car. Okay?"

"Is this Herman Peters we're talking about?"

I wanted to say, "No, you lunkhead, the King of England," but I didn't.

"Yes."

"I'll be there as soon as I can," he said and hung up.

I began to apply cold compresses to Herman's face to reduce the swelling. I didn't want to touch his arm. I might do more damage. At some point, he came to.

"We're set. Al's coming to help me get you into the car, and we're taking you to Ma's. Doc Chase is going to see you. No hospitals."

"Good. I need to call my mother. She'll be worried if I don't come home," he mumbled around his fat lip.

I dialed, and Herman managed to pull it together and sound normal. Yes, he was on a job for Mr. Vance. He couldn't talk about it, but he'd be gone for a while. No, he didn't know how long, but he'd try to call every day. He was fine. He said a few words in Polish, hung up the phone, and then physically crumpled into the couch cushions, like those two minutes of sounding normal had taken all the stuffing out of him. I cobbled together a sling out of a bandana and two pairs of socks.

Al's face was pinched in that mulish Maggie's-just-being-dramatic frown. Until he saw Herman.

"Jesus," he muttered to himself. "We need to take him to the hospital, Mags. He's—"

"No hospital, Mr. Al," Herman insisted. "Doc Chase will fix me up."

"Herman, you—" Al began, but Herman didn't let him finish.

"I'm not busted up inside, Mr. Al. It's just my face and my arm. I swear."

"He wouldn't listen to me either. Let's get him home and let Dr. Chase evaluate him. Okay?"

Al nodded because we didn't have any choice. We couldn't force Herman to go to S.F. General. Between the two of us, we managed to slide Herman's wrist into the sling without him passing out again. No one said a word the entire drive to our house, although I'm sure Al had a million questions on his lips. My mother had been a nurse, so little rattles her. Between the two of us, we got Herman into the house. Doc Chase was already there and gave Herman a hypo of something that wouldn't quite knock him out, but he wouldn't care even if he was in agony.

Al and I sat in the living room, staring at our hands while the doctor plastered up Herman's wrist.

After about thirty minutes of total silence, Al said, "Do you know what happened?"

"No. I found him slumped against the door to my apartment."

There was another long silence.

"Is it something to do with a case you're working on?"

"I don't know. There's a push to undermine the unions, and the Wobblies are trying to make inroads with the cabbies. This could be related."

Al scratched his head. "I can't see Herman getting involved in a union beef."

"Vera dumped him. He'd have done anything to win her back. If it meant more money, he might do something stupid."

"Yeah." He waited a couple of minutes before saying, "How involved are you? How much do you know about this union beef?"

"I've been haunting the morgue at the *Examiner*, learning about the cabbie strikes in 1921 and 1922, but nothing more than that."

"If something happens to you, it will break Ma's heart."

"I know."

"It will break my heart, too. It was hard enough to see Herman beat up like that. What if it'd been you?"

"I know."

Chapter Thirty-One

With Herman conked out in my room, I shared a bed with my mother. I have to admit it was nice listening to the in-and-out of another person's sleep. It hammered home how lonely I was. I thought about Nick. He knew a million people in this city. He'd never have to sit alone at a bar if he didn't want to, but what about in his quiet hours? When you can hear the ticking of a clock and the easy feeling of sharing a cup of coffee with someone across a kitchen table. I had a hard time seeing Eileen Taylor lazing around on a Sunday morning with one of her chumps, never mind Nick. More like spending the morning copying someone's signature so she could forge checks.

Al and I were thawing out, slowly. At some point, I hoped we could get back to our normal bonhomie, but I wasn't sure. Being so much older than me and with my father's death, Al had always straddled the line between being both a brother and a father figure, but I didn't need a father figure anymore. I wanted a brother. I didn't know how to define the line between being overbearing and being brotherly, but he had crossed it and then some. At least we weren't snarling at each other, but we were as leery as two jungle cats circling one another. We didn't talk much. Mostly because I was afraid of saying something in the wrong tone and sparking another ugly confrontation.

We sat at the kitchen table and had breakfast together before Al rushed off to the library to study for the bar. Although we handed each other the newspaper back and forth as we finished a section, like we always had, the tension between us was palpable. My mother acted like everything was jake, except she kept dropping spoons and almost broke a plate. Finally, she said to me, "Here's some oatmeal for Herman. See if he's awake," if only to get me out of the kitchen.

The dope had made Herman too groggy to talk the previous night, but he was awake and sitting up when I knocked on the door jamb. I offered to feed him some breakfast—with his arm in a heavy cast, he couldn't reject the offer. Plus, his other arm, although it wasn't broken, was black and blue and must have hurt like the dickens. This gave me a perfect excuse to grill him about what happened.

In between bites of oatmeal, I bombarded him with questions.

"How is the wrist this morning?" I asked.

"Oh, not too bad," he lied. Pain lines bracketed his mouth. His shiners were one long bruise across the width of his face, but his lip didn't look too bad this morning.

"The doc will be here later to give you some pain meds. Did you see who attacked you?"

"No, miss. It was too dark. I was checking my tires. A lot of the guys have been finding their tires slashed. Someone's been draining our gas tanks, too, so we're all running our cabs on the minimum amount of gas. Mr. Waters is pretty upset about it."

"Were you by yourself? Weren't there other cabbies around? More oatmeal?"

He nodded. "Your ma's a good cook."

"I'll let her know. So the rest of the crew weren't around?"

"No, miss. Most of the guys on the day shift had packed up already, and the night shift had headed for the docks. There was a passenger ship due in at Pier 39 last night, so there was some money to be made. I was parked down on Battery and thinking I might drive to the waterfront. Maybe see if I could get one last fare for the day when someone came up behind me. He swung a tire iron at my head, but I saw his shadow first and was able to duck."

I managed to keep my face neutral. This wasn't vandalism. Someone was trying to kill Herman.

"I guess he thought I saw him trying to slash my tires."

"Yeah. Sure."

In some ways, it was better if Herman didn't know he was the next victim on Pinkerton's list. The only way to connect Vera to DeSoto was through Herman, so he needed to be silenced, too.

"This guy's good, miss. As you know, I'm no slouch, but he's even better than Mr. Al. He got my face but good before I got in a punch to his gut. It didn't take him down, though, and the force of my hit sent me back, and I fell. He came at me with the tire iron again, and that's how my arm got broken."

I could envision what happened. Herman was on the ground and still dazed from the punches to his face, but with his arms up and crossed to protect himself. This guy would be standing over him with the tire iron and smashing it into Herman's arms to take them out before beating him to death.

"Someone started yelling at us, and he dropped the tire iron and ran up Battery and turned left down Jackson."

"How did you get to my place?"

"The guy who stopped the fight was another cabbie. He drove me to your apartment. To be honest, miss, I don't know how I made it up the stairs. I just did. If Mr. Al wouldn't mind, could one of you drive down to Battery and get my cab? I don't want to leave it down there."

"He's at the library today, but the minute he gets home, I'll make sure he drives it back here. Key?"

"On your dresser."

"Can you remember anything about the guy who attacked you?"

"It's pretty dark on Battery, so I never got a good look at him. The guys like to park there because it's close to the docks. You know, now that I think of it, he was wearing a handkerchief tied around his head, so I couldn't see his face."

"Was he short, tall, a big man?"

"Tall, slender, sort of a drink of water to be honest, but fast. And strong. I think I might take a nap now, miss, before the doc shows up again."

"Sure, Herman, I'll turn out the light."

After making sure the curtains covered the window so the room was as dark as possible, I took the half-finished bowl into the kitchen and put it on the counter. With that lip, oatmeal was probably the only thing he'd be able to eat over the next week.

"How'd he do?" asked my mother.

"Not too bad." I joined her at the kitchen table. "Ate half of it. Doc Chase's coming by this morning, yes? He could use another round of pain meds."

"Oh, yes." She blushed. I needed to talk to Al to get the scoop on Dr. Chase. "Maggie, do you know what is going on?"

"I'm not sure, but I think it has to do with the union and the cab companies wanting to bust the union contract. Red Cab has brought in Pinkerton ops, and they're sabotaging the cabs of the DeSoto drivers."

She made a few figure eights on the tablecloth with her finger before saying, "How are you involved in this?"

"I'm not," I lied. Not yet. Sort of. "I think Herman got beat up by someone who was going to slash his tires, and the guy attacked him with a tire iron. Do you remember the strikes in 1921 and 1922?"

"Not really. Your father was dead, and I was more concerned with keeping a roof over our heads than what was happening downtown. It was a... A hard time. Promise me you won't get involved in this... This fight. Herman could have been killed."

"Ma, this is between Red Cab and DeSoto. Herman needs his cab picked up. When Al gets home, would you ask him to take a cab down to Battery and Jackson and pick up Herman's cab? The key is on my dresser."

She seemed satisfied with the evasion or pretended she was.

"What a fancy car you drove up in. Did you borrow it from someone?"

"No, I told you. It's mine. Catherine Washington gave it to me before she left town."

"Oh. The 'Catherine' Al was sweet on?"

"Yes."

"He's dating Bridie O'Neill these days."

Bridie was pretty, I'd give her that for free, but she wasn't a patch on

Catherine. She giggled a lot.

"Do you think Catherine is coming back any time soon?" She was making more figure eights on the tablecloth with her finger.

"No."

"Good," she said. "Would you like another cup of coffee?"

Chapter Thirty-Two

I stayed until Doc Chase arrived. He assessed Herman's condition, proclaimed him okay, and then sat at the kitchen table in what was usually my seat. He acted as if he'd sat in what used to be my chair many times and, even worse, that he belonged there. With Al and I now grown, it was selfish of me to expect her to be a martyr to the memory of my father. I wanted her to be happy. I didn't want her to be lonely, but I didn't want that man sitting at our breakfast table either. I kissed her, said goodbye to the doctor, and told her I'd call her later.

I drove to the nearest Catholic church and sat in the last pew. I didn't need to pray. I needed to think. The IWW was meeting again down on Folsom Street tonight. Do I go back? I thought of my mother and my soft lies about not being involved. I remembered Vera in her white dress, surrounded by flowers and the people who would mourn her forever. Herman's battered face and broken arm. Vera's murder. Big forces were at play here. No one would approach Herman's cab to siphon off some gas or slash his tires with him standing there. His attacker *knew* it was Herman, *knew* he could box, which is why he bashed Herman's hands. Herman only survived due to luck. I had no doubt he'd have been killed if his attacker hadn't been interrupted.

Those same jumping beans in my stomach I got when the Washington case was about to break were now doing the mambo. Call it intuition or the heebie-jeebies. After some careful reflection, I decided to attend the meeting. I'd be careful. I'd take a nap this afternoon so I'd be alert, and I wouldn't take any unnecessary chances.

Once I reached my apartment, I laid out my usual kit. Just for good measure, I filled a sock with quarters and tied a knot above the quarters so if I needed some extra heft in my punch, I could hold it in the palm of my hand or swing it like a sap. I was ready.

I wanted to lie down there and then, but I needed to do two more things: see Dickie and update him on Herman and talk to Matt Doyle.

I didn't pick up the tail until after I'd left the church. They kept their distance but never lost me, even though I drove down several alleyways and not a few one-way streets. It didn't help that I drove a yellow roadster convertible as long as a city block, which stood out a mile in a sea of black Model T-Fords. I ran a couple of red lights and managed to ditch them somewhere around Van Ness. I parked the car in front of my apartment and went up the steps like I was going home. I snuck out my back door to the tiny yard where we hung our laundry, which abutted the equally tiny yard of the apartment building behind mine. The back door to the apartment block was open. I strolled through their hallway and out the front door to the street parallel to mine and then walked like the devil to catch Dickie before he finished his lunch.

On Saturdays and Sundays, he ate in the dining room of the Mark Hopkins Hotel. I'd never met him here for business, and my presence would signal to him that something dire had happened.

Dickie had just finished lunch, and I caught him just as he was throwing his napkin on the table. When he saw me walking across the room, he picked up his napkin, placed it back on his lap, and said to the waiter hovering over him, "William, I'm afraid this is a three-piece of pecan pie day. Sigh. Some days?" He shrugged. "Shall we leave off the ice cream this time? I believe so. Margaret, would you like a piece of pie?"

"No, thank you."

"A tea for the lady?" I nodded. "And a coffee for me. Real coffee, if you please."

The waiter pulled out a seat for me and then bowed.

I waited until he'd moved away enough so he couldn't hear me. I also did a quick reconnaissance of the restaurant. Almost empty. Good.

"What has happened? Do not beat around the bush."

"First of all, you should know he's okay. He's staying at my mother's house for the next couple of weeks."

"Is this about Herman?"

I nodded.

"Someone with a handkerchief tied around most of his face attacked him with a tire iron. They broke his arm, and he's got shiners on top of his shiners. Another cabbie stopped the attack before they could kill him. He thinks it's part of the general sabotage going on with DeSoto cabs. It is, but also more than that."

"Agree. What is this about DeSoto cabs being vandalized? I have not heard anything." He sniffed in irritation. "I have half of the cabbies in this city on my payroll."

"DeSoto cabs are getting their gas siphoned and their tires slashed. I think Waters has been keeping mum about it, maybe leaning on his fleet until he had a better idea of what's going on. It could be the IWW trying to muscle out the Teamsters or the CLP trying to muscle out both the Teamsters and the IWW, or any combination of the above, blaming each other and riling up the members to switch representation. I spoke with Waters yesterday and told him about Barnes, Sr., sending Pinkerton ops out west to both bust the unions and Waters' hold over most of the cab business in town. You sent him to me, didn't you?"

"I did. Now I am not sure it was such a good idea."

"At least he now knows Barnes is making a dirty pitch for his business. But that's only half of the equation."

He looked at me over a stern, lowered brow.

"And the other half?"

"There was a secret meeting of the IWW at a defunct sheet metal shop over on Folsom the other night, and it was filled with cabbies wearing Red Cab and DeSoto caps on their heads. The IWW is making a pitch for a strike as Barnes is starting to lean on the union. If DeSoto goes out on strike as well, that helps Barnes. He doesn't care if Red Cab drivers go out on strike. I bet he's lining up scabs as we speak. The cabbies might be torn on whom to trust."

"And you know this how?"

I could sort of lie to my mother, and I didn't want to lie to Dickie, but—

"Margaret, come clean, or I will call your mother this instant."

"That's blackmail, Dickie," I said, more than a little outraged.

"Yes, it is. Speak or I will ask William if I may use their phone."

"Fine!" I huffed. "There's a secretary who works at Hardesty's. I met her when I was working the Washington case. Her brother has been sneaking out at night. She asked me to tail him and find out what he's been doing. She thought he might be stepping out on his fiancée. He's attending these meetings of the IWW. He's a cabbie, too. Drives for Red Cab."

"This is not optimum. Did you get into the meeting?"

"No, they've got a secret knock to let you in the door. I climbed onto the roof." He gave me another stern look. "It was a breeze. Don't worry." A breeze if you're a mountain goat with opposable thumbs. "Fortunately, several of the panes of one of the skylights were busted out, and I could hear. Herman wasn't there," I assured him. "So I don't think Herman getting beat up is about whatever strike effort is looming. I think it's about Vera."

"I assume he can't identify this thug who attacked him."

"No."

"How badly is he hurt?"

"Black eyes that go on for days, a fat lip the size of Alcatraz. The worst thing is a broken wrist. Herman refused to go to the hospital. I got Doc Chase to set it."

"Ah, Chase is a good man. He will not speak of this to anyone."

"What about Waters? I don't want Herman to get fired if he doesn't show up to work."

"I shall give John Waters a phone call. He owes me a favor."

"Oh?" In all our previous interactions, Dickie had mentioned Waters as nothing more than an acquaintance, someone he ran into at parties, shook his hand, and then went to find a drink.

"Yes. Oh. And you may not know why he owes me a favor. I would only lie to you. As you will lie to me when I ask you if you plan on going to any more of these meetings." He lowered his brow again to visually chastise me.

CHAPTER THIRTY-TWO

"If you were to go to one of these meetings—"

"Which I'm not."

"But if you were, you would be especially careful, and you would call me, no matter what time of night, to let me know you are home safe."

"This meeting I'm not going to? It's tonight."

"I shall expect a phone call."

"You'll get it. I'm going back to the office and call Matt Doyle after I leave here. I'm not telling Doyle about the IWW stuff, but he should know about Herman. I'm going to force his feet to the flames. If he tries to palm me off again, I'll call Terry Richards and see if she can use her byline at the *Call* to get City Hall to at least acknowledge that various forces are on a collision course."

"I am sorry to admit this, but the *Examiner* will not run any story criticizing Smiling Tim, even peripherally. Any hint he is not in complete control of this city will not be printed. He is Hearst's man."

"And Hearst hates labor."

"And Hearst hates labor. Anything else?"

I took a deep breath, "Someone just tailed me from St. Ignatius's right now. I lost them somewhere around Van Ness, but they were good. I'm going to assume they know where I live."

His pie and our beverages arrived. He pushed the pie away.

"William, another coffee, but this time, the one spelled c-o-g-n-a-c. Thank you, my good man."

Dickie toyed with the salt and pepper shakers for a minute or two.

"Make? Model?"

"I don't know cars, Dickie. It didn't look like mine. It was black, kinda squat, and the driver knew what he was doing."

He waited a few seconds before saying, "I do not like this development."

"I can't say I'm thrilled."

"This attack on Herman and Miss Kowalski's death must be tied together. It doesn't make sense otherwise. Do you think this is about tidying up loose ends?"

"Yep. There is no way for Pinkerton to know that Vera didn't go to Herman and blab to him about Barnes using her to get dirt on DeSoto. I don't think she did; otherwise, Herman would have come to me." I paused. "At least I think he would have."

Dickie waved a hand. "Undoubtedly." He took a long gulp of his drink. "You will call me when this meeting is over."

"I promise."

Chapter Thirty-Three

I called Doyle's house, and his wife answered the phone.

"Hi Moira, is Matt home?" I could hear kids fighting in the background.

"Sorry, Maggie. He's working today. He's supposed to be home by now." She didn't sound pleased.

"Okay, I'll try to catch him there. Thanks."

My office wasn't far from City Hall, so I decided to walk. Most city employees parked their cars in a lot on Golden Gate. I leaned against the fence and waited for him. It wasn't more than ten minutes before I spotted him crossing the street. He'd yanked off his tie and unbuttoned the top button of his dress shirt. With his jacket slung over his shoulder and sweat stains under his arms, he looked a lot younger.

He didn't see me right away. With his keys in hand and staring down at the ground, he walked right past me to his car, a brand new 1930 Cadillac in a dreamy green color. For the first time since I'd met him, Doyle didn't exude confidence and power. I liked him this way. His arrogance was in check for once.

"Hey, Doyle!" I shouted and walked up to his car.

Doyle didn't look too pleased to see me.

"Maggie, what in the hell are you doing here?"

"Gee, Doyle, I'm happy to see you, too."

"I've had a stinker of a day, and I need a smoke. If you have an ounce of sympathy for me, come back on Monday."

I sidled in between him and the car, blocking the driver-side door.

"Jesus, Mary, and Joseph," he muttered. "Get in. Give me five minutes to myself before you start yammering at me."

I slid into the passenger seat and sat there for a while—longer than the five minutes he requested—while he leaned back in his seat, closed his eyes, and smoked down a couple of cigs.

"Okay. What's bothering you that can't wait until later?"

"You look beat, Doyle. You okay?"

"No, I'm not okay. There are…things happening behind the scenes. I can't tell you what they are, so don't bother asking. Butt out. I won't ask you again."

"What are you going to do? Send me to bed without my supper? I'm not one of your kids, Doyle."

"Step back. Please. I'm not telling you; I'm begging you. Second, I've just come out of a four-hour meeting with the mayor. I'm hanging onto my job by a thread. I haven't had lunch and I need a drink. I'm going to drive home, and the second I step over the threshold, the kids will start crawling all over me. I'm going to get a sandwich for dinner. Moira is going to be in a miserable mood because I'm working on a Saturday and she's dealing with the most colicky baby ever born. Her mother helps out, but this kid will not shut up. I will try to smile and take the kids off her hands so she can fix my sandwich. But what I really want to do right now is walk over to Fior D'Italia, order a plate of pasta the size of a Crissy Field, and a gallon of their best red to wash it all down. Then I want to stagger back here and drive home to a quiet house, where my wife greets me at the front door in the filthiest negligee imaginable."

We sat there in silence for a few seconds.

"I'll make a deal with you, Doyle. Listen to me, really listen to me this time. I'll babysit for you and Moira one night. I can deal with a howling baby for a few hours. Take her out to Fior D'Italia for dinner so she can order her own plate of pasta the size of a football field. The negligee? You're on your own."

He laughed. "I might take you up on that offer. The babysitting, not the negligee."

"I'm serious."

"I'll think about it. I'm not very happy with you right now. My four-hour meeting? On a Saturday? John Waters had dinner with the mayor last night at the Pacific Union Club, and Waters threatened to pull his business out of San Francisco if the mayor didn't find out who was vandalizing his fleet. The mayor went nuts on me, and I have one week to find out who's sabotaging DeSoto cabs. And do you want to know why I'm not overjoyed to see you? Waters asked the mayor why the caddies at Lincoln Park know more about what's happening in this city than the mayor or the D.A. Now, who do you think that caddy might be?"

"No idea," I replied. Wow, Waters worked fast. I'd only caddied for him yesterday morning.

"You're not fooling me with those big doe eyes, Maggie. I *know* you caddy at Lincoln, and he *told* me he spoke to you. What did you say to Waters?"

"How about you dial it down?" Doyle was getting all itchy with me. When that starts, he gets my Irish up, and I end up slamming doors and stalking off into high dungeon. No one does high dungeon better than the Irish. I took a deep breath. *Think Herman, Maggie.*

"First of all, you should know he's a lousy golfer. If you ever play with him for money, bet high because he tends to undershoot, and his shots curve to the right. Anyway, we started talking about Winston Barnes and his death, which led to a discussion about Barnes, Sr., taking over Red Cab, which led to another discussion about Pinkerton sending out some hard boys to run the company because his son wasn't mean enough. Like I told you. Several days ago."

He ignored that last dig.

"Moore's in contact with you?"

"No. Not that there's an echo in this car, but I told you all this the last time I saw you, and you weren't interested. Don't get all high and mighty with me. I didn't know about the sabotage until Waters told me."

"Is that the truth?"

"On my father's grave."

"How bad is the sabotage? Waters didn't give me any details, just the orders to stop it."

"Guys are driving around with a thimbleful of gas in their tanks because their tanks keep getting raided. There's been a lot of construction around town, so a bunch of tires getting blown wasn't noticed at first. But word must have got out about all these tires going bad, and the cabbies started to realize these weren't punctures but slashes."

"So how many Pinkertons do you figure?"

"I don't know," I admitted. "It only takes two seconds to slash a tire. Siphoning gas?"

"Five minutes."

"Good to know."

"I sincerely hope you're not considering adding raiding gas tanks to your bag of tricks. And you're learning how to box now?"

I narrowed my eyes.

"Who told you that?" I demanded.

"You're not the only one with 'sources.' Moore didn't say how many goons Pinkerton sent out, did he?"

I gave him a look. "Do you think I'm stupid?"

He smiled. "Worth a try. I'm thinking at least two guys, maybe three."

"It's at least two. A couple of guys appeared in Red Cab's office. They're supposed to be accountants, but all they seem to be counting is the number of guys they rough up if the cabbies don't turn in their receipts on time. I don't see guys in suits slashing tires at night."

"I agree. Four then. Two in the office and two on the street."

"How much juice does Smiling Tim have in his smile? Can he tell Pinkerton to back off? Go home? Tell Barnes to stuff it?"

Doyle rolled another cigarette, but this smoke was leisurely, and he had a thoughtful crunch to his brow.

"I think so. Did you want to warn me about Waters? Is that why you ambushed me at my car?"

"I didn't ambush you. Consider the offer to babysit off the table."

"Come on. Calm down. What gives? Why are you here?"

"First of all, I came here to tell you about the sabotage going on. Second? Someone's tailing me. Third? Whatever secret you've got running, it's turning ugly. I don't know if it's part of the sabotage plot, but it's related to Barnes and Red Cab. One of DeSoto's cabbies is parked in my bedroom with a broken arm and a face that looks like he went ten rounds with Dempsey. Someone went at him with a tire iron. He's lucky he wasn't killed. Another cabbie stopped the guy wielding the tire iron, but this bad egg ran off before anyone could get a bead on him. Tire-iron guy was wearing a handkerchief tied around his face. This cabbie thinks the guy was going to slash the tires on his cab, but the cabbie surprised him and attacked him with a tire iron."

"Let me guess. You don't think so."

"No, and if you have a working brain, you won't either. This cabbie was the ex-fiancé of Vera Kowalski, the woman shoved into traffic last week. Who happened to be the woman Win Barnes was sweet-talking to get information about DeSoto. Barnes, Sr., is clearing up loose ends. I think this guy with the tire iron was trying to kill him. Have you found the Red Cab driver who ran her over?"

"No, he's gone missing."

"Surprise, surprise. Maybe my hare-brained theory isn't so hare-brained after all. Maybe someone did shove her into traffic because Barnes didn't want her spilling her guts to Waters. Maybe Barnes ordered one of his Pinkerton thugs to eliminate the only other person whom Vera might have gone to in a panic. Her ex-fiancé."

"Did she?"

"I don't think so, but I'm not one hundred percent sure. It doesn't matter. Barnes thought the cabbie might know something, so they put a hit out on him. He's not driving a cab any time soon. If you want to question him, he's parked at my mother's house for the next two weeks. By the way, will you teach me how to fire a gun?"

"Doesn't that beat all? Are you out of your mind?"

"I thought you'd say that, but I wanted to make sure. If I'd had a gun in the speakeasy—"

"You'd be dead."

"You don't know that."

"Neither do you," he countered. "Anything else you want to spring on me?

I'm all ears."

"That's a first," I grumbled. "Just this. Smiling Tim can't sit on this if he wants to run for governor, which means you can't sit on this. Have the D.A.'s office work with the churches to get those men sleeping on Market Street some food and a warm place to sleep. Winter's coming. One good square meal a day might stop them from joining whatever labor unrest the IWW or the CLP have in mind. At least for a little while."

He pressed my shoulder oh-so-briefly. "This gig is making you older than your years, Maggie."

"You say it like it's a bad thing. The offer for babysitting still stands. Enjoy your sandwich."

Chapter Thirty-Four

I hailed a cab to take me to the defunct sheet metal shop and had it drop me off on Bryant. I walked the rest of the way to Folsom Street. The sun was dropping fast, but it was still light enough to scope out the building and its environs. After giving it some thought, I decided that another go at the roof was a bad idea. I shook the fire escape. It seemed a lot less secure than it had been last week, and I wasn't sure it would hold my weight again. Plus, my vantage point on the roof had given me a limited view of the room. I needed to be *in* the room for this round.

I moved the garbage can on the west side of the building and parked it next to the garbage can on the east side. I'd hide in the gap between the two cans. I hoped I'd be able to hear the secret knock, memorize it, and then enter the shop myself using the code. If not, I'd brave the fire escape one more time.

I walked back to Bryant and hailed another cab. I had him drop me off at the Old Clam House on Bayshore, ordered a bowl of clam chowder, stuffed my purse with several slices of sourdough, and hailed the third cab to drive me home. I knew Dickie had more than one cabbie on his payroll, although Herman was his personal favorite. These guys drove all over the city. They were everywhere. A strike would cripple the city. It had grown exponentially since the 1906 earthquake, and the cabbies were integral to that growth. I didn't think Barnes had much leverage. The city was too dependent on the cabs. Of course, if Waters started selling Plymouths cheap, he'd reduce the city's reliance on cabs and mop up on selling cars.

I dressed in my disguise and packed my usual assortment of tools in the pocket of the peacoat, plus the bag of quarters. Except for Tommy and Hank, I doubted I'd recognize anyone there. I'd stand in the back of the room, as far away from him as possible, my scarf hiked up to my eyeballs so he wouldn't be able to see my face. With my tools in one pocket and slices of sourdough bread in the other, I was ready.

A ten-minute drive took me over forty minutes of circling around blocks, turning down alleys, and parking in the back of deserted buildings to make sure I wasn't being followed. Once I was certain no one was trailing me, I headed to Folsom Street several hours before showtime. I'd driven to the sheet metal shop in case I had to make a quick getaway. I parked around the corner and down the block, as far away from a streetlamp as possible. Even in the dark, the car stuck out like a cannonball on a snowbank, but I wanted my car nearby. Hopefully, when the sun went down, it wouldn't look so obvious.

The alleyway was dark, and my outfit was dark. I noted with satisfaction that the fog was rolling in. I'd sit there, nibble on my bread, and wait for men to start arriving. And knocking.

Sometime around nine, a sleek black roadster—far too swanky for that neighborhood—parked in front of the building. I poked my head above the garbage can. Two men sat in the front seat and were talking. I couldn't hear a word, but I didn't dare try to get any closer. After about five minutes, the passenger got out. There was no mistaking who that was. The driver waited until Tommy was in the building, and then he lit up a cigarette, the lighter illuminating his face for a split second. I knew him, but I couldn't place him. Who was he? Then he drove off with me none the wiser. I replayed that brief glimpse of this man's face several times, but I still couldn't identify him. He was much older than Terry, with graying temples. Tommy didn't strike me as the kind who palled around with men who drove cars like that. Drinking horrible coffee in down-and-out diners seemed more his style.

It was cold and damp enough to keep me awake. At around ten-thirty, men started arriving in waves. It must have been coordinated so there wasn't a crowd of people standing in front of an empty storefront at eleven o'clock at night in a desolate part of town. I waited until I thought the room was full.

The worst thing to do would be to walk in and have Tommy spot me. By 11:30 p.m., I tapped out the secret knock and was let in. I wove in and out of the crowd until I reached the very back of the shop. No one gave me even a passing glance. I began to scan the room and spotted Hank right away. The room was crowded, and the door kept opening to let more people in.

Although I kept my eye on where Hank was standing, I recognized several men in the crowd. They were cops. O'Brien. Delancey, Brandi, Lazzo. Blazer. Brott. And those were the ones I recognized. How many of the beat cops I didn't know were here? This was going to get bad. Really bad. All those newspaper stories I'd read about cops and Pinkertons infiltrating labor meetings and strikes and then turning on the strikers ran around in my head like rabid squirrels. I inched my way to where Hank was standing. I tugged on his coat, and he turned toward me.

"I'm a friend of your sister's," I said in his ear. "This place is crawling with bulls. We need to get out of here."

"A friend of Janie's? I don't—"

"The fists are going to start flying, and the saps are going to start busting heads. With your bum leg, you won't be able to get out of the room without getting the hell beaten out of you. Move, Hank," I said as loudly as I dared.

I started shoving him toward the door. He didn't fight me. Luckily, Tommy had started his spiel, so no one paid attention to us as we moved closer and closer to the door. It was no different from the last time; his speech was nearly the same. Capitalism is evil. The banks and industry should be nationalized. It is only fair that a more equitable distribution of income and better living conditions for the working classes be a goal for society. I'd heard it last week; this was no different. The delivery was the same, with the stops for humor and the rise in his voice when he wanted the crowd to react. If I hadn't heard this before, I'd have been wowed. Now it felt rehearsed. What *was* different was the crowd. No longer silent, men started cheering and clapping, the cops in the crowd the loudest. Feet began to stomp, and fists were raised. At a certain point, he lost control of the crowd and had to shout to be heard. The anger in the room was palpable. *Dear God*, I prayed. *Let us get out in time.*

We made it to the door, but then my luck ran out. Who was manning the door in civies but O'Malley and Murphy. I hadn't seen who'd opened the door because I'd kept my face downcast, my cap pulled low over my forehead, and my scarf high up against my face.

"We need to take a piss," I said in a gruff voice, trying to bluff my way through. I reached for the door handle and opened it. Hank managed to get out, but O'Malley grabbed my arm, and the scarf dropped.

It took him a second, but then he recognized me.

We stared at each other.

"Jesus, Maggie. What in the hell are you doing here?" Murph said in a frantic tone.

O'Malley shook my arm, demanding an answer. I tried to pull away, but he held me fast. "And why are you dressed—"

"Let me go! All hell is going to break loose—"

And then it did.

There must have been a word, a sign, because all of a sudden, fists started flying, and billy clubs and saps appeared out of nowhere. There was screaming and shouting, and men were going at each other like animals in a cage. Someone grabbed the end of my scarf and pulled me deep into the crowd. I grabbed the bag of quarters in my pocket and hauled back with a haymaker that dropped this guy to his knees. Someone yelled my name. A fist flew past my head. I whirled around and, with a one-two punch to the jaw, I felled the guy trying to deck me. I punched, pushed, and flailed my way back to the entrance, desperate to escape this carnage. When I was about twenty feet from the front door, I saw someone clubbing Murphy over and over with a sap as he lay on the ground.

With what I can only attribute to God-given strength, I shoved my way through the crowd with my fists and elbows. I kicked people out of the way, kneeing them in the groin, heedless of their cries and moans. I went at them with everything I had.

"O'Malley!" I screamed over and over again. I grabbed the man who was clubbing Murphy by the collar and hauled him back. I smashed my fist into his face, over and over again, until he collapsed. As I turned around,

O'Malley was dragging Murphy out the door. The amount of blood he'd left behind made me sick to my stomach.

"My car!" I shouted. "It's around the corner!"

O'Malley hauled Murphy over his shoulder, and we ran to where I was parked. I opened the door and snapped back the front seat.

"Throw him in the back seat!"

I started the engine, shoved the car into gear, drove three blocks over, and stopped in the middle of the street. I could hear sirens in the distance. Ambulances or paddy wagons, I didn't know which.

"What in the hell are you doing?" screamed O'Malley.

I didn't answer. I tore off my coat and then my shirt, and opened the back door to the roadster. I wrapped my shirt around Murphy's head, trying to stop the bleeding. At a minimum, he had a skull fracture. I pulled the sleeves of my shirt around his head as tight as I could and then did the same with the shirt tails. It was crude, but it would have to do. I started up the roadster again and made it to San Francisco General in five minutes flat. When we pulled into the emergency entrance, I blasted my horn long and loud, and a crew of doctors and nurses came out to see what the hullabaloo was about. They ran over to the car.

"Backseat. Head injury!" I shouted. "He was attacked with a sap and has lost a lot of blood."

Someone shouted for a gurney. Someone shouted for a surgeon. O'Malley shouted that he was a cop. They pull out all the stops for cops. I sat on the running board, unable to stand another minute, my hands shaking so badly that I dropped the car key onto the pavement.

I looked up at O'Malley and pointed to the entrance to the ER. "Go with him. I'll go get his mother."

O'Malley nodded and went inside the hospital.

I sat there for God knows how long before I was confident I could drive. It was then I realized I was down to my bra and began to shiver. Somehow, I managed to thread my arms through the sleeves of my pea coat. The buttons were gone. I wrapped it around me as best I could. Then I started the car to drive out to the Avenues so I could tell Mrs. Murphy that her only child was fighting for his life in San Francisco General and ask if she needed a ride to the hospital.

Chapter Thirty-Five

When I arrived at the house Murphy shared with his mother, I leaned on the doorbell for a good two minutes until she opened the door. The constant buzz of the doorbell had told her all she needed to know. She didn't seem surprised to see me, even though I was standing on her porch in the middle of the night, my coat barely hiding my bra. Already dressed, wearing her coat, her handbag slung over her wrist, she asked two questions, no more. When you're the mother or wife of a cop, it's better not to ask too many questions, or you'll never sleep again.

"Maggie, is he alive?"

"Yes."

"Do you have a car?"

"Yes."

She followed me down the steps and got into the passenger seat. She recited the rosary on the drive to San Francisco General, and I joined her. I didn't stop for anything. I kept the car in third gear the whole way, blasting the horn as I drove through stop signs and red lights, my foot pressing hard on the accelerator.

Like my mother, Mrs. Nora Murphy was one of the mainstays of the parish. The ones who volunteer, decorate the altars for the holidays, and help raise money through bake sales for stained-glass windows, orphans, and missions abroad so those pagan babies won't go to hell. Their faith is immovable despite the tragedies of their life. Her husband died the same week as my father, both victims of the Spanish flu epidemic. She'd never remarried, devoting her time to raising her only child and scraping out a living as the secretary to the local bishop. Those must have been lean years, but I never heard her complain. Murphy had never married, and I couldn't remember him dating anyone in the parish. He was the perennial Irish bachelor, living with his mother and attending mass every day.

O'Malley was waiting for her at the entrance of the hospital to escort her upstairs.

I raised a questioning eyebrow.

"They're working on him," was all he said.

It was past four a.m. before I made it home. So tired even my toenails were yawning, I phoned Dickie.

He picked it up so fast it didn't even ring.

"I had given up hope and was about to call the hospitals. I trust this means that the evening was a disaster. First, assure me you were not harmed."

"I'm fine. Others aren't so fine."

I gave him the *Reader's Digest* version. Speech. Cops. Fight. Riot. Murphy getting sapped. Hospital. Home.

"You are aware that this business will not appear in the newspapers."

"Smiling Tim must have approved this. The place was crawling with buttons. People were hurt, Dickie. Some might have been killed. How are they going to embargo this with half of the cabbies in this town beaten to a pulp?"

"Hearst will not print this," he reiterated. "Other papers might, especially if they want to scoop the *Examiner*. I shall name no names. Now get some sleep. You sound utterly spent."

Terry Richards was a name. I'd give her the details and let her take it as far as she could.

I forced myself to take a shower, even though I was crying from exhaustion. My hands and torso were painted with Murphy's blood. The skin on my knuckles was raw, and a shiner was rising on my left eye. Someone had gotten me, although I didn't remember it happening. As I watched the water run pink with Murphy's blood, I yanked back the shower curtain and began to vomit into the bathroom sink.

I woke up at one o'clock, dressed, grabbed a bucket, and cleaned the back seat of the roadster before heading back to the hospital. I'd never get the bloodstains out of the stitching in the leather, but I did my best.

The nurse at the front desk told me, "Detective Murphy is out of surgery and is in a private room. Are you related?"

"I'm his sister," I lied.

"Room 304. Ten minutes only. He's critical."

I gave the desk clerk a mock salute.

At least four nurses warned me that visiting hours were over in ten minutes and admonished me that patients needed their rest, so please do not overstay my visit. By the time I encountered the fourth nurse, I was finishing her sentences for her. Murphy was in a private room at the end of a ward filled with beds on either side. I tried not to think about my father dying in a ward identical to this one, the long room smelling of illness and starched sheets, his fellow flu victims lined up like soldiers, all wheezing out their last breath.

I was at the entrance to the private room when I heard sobbing. I opened the door very slightly, and it wasn't Murphy's mother like I expected, but O'Malley. Murphy lay there, his head encased in some gigantic bandage. He was whiter than the sheets, and the skin around his eyes, not covered in bandages, was black and swollen. His nose had been broken and set, and his lips were pinched and pulled tight over his teeth. O'Malley was seated next to his bed in a chair, and based on the blood all over his shirt, he hadn't gone home yet.

"Murph, goddamn you, please come through. Just…I can't…if something happens to you, I'll…I don't know what I'd do…I know we can't…you and I…God, please, please…"

He began kissing Murphy's fingers, his palm, his wrist, and then buried his head against Murphy's chest and cried those silent tears that are so much worse than those you cry out loud.

"Maggie," someone called to me. It was Bree, O'Malley's wife, with her arm through Mrs. Murphy's arm as they made their way slowly down the corridor.

I edged the door nearly but not quite closed so O'Malley could hear me.

"Hello, Mrs. Murphy, Bree," I said this very loudly, so loudly, I hoped it cut through O'Malley's grief. This was not something either woman should see. I did everything I could to waylay them to give O'Malley time to pull himself together.

"Did you get some shut-eye, Mrs. Murphy? They told me visiting hours were almost over, but I doubt they'll throw you out. Wasn't it nice of them to give him a private room?" All this was said in a loud and false voice, but they didn't seem to notice.

"Is he awake?" asked his mother in a shaky voice.

"Not yet," I boomed.

Bree brought a hand up to my eye. "What happened to your eye? Does it hurt?"

"Golf ball," I lied. At some point, I needed to sit in a pew and do some serious meditation on what a first-class liar I was becoming. Not today. "Your husband is with him. Try to convince him to get some sleep. He looks done for."

I couldn't keep them out of the room any longer. I went into the room first and sighed an internal sigh of relief. O'Malley had pulled himself together, and his red eyes might be because he'd been up for over twenty-four hours.

"I'm going to go now," I said to no one in particular. Bree and Murphy's mother began fussing over the bedclothes and talking in whispers so as not to wake up Murphy. Fat chance. I didn't say anything. It would be a blessing if he woke up.

"You going home, Maggie?" O'Malley said in a quiet voice, so unlike his usual belligerence when talking to me.

"In a bit," I replied. "I need something to eat."

"I'll come by in a couple of hours."

I nodded. "Meet me at the office."

This was not a conversation I wanted to have with him, but I knew I didn't have a choice.

Chapter Thirty-Six

Upon opening the door to my office, I discovered that someone had picked the locks to the outer office and tipped over the file cabinet. Paper and files lay like a carpet all over the office floor. I immediately ran to the inner office, but it remained locked and secure.

"Nuts and nuts squared!" I screamed. Someone had threaded a piece of paper through the typewriter and had typed in caps: "STOP YOUR MEDDLING."

I ripped the paper out of the typewriter, tore it into shreds, and threw the pieces into the wastepaper basket. Although it was a long shot, I called four locksmiths, hoping like hell someone needed the work. Locksmithing must be lucrative because it didn't seem like anyone wanted to work on a Sunday. Fifth time was a charm. Lenny the Locksmith said he would be over as soon as he finished his lunch.

"Whatcha got on there now, lady?"

"A Chubb. Doesn't look damaged, but someone sure picked it easily enough."

"Hows about I replace your Chubb with a Zephyr combination lock? No one's going to break into your place with that puppy. I'll be there in ten, miss…"

"Laurent. Maggie Laurent."

The Amazing Victor was the most obvious suspect for vandalizing the office, unable to resist a parting shot before he moved to Los Angeles. That's why he came by the first time. He wanted to scope out the office and see what kind of lock he'd be dealing with. Like an idiot, I told him we had a file on him. A hundred dollars says this is the one file that will be missing. Upending the file cabinet and its contents but leaving the inner office alone said this was plain old-fashioned malice, and Eddie struck me as the malicious sort.

The note told me a different story. That wasn't malice, but a warning. I didn't think the same person who'd tipped over the file cabinet was the same person who'd typed the note. I had no intention of exposing Victor's grift. I made that pretty plain. So who left the note? Doyle? Nope. I couldn't see Doyle picking the locks to my office door. He'd call me to his office to bawl me out in person. Then who?

I'd barely made a dent in picking up the paper before Lenny arrived with a drill hanging from his belt and a bag of locks that jingled when he walked.

"Oooh, lady. You've got a hell of a mess."

"Thanks. I got the memo."

I kicked a space clean in front of the door so he could work.

"They'll have to take the door off the hinges next time. This new lock will keep you safe. What do you do?" he asked as he began to replace the lock.

"I'm a detective."

He glanced up at the door and the lettering that said *The Moore Detective Agency*.

"I thought this was Nick's place?"

Truly, Nick knew everyone. As I was finding out, that worked for me and against me. I hope this was one of those times it worked in my favor.

"He's in Chicago for a few months. He'll be back. Say, could you teach me how to pick locks? The lock on my front door keeps jamming."

He didn't blink an eye.

"Sure. Come by any time. For Nick, anything. He got me out of a bad jam once. I owe him."

Yet another criminal I'd run into that Nick had helped go straight.

The phone rang.

"Are you alone?"

It was Nick.

"Hey, long time no hear, pal, and no, someone trashed the office. Upended the file cabinet. I've got Lenny here putting a new lock on the door. Says you know him."

"Lenny Swartz? Good egg. Tell him I say hi. You sure it's not serious?"

"Sure. It's just the outer office. Whoever it was, didn't touch the inner office. Just spite. Could be anyone, although I have my suspicions."

"Yeah, me too, but it might be more than just spite. I'm hearing things, and none of it is good. They sent out a few heavies like I told you, but they're small fry compared to this guy. He's something of a fixer, a freelancer. He doubles as a killer for hire." Nick was speaking in a low, muffled voice, like he didn't want anyone to hear him.

All of a sudden, my cavalier assumption that Eddie, con-artist *extraordinaire*, had been behind the file cabinet caper looked too cavalier. Maybe the file cabinet and the note in the typewriter *were* connected. I remembered Victor's threat about his nasty friends in nasty places.

"You at the office?"

"I'm calling from a broom closet. Just heard about this guy and I wanted to give it to you fast. He's got a hundred aliases, so I don't know his current name, but his real name is Kevin McCarthy. You got that? We'll talk soon. Be careful."

Then he hung up. I needed to chew on this, but with O'Malley coming by, it would have to wait.

"Nick says hi."

"Nick. He's the best," he mumbled around a mouth full of nails. "Named my first kid after him."

When he'd finished, he handed me a piece of paper with the combination on it. I paid him, thanked him for coming out on a Sunday, and stuck the paper in my pocket so I could memorize it later.

I separated the file folders from the papers, put the folders back in the file cabinet, and painstakingly began to reconstitute all our files for the last six years. Whoever had done this had meant business. Some of the letters had footprints on them. The bill for the Heldman job was halfway across the room from the notes on the Heldman job. I'd grab a bunch of papers and then refile them. Grab another bunch and refile. I'd been at it for an hour when O'Malley arrived.

He'd shaved and showered, but it didn't look like he'd gotten any sleep. He wasn't staggering, but he was close to it. His face had that gray cast when you've been up for too long. There was no trace of the looker he'd been when he was younger. Old, tired, and jaded, I felt sorry for him. That was a first.

"Someone getting their own back?" he asked.

"Yes, and if they walked through the door right now, I'd kill them with my bare hands."

He began to pick up the paper and organize it into neat stacks.

"Don't bother, O'Malley. Have a seat. How's Murph doing?"

"Okay," he nodded. "His vitals are improving, and although his face looks like yesterday's hash, he pulled through with nothing more than a broken nose. They don't know yet about any brain damage, but he's talking, and it's not gibberish. They think it's just a simple skull fracture. Head wounds always bleed like crazy. Fell back and hit his head on the floor when that guy sapped him."

"Glad to hear it." I turned back to the file cabinet. "You look terrible. Go home and get some sleep. What comes first, 'm' or 'n'?"

"Maybe *you* should get some sleep."

"Not going to argue that point. Go home."

"Doc says you saved his life."

I stopped filing to lean against the file cabinet for a few seconds. *Thank you, God. Thank you.* I was terrified that the stop I made to wrap his head in my shirt might have sealed his death warrant. That I didn't drive fast enough. A thousand things I should have done so that he'd live, but I hadn't done any of them, and he'd die because of me.

"Then my prayers were answered," I replied in a wobbly voice and used my hand to wipe my eyes.

"You saw, Maggie. Didn't you?"

I had wrestled with this since I'd woken up. Nick had bandied about terms like faggot, queer, fairy, and punk, and I understood what they meant, but I'd never connected that with men I knew. Yes, there were streets in North Beach my parents avoided and bars with no names they'd scurry by, dragging me and Al by our wrists. I knew what the Bible had said—the tale of Sodom and Gomorrah, a personal favorite of Father O'Flaherty—but what I'd seen between O'Malley and Murphy hadn't looked like sin. What I saw was more than friendship, and yet I didn't have the words to name what it was. I thought about Terry Richards and Lorna, and how their flat looked like a home, not two people just living together and sharing the rent. Lorna's hand on Terry's shoulder, and Terry shrugging it off.

"You saw, and that's why you were practically screaming at Bree and Mrs. Murphy. You were warning me, weren't you? Murph's not part of this. It's just me. I don't have much money, but I'll pay you what I can."

Murphy never marrying. A daily communicant. Always in confession. Best buddies. You rarely saw one without the other. I turned back to the file cabinet, my hands crumpling the letter I had in my hands. *Please, dear Jesus, please make him stop talking.*

"I have no idea what you're talking about," I said to the wall.

"You saw, Maggie." His voice now had that hard cast to it.

I turned around to face him.

"I didn't see anything, O'Malley. Not. A. Thing."

He stared at me. I stared back.

"Go home," I said.

He stood up, his shoulders back, his posture straight.

"Wait a minute."

He turned slowly, his face flushed with a familiar rage. "What?" he snarled.

"Can you teach me how to fire a gun?"

"Now?" he said and barked out a laugh edged with hysteria.

"Yeah. Cars have been tailing me, and I've been getting threats. And then this." My arm swept the room. I didn't mention the typewriter. "Let's cut out the fiction. Barnes is dirty. He's using Pinkertons to force a strike so he can break the contract. A good quarter of the men in that machine shop were cops. I'm asking questions, and certain people are getting anxious."

I waited for his denial.

He didn't say anything.

"I already asked Doyle to teach me, and he said no. I have a gun that belongs to Nick. How'd you get here?"

"Took a cab. Car's in the shop."

"If we hurry, we'll have just enough light for you to show me the basics. How about I drive you home, and along the way, we stop at Land's End and you show me how to shoot."

"You sure?"

That question encompassed a lot more than learning how to shoot a gun. "Yes, I'm sure."

"Okay," he agreed. "You were pretty impressive in that fight."

"It wasn't a fight. It was a riot. I've been taking boxing lessons."

He smiled and looked ten years younger.

"Maggie Laurent, I might find myself almost liking you one day."

"Your worst nightmare. Give me a second."

I retrieved Nick's gun from the desk drawer and a box of ammunition. I put the gun and the ammo in my purse. We drove to the Cliff House, parked the car, and walked down to the beach, all in silence. By this point, O'Malley was staggering a bit from exhaustion, but he didn't complain. We found a deserted spot filled with ragged pines.

I took the gun out of my purse and handed it to him.

"Did you know this was loaded?"

I shook my head.

He blew out a huff of air.

"Luckily, the safety's on, or you could have killed yourself."

"Or you."

"Or me. First of all, you need to assume that any gun you pick up is loaded. Even if you know it isn't loaded. Two. Always keep the gun pointed away from people. Three. Keep your finger away from the trigger until you are ready to shoot. Four. Know who or what you're shooting and what's behind it. Got it? Those are the basics."

He showed me how to pop the cylinder, empty the slugs currently in there, reload it, and snap it shut.

"Now, grab the gun with the web of your hand high up on the back of the grip. No, your right hand."

"I'm left-handed. The nuns tried to beat it out of me, but the older I get, the more I'm using my left."

"Good to know. Gives you an advantage. No, higher. Put your index finger along the base of the cylinder, above the trigger but away from the trigger. Good. Wrap the other fingers around the front of the grip and tuck your thumb against your index finger. With your other hand, wrap it around the base of your right hand. You're going to pull the trigger with the forefinger of that hand. Squeeze tight because the gun is going to kick back on you when you fire. Bring the gun up to eye level. Pull the trigger. Aim for one of those pines."

Aiming the gun wasn't a problem; it was getting used to the kick from the shot. But soon enough, I'd mastered the rudiments, at least enough so I felt confident enough to fire it without shooting myself in the foot.

"It doesn't seem very accurate," I said as I reloaded it, flipped the safety on, and put it all back in my purse.

"Nope, but it will get your point across."

"Let's get you home. Bree will be wondering where you are."

It was a silent trudge up to the car and a silent drive to O'Malley's house in the Aves. I parked in front of his house, a small three-bedroom bungalow, which was identical to my family's home in layout, except his housed five kids.

He paused before getting out of the car.

"Thanks, Maggie."

I faced the street, not wanting to look at him when I said what I had to say.

"O'Malley, I don't understand much or any of this, okay, but—"

"Welcome to the club," he said. "If you think I don't—"

"It's none of my business, O'Malley. None of my business," I repeated. "There's a really good joe in the hospital right now, and that's the part I understand. But," I paused and took a big breath. "Stop beating your wife because she isn't him."

He got out of the car without making a sound. I saw the back of him as he struggled to make it up his front steps. Bree was waiting at the front door for him.

I went to the church I'd been baptized in, where I'd received my first holy communion, and where it was anticipated I'd marry, and have my children baptized in the same font. I sat in a pew but didn't kneel. The glimmer of the candles lit for the souls of loved ones cast deep shadows, their flames dancing merrily, oblivious to the anguish they represented. I thought about the scene in the hospital room. Much to my chagrin, I realized that O'Malley, and maybe Murphy, might be "others" like me. Like Dickie Vance. Square pegs in a community of round holes.

I couldn't talk to my mother about this. What I saw didn't feel wrong, although Father O'Flaherty would condemn O'Malley to hell on the spot. If I broached it with her, it'd be just another reason for me to come home. *I won't have you exposed to that sort of filth*, she'd mutter, not realizing we were talking about two men she'd watched grow from boys to men.

Six years ago, I might have reacted the same. Disgust, maybe even horror. But over the years, I'd seen good men do bad things, and bad men do good things, and what was a sin wasn't so clear anymore. I did know what evil was. I'd witnessed that first-hand. But sin had become murky. What I saw between O'Malley and Murphy, I wouldn't classify as sin. I didn't know how to classify it. I didn't have any answers, and the only person I could talk to about this was in Chicago. And maybe Dickie, but that felt too close to home.

I drove back to my apartment, pulled the gun out of the purse, and shoved it under a pillow on my couch. Things were about to blow. I felt it in my bones.

Chapter Thirty-Seven

A week passed. There was no mention in the newspapers about the melee at the machine shop, no more threatening letters in my typewriter, and no word from O'Malley or Doyle. Or Tommy. I filed, making a little headway on the paper covering my office floor. I took excellent photographs of a man kissing a woman with his hands underneath her skirt. Too bad she wasn't his wife. I took lock-picking lessons from Lenny. I played a few rounds of golf. I caddied for the surgeon whose ball landed in the sand trap four times.

I got angrier and angrier.

On Sunday, I attended mass at St. Ignatius for the first time in weeks. I slid into the pew where my family always sat and inhaled the gentle scent of my mother's perfume, a medley of roses and lilies. My mother gave me a tremulous smile, kissed me on the cheek, and then saw my eye.

"What happened?" she whispered, pointing to my eye. It was getting better, but with black eyes, they always looked worse the better they felt.

"Golf ball. Where's Al?"

She shifted her gaze across the aisle and up.

Al was sitting with the O'Neill family. I elbowed my mother in the ribs, gently, and hiked my eyebrows in Al's direction. "What gives?"

"They're dating." She obviously approved.

I didn't. Bridie O'Neill was nice enough, but nothing special. She'd been sweet on Al for as long as I could remember, but he'd never paid her any mind in the past.

My prayers on Sunday were all for Murphy and Herman, expressions of gratitude to God for having spared their lives. I asked the Virgin to intercede on my behalf, that my mother and brother accept and respect the person I was becoming. I prayed to Jesus to welcome Winston Barnes into heaven, even though the church thought suicide was anathema; this poor man needed God's grace. My prayers were so fervent that my mother had to poke my shoulder to stand for the final Blessing. I think she thought I was falling asleep on my knees.

Using the excuse to check up on Herman, I decided to ditch the post-mass social hour in the church basement. I needed to ask Herman more questions, and I didn't want my mother or Al in the house. I searched the crowd for Mrs. Murphy, but I didn't see her. She was probably at the hospital. Before leaving, I went up to O'Malley.

"How's Murphy? Any word?"

"He's doing okay. They say he'll be there for another week and then he can go home."

O'Malley's body language was wary, his posture too straight. His face had lost the gray shadow of exhaustion, but there were grim lines around his mouth that hadn't been there the week before. Had I reconsidered my stance from last week? He wasn't his usual belligerent self, but he was poised on the balls of his feet, just a little.

"Great. I might go see him later today. Did you get some rest?"

He nodded.

I gave him a brief punch on the shoulder—Irish affection—and then told my mother I was leaving to check up on Herman.

He was sitting in the living room, trying to catch a little of the morning sun. Al must have helped him dress. He was wearing his pants but Al's bathrobe, probably the only garment whose sleeves were big enough for his cast. Most of the swelling had gone down. His face looked worse, but it probably felt better. I'll never understand black eyes.

"Hey, Herman. Want a warm-up on your coffee?" I pointed to an empty coffee cup on the table.

"Yes, miss. Thank you."

While a fresh pot was brewing, I made his bed. It wasn't my room anymore.

With the overly floral wallpaper and the frou-frou lace on the curtains, it reflected a teenager I'd never been, perhaps the teenager my mother thought I was, or the one she wanted. My tennis racket and clubs were in the trunk of the car. Most of my clothes were already at the apartment. I swept the dresser clean of its few knick-knacks and a framed photograph of my father, sitting in a café in Paris, young, handsome, and holding a glass of champagne, the world in the palm of his hand at that moment. He'd just finished medical school. Six months later, he'd be on an ocean liner, and in another six months, he'd be married to my mother. Looking at him, dapper in his sharp suit and a straw boater, his smile broad and confident, I wished I'd known him then, on the cusp of a great adventure. Most of the time, I felt I was on the cusp of a great adventure, too, but I didn't feel very sure I'd succeed.

I bundled all of it up in a towel, emptied out what was left in the closet and the dresser, and took it to my car. The only thing I'd regret leaving behind would be the wedding ring quilt my grandmother had made for me when I was ten, made for a girl I didn't recognize.

When the coffee was ready, I returned to the living room with fresh cups for both of us.

"How are you feeling today, Herman?"

"Really good."

Some of his enviable equanimity had returned. Tommy was right. He'd find someone else to marry. He might not love her as much as he'd loved Vera, but he would love her enough.

"Doc Chase says I might be able to get a lighter cast on my left arm next week. Then I can drive again."

I looked at him.

"Herman, your face needs to calm down first. I assure you, no one is getting in a cab with you until those black eyes heal."

"Fair enough. miss, you have a black eye, too. What happened?"

"Golf ball. Herman, how did you meet Tommy Morgan?"

"Oh, you know, around."

This was a revelation. Herman was proving to be an excellent liar, which surprised me. His life was a circuit between his family, his cab, and the church. Herman did not go to speakeasies or even order a tuna sandwich at the Pig n' Whistle. There was no "around" in Herman's life, and he liked it that way. Still, this was another instance of me underestimating people. If I were going to make a go of the detective business, I needed to accept that even decent people like Herman would tell bald-faced lies if it was in their interest.

"Do you know where he lives?"

"No."

"Does he have family here?"

He lowered his eyes and tried to scratch an itch under his cast.

"I don't think so."

This Mr. Morgan was becoming more of a mystery.

"If I needed to get a hold of him, do you have a phone number or somewhere I can reach him?"

Herman refused to meet my eyes.

"No, miss, can't say I do."

"You met him at a Wobblies meeting, didn't you?"

He didn't reply and kept his gaze on the vase on the dining room table, sipping his coffee even though the hot liquid must be hell on his bruised mouth.

"There was a meeting on Friday night at the sheet metal shop down on Folsom. There must be a snitch. They salted the place with cops, and it turned into a riot. Tommy was speaking. He's working as a labor organizer, isn't he? That's how you met him."

I hoped never again to see shame on Herman's face.

"I... You know, miss. I really like working for Mr. Waters. He's a fair man. I don't want to lose my job, but I was thinking. If I earned more money, then Vera might come back to me. I could buy our house sooner, and give her the things she wanted. I just thought...I only attended a couple of meetings. Tommy's been wonderful to me since Vera died. My brothers are great guys, but they didn't understand Vera. Thought she was uppity. Had stars in her eyes. They never saw her like I did."

Vera's personality was probably somewhere between the two extremes.

Not a gold digger exactly, but she never would have been happy with Herman. Win Barnes had opened her eyes to another world. Once you see that world and put a foot across its threshold, you can't go back. I could relate.

"Please don't tell anyone, Miss Laurent. Not even Mr. Vance," he begged. "If Mr. Waters found out, I'd lose my job for sure," he insisted.

"I promise," I said, not that I thought Dickie would mind.

"Your mother and Mr. Al have been so wonderful to me. You have a great family, miss."

"Yeah, I do. How about an ice pack for your face?"

It was a small blessing that Herman had been beaten up on Thursday; otherwise, he'd have been at the meeting. When God closes a door...

Chapter Thirty-Eight

I hit the office and typed a recap of what had happened at the sheet metal shop. I didn't name anyone but made it clear it was a setup. The cops had infiltrated the meeting, and a fight had ensued. It was violent and it was planned. Four sheets of single-space typing later, I was done. I folded it into thirds and stuffed it in an envelope.

I drove to North Beach and rang Terry's bell. Lorna answered the door with a subdued, "Hi, Maggie." I noticed she didn't open the door more than a crack.

"Who is it, honey?" said a voice from inside.

"Maggie Laurent, Terry."

"Hi, Lorna. I need to speak to Terry. Right away."

Lorna stepped away, and Terry appeared, angry and hostile.

"Look—"

"You didn't get this from me." I held up the envelope. "Read it and then burn it. Things are starting to blow up."

I handed her the envelope with my write-up in it.

She squinted at me. "How'd you get the black eye?"

"Like I said, things are starting to blow up." I turned away and walked down the stairs.

I returned home. Although I kept my eyes on my rearview mirror, I didn't sense I was being tailed. Luck was with me, and I found a parking spot in front of my apartment building. I managed to haul all my clothes and the towel to my apartment in one go. The first thing I retrieved was the photograph of my father. I set it up on the nightstand so I'd see his face when

I woke up. I put away the rest of my clothes and gewgaws. I should have done this three months ago. Although Nick's presence still hovered in the corners of the apartment, this helped to make it more mine. The photograph made it more real.

I phoned the Mark and left a message with the desk clerk: "Mr. P. is doing fine." Then I called the answering service to see if I had any messages.

Just two.

Gertrude from the answering service said to me, "This first one is weird. They refused to leave a name but said, 'Tell her this is her last warning. She'll understand.' It was a guy. Deep voice, but it sounded fake to me. Like they were pretending to have a deep voice."

Sounds like Terry was rattling some cages that didn't want to be rattled.

Yes, things were heating up, but unlike the Washington case, there wasn't anything to resolve. What was I getting close to that I didn't know I was getting close to? Vera's death would forever be labeled an accident. How do you put a crowd of people on trial for murder when you can't identify anyone in the crowd? The labor unrest would be ongoing and probably get worse, but that was so much larger than my little detective agency. And yet, I could feel it, danger pricking at my bones. Why the repeated warnings?

"Oh, that's from the phone company. I paid the bill. No worries, Gertie." Lying was now so easy. "What about the second message?"

"From a Theresa Richards. 'Thanks, Maggie. Just so you know. Barnes, Sr., has been in town for the last week. Will contact you when I hear something.'"

Talk about a punch to the gut.

"You got that, Maggie?" asked Gertie when I didn't respond.

"Yeah, got it. Thanks, Gertie."

I hung up, my hand fumbling as I tried to put the receiver back on the hook.

The man in the roadster talking to Tommy was Barnes, Sr. His son was the image of him, but thirty years younger. My mind began to race so fast, I put my hands to the sides of my temple because it felt like my head was going to explode.

Oh, there were gaps, but now I knew. Tommy Morgan was the Pinkerton plant, the freelancer. He even admitted to me that he was a vagabond, which was his code for traveling the country, infiltrating various labor organizations, ginning up the mob, and then coordinating with the law to break heads. He didn't have a known address. No one knew his family. He moved "back and forth." He was glib, oh so glib, and charismatic. *He* was the snitch. He'd befriended Herman so he could get the dirt on DeSoto and…

Oh, dear God, he was the hitman. I staggered to the edge of the sofa and collapsed. He'd shoved Vera under that racing cab. He'd beaten up Herman. He'd tied the handkerchief over his face so Herman couldn't identify him if he weren't successful in killing him.

I was such a fool. Appearing at Vera's funeral and going right up to Herman to speak to him about Vera put a bullseye on my back. He needed to find out how involved I was. He was *waiting* for me to leave the church after Vera's funeral to drill me about what I knew. All those questions about Herman and Vera. How well did I know Herman? Did I know Vera? Why would I go to the funeral of a shopgirl? All those questions had seemed so random at the time, but now they added up. He sweet-talked me and kissed me, all the while wondering how much I knew. I bet he nearly had a heart attack when he discovered I was a detective.

Someone was knocking on my door. I hadn't heard the buzzer of the front door to the lobby. I stood up on shaking legs and made my way to the front door to look through the peephole.

Tommy.

"Open up, Maggie. I know you're in there."

He'd been tailing me. Saw me at church. Saw me at my mother's house. Saw me through the front window, talking to Herman. Followed me to the office, then Terry Richards' apartment, and finally home. I stood there, silent, praying he'd go away.

Then he began to pick the locks.

Chapter Thirty-Nine

I lunged for the telephone to call the police, but he got in before I could grab it.

Anger, Maggie. You have a right to be furious.

"What in the hell are you doing?" I screamed. "Get out!"

He shut the door gently.

"Now, darling, I'm sorry, I was worried about you. I heard you talking on the phone and thought something was wrong when you didn't answer."

My windows were shut. There was no way he could hear me talking through the door.

"And you decided to pick my locks? What if I weren't dressed?"

"No harm done there." He wriggled his eyebrows.

He was still playing the game. Could I bluff my way out of this? He sidled up to me, close.

"How'd you get the black eye?" He ran a soft forefinger along my cheekbone.

"Golf ball."

"Oh, I don't think so. Do you know what the first thing I noticed about you? Maybe the second thing. You have such a lovely mouth. The second thing? You're such a good liar. People who are good liars can spot it in others," he said, his voice warm in admiration.

I stood still. He smelled of cigarettes and burnt coffee and lies.

"Catholic school."

He ignored my attempt at evasion.

"You were at the meeting. At the machine shop."

"No," I lied. "You're mistaking me for someone else."

"Another lie. I *saw* you, Mags. Didn't you hear me call your name?"

So it was him, calling out to me. If he knew I was there, I was done for.

"No, it was too crazy."

"I'll grant you, it was crazy. What were you doing there?"

His voice, gentle and easy, told me he still wasn't sure of me or he was pure evil, toying with me, lulling me into believing he was asking a simple question. By this point, no questions were straightforward, no answers were simple.

"I had a tip from a cabbie that the IWW was holding meetings there. It was a hunch. I told you I was researching labor unrest. How did you get away? You don't have a scratch on you."

"Fast on my feet."

He dragged his forefinger the other way.

"Did you hear it from Herman?"

"No, it was someone else. I didn't see Herman there that night. Did you?"

"No, I didn't."

"So, in addition to being a carpenter, you're a labor organizer." Maybe if I played to his ego, he'd back off. "You're a wonderful speaker."

"Thanks, darling. Keep it under your hat. I don't want to get in trouble with the Garda. They'll ship me to prison for sure, but it'd be even worse if they put me on a boat for Ireland. So keep mum, eh?" He dragged a finger across my lips. "But why were you dressed like a boy?"

"Don't be stupid, Tommy. If I'd appeared in a suit, heels, and a hat, would I have been let in?"

He laughed, and the mood shifted, just a little. I might have a chance.

"Not likely. You're lucky you weren't hurt. Those damn bulls."

I don't know how I said this with a straight face. "Someone tipped them off."

"You?" he joked, trying to keep the interaction between us easy and light to keep me pliant and unsuspecting.

"No. Ask around. I don't get along with the D.A.'s office."

"Not what I've heard."

He was so good at lying that I didn't know by this point if I was wrong about him. I didn't know what the truth was.

"Ready for some sparring?" he asked. "You're getting pretty good. You might KO me one day."

"Very unlikely. We don't have the gloves." Where was he going with this? "Let's go to the office."

If we walked to the office, I could scream, I could punch him hard enough to get away. Plead with a traffic cop to help me.

"Oh, I don't think we need gloves. Not the kind of boxing I had in mind." Tommy cupped my cheek. He had no intention of leaving my apartment. "Let's box, shall we?" he said, drawing me toward him, a teasing note on the word "box."

I sidestepped his mouth. "Not yet. Boxing first, kissing later. Help me with the table, will you? We need the extra room."

He mock-pouted for a second and then gave in. We pushed the kitchen table and chairs against the wall, giving me a clear path to the front door if I got the chance to run for it. I held up my fists.

We parried, ducked, and side-stepped each other's punches. I didn't let him back me against the wall like last time, but held my ground. Every time I pulled back my arm, I thought of Vera. Every time I blocked a punch of his, I thought of Herman, his arm in a cast and his face busted up. This wasn't the boxing match of a couple of days ago, where it wasn't so much boxing as caressing. I meant business. His eyes widened as I threw punch after punch and easily blocked his punches.

"You've been taking lessons from someone else?" he accused.

"No."

This time I was telling the truth

He tried a cross and I blocked him.

"You still mad at me about breaking into your place?" he panted. "I was worried."

"No," but I said it with an edge to my voice to make him think I was still furious about him breaking into my apartment. I needed time.

We parried like this for a couple of minutes while I tried to figure out how to get out of my apartment, and failing that, how to get to the couch and the gun. When my opening came, I took it. I let him have it with a left hook that I hoped broke his nose. He fell to the ground and curled up into the fetal position, with his hands covering his face. I'd gotten him good. I should have run out of the apartment there and then. But I didn't. I wanted proof. I needed to know if this man, whose kisses completely unnerved me, was a murderer.

"Oh, Tommy, I'm so sorry," I gushed, expressing contrition but secretly pleased. I'd done a number on his nose, and it was bleeding. "Do you have a handkerchief?"

"Pocket," he groaned.

I fished in his pants for his handkerchief and took out his wallet as well. I handed him his handkerchief and opened his wallet. There was a driver's license issued by the state of New York to one Kevin McCarthy. I left the wallet on the carpet. I ran to the bathroom, rinsed out a washcloth with cold water, and handed it to him.

"This will be better than a handkerchief. Did I break anything?"

He sat up and pressed the washcloth to his face. I could have used those two seconds to run out the door, but he grabbed my ankle with his free hand.

"I don't think so. Wasn't expecting that." He tried to smile. "Help me up?"

"Your wallet's on the ground. It fell out when I grabbed your handkerchief. Come sit on the couch. I'm so sorry."

I guided him to the middle of the couch, and I sat on the side where I'd hidden the gun under the pillow.

"Here, let me." Using my right hand, I daubed his face with the washcloth, and with my left hand, I shoved my left hand under the pillow and thumbed the safety off. Just in case. I didn't know what he was going to do, but I wanted to be prepared. It was just a matter of time. Today. Tomorrow. I was a liability.

"S'all right. I'll live. Come here, you little hellcat," he ordered in a sultry voice and pulled me to him. I went to him, my left hand clutching the grip of the gun, my other hand raking his hair. I knew he'd killed Vera and had nearly killed Herman, and yet I bent into his gentle kisses and let his hands roam over my body. It felt so wonderful, and I committed how this felt to my memory. To desire and be desired.

He pulled away for a second and murmured, "You kiss like a French woman, not an Irish woman."

"Is that a compliment?" I tightened my hand around the grip of the gun, hoping I wouldn't have to use it.

"Oh, yes, my lovely. Oh, yes," and he kissed me some more. My toes were curling from desire and want, even as I hated myself, and then his hands went to my neck. With anyone else, I would have thought he was caressing my neck as a prelude to moving his hands down my body. But I'd been waiting for it. His hands started to tighten.

"Kevin," I breathed into his ear.

He pulled back and dropped his hands. "What did you call me?"

"I called you Kevin. That's who you are, isn't it? Kevin McCarthy, Pinkerton thug."

He pulled away even further, and his breathing became harsh and ragged. And it wasn't because he wanted me.

"Why did you murder Vera?"

"I have no idea what you're talking about. Have you gone stark raving mad?" His face went blank like every Catholic school kid I knew when accused of something they most definitely had done. Who was lying now?

"Why did you murder Vera?" I repeated.

We stared at each other. He blinked first.

"I'll answer for you. You killed her because she confronted Win Barnes. He was only going out with her to get the dope on DeSoto. Barnes panicked and asked his father for advice. Barnes, Sr., calls up Pinkerton and orders a hitman to silence her. Pinkerton already had you in town working as a labor organizer for the IWW, and you moonlight as a hitman. How convenient. The IWW don't know you're a snitch, do they?"

"Maggie, you've got this all wrong," he insisted.

"No, I don't. Barnes wants to challenge DeSoto for the lion's share of the cab business and thinks that by breaking the union, he'll get there faster. He pays top dollar for Red Cab and is now smarting since the stock market crash. He's desperate to cut his labor costs and appeals to the mayor, who's running for governor in November. Barnes, Sr., says, 'Hey, Tim, let's join forces. The last thing you need is a gigantic labor strike two months before election day, and I need to cut costs. For some stupid reason, this flies with City Hall. Pinkerton sent you out to the West Coast to sell your baloney about workers' rights, setting them up to be beaten up by the bulls, and hoping they'll stay quiet and not buck the system when Barnes makes his play. But if they do strike, he's got scabs all lined up. All he needs to do is walk down Market Street and tap on the shoulders of all those men sleeping on the sidewalk. He's got all the bases covered. I—"

"Maggie, I don't know where you be getting this malarky—"

"Save it for someone else. I'll give you a tiny break. I don't think you iced Win Barnes. I think he tried to swim out as far as he could and put a gun to his head because he couldn't stand the thought of his father putting a hit out on Vera. I don't imagine he got very far, given how cold the water is, never mind the waves, and he plugged himself before he drowned. If he shot himself with the outgoing tide, he'd end up at the Farallons."

"You're crazy," he protested, but his voice was getting harder and there was a nasty edge creeping into it. "Don't know where you're—"

"Stop it, Tommy! I'm the one with her head on straight. Remember? You even had the IWW fooled, Mr. Union Organizer. I *saw* you get out of Barnes, Sr.'s car the night of the riot in the machine shop, all chummy and hail fellow well met."

He blanched at that, visibly blanched, his face as white as a piece of paper on a snowbank.

"As if that wasn't bad enough, I'm damn sure you took a tire iron to Herman and tried to kill him as well. You befriended Herman to get more dope on DeSoto and see if Vera had talked to him about Barnes. Did you meet him at one of your stupid meetings? I can see by your face that's exactly what you did. He's loyal to DeSoto, but he'd have done anything to win Vera back, even joining the IWW if it meant bigger wages so he could buy her a house in the Sunset. Fortunately, he's made out of rock. You only broke his arm."

"You're so wrong, Maggie. About all of it. So wrong," he insisted. He was such a good liar, but it was beginning to fall apart for him, and he knew it. His face had lost the outrage, and now he began to frown. I kept my hand on the gun.

"Then you tried to sweet-talk me to steer me away from Vera, Herman, DeSoto—"

"You know that's not true. You *know* it!" he shouted.

Worse for me, I believed it, but I didn't let it stop me.

"Yeah, I do. But the rest of it is true. Why the alias?" I countered. "Why are you on Pinkerton's books as a fixer, a murderer for hire?"

He moved in and began to run his hands over me again, kissing me, talking in between kisses.

"Why did you have to ruin everything? I wish…wish you hadn't done this. I'm so sorry," he whispered in my ear.

I had just enough time to pull the gun from behind the pillow and hide it in the fold of the couch cushion. He fell on me, using his weight to pin me to the couch cushions.

"You're amazing and…know that I didn't…really, really sorry…" he said as his hands moved down to my throat. He began to squeeze even as he was kissing me. I tried to bring up my knee and shove it into his groin, but he shifted his weight. His hands tightened. "So sorry, my Mags," he whispered, and I had to fight for breath. I went for his eyes with my free hand, but he ducked and slapped me across the face, hard, easing up for a fraction of a second on my throat. I took as big a gulp of air as I could.

Herman's voice floated through my rising panic. "You only have eight seconds before he crushes your windpipe."

I had four seconds before he killed me. Fighting my instinct to claw at his hands with both of mine to stop that relentless pressure on my throat, I went slack, hoping it would lull him into thinking he'd already half-killed me. I only needed one second. So intent on tightening his hands on my throat to finish the job, he ignored my moving arm. I guess he thought I was flailing, one last-ditch effort to save myself. It was. I brought the hand holding the gun up to the side of his chest. I don't know if I said it out loud, but I said it in my head. *I'm so sorry.*

I hooked my index finger around the steel of the trigger and pulled.

His hands slackened, and he fell on top of me, gasping out my name. I lay there sobbing as he died right on top of me, his body twitching as it fought for life, even as his hands never left my throat. Horrible gurgling sounds filled my ears. He kept getting heavier and heavier, and then his hands went slack. Finally, there was no movement, no sounds.

He was the first man I'd loved and the first man I'd killed.

Chapter Forty

Even as I sobbed, I shoved him off of me and onto the floor, clutching the gun to my chest. Someone must have called the police because a couple of bulls battened down the door. One of them used the phone, and I heard him say, "Bag the ambulance. Send the coroner. Vic's a goner." Then there were sirens and lots of people in the apartment. I turned toward the back of the couch and continued to sob.

Eventually, someone hauled me to my feet, led me to the landing of my staircase, told me to sit, and bumped up against me so I wouldn't fall over. It was Dickie Vance. He didn't say anything, but his enormous bulk made me feel safe, and I stopped crying.

"First of all, I'm flipping the safety on the gun. No, I won't take it away from you. Don't worry. I just need to…there. Here's a handkerchief. Blow your nose and dry your tears. Now listen to me. I've asked Mother to come over and pack your suitcase. I'm sending you away for two solid weeks. Do you understand?"

Before I could answer, Doyle spoke up.

"Get up, Vance. I need to talk to her."

"Look at her neck, you cretin. He obviously tried to kill her."

"I still have to do the goddamn paperwork. Get up, Vance. If that worthless Chief of Police O'Sullivan ever gets his ass here, he'll screw it up and probably arrest her for murder."

Dickie stood up, even as I clung to his jacket.

"I'll be back soon, *ma petite*." He patted my hair.

Doyle took his place, sidling up against me. "Maggie, can you give me the gun?"

I hadn't let go of the gun. I was still clutching it to my chest.

"No."

"Whose gun is it?"

"Nick's."

"O'Malley," he shouted. "Get over here and get this gun away from her before she kills herself or me."

O'Malley stood a few steps down the staircase so we were eye to eye.

"I need the gun, Maggie. Can you give it back to me?"

He was speaking to me in the soft tone you use with children.

"Will you keep me safe?"

"You bet."

I handed it over reluctantly and then crouched into a small ball against the wall, trying to stop my teeth from chattering.

"Someone bring me a blanket, stat," Doyle shouted. Soon, he'd wrapped me up tight. When I stopped shivering, he said, "I need to know what happened."

I said, "Did you ever find the cabbie who ran down Vera?"

"Yeah, a floater around Pier 33."

I'd been talking into my lap. I raised my head. "Why didn't you listen to me?"

"What happened in there?"

"I shot him because he tried to kill me."

I'd already told Doyle my suspicions about why I thought Vera had been murdered, so I started with the melee in the sheet metal shop. "Tommy, or I guess it's Kevin, shoved Vera into traffic to stop her blabbing to either Waters or the newspaper about Barnes."

"I don't know what you're talking about."

"Go to hell, Doyle. It's only part of why he was sent out here. He'd been posing as an IWW rep so that you and others could identify potential strikers. Why am I telling you this? You salted the crowd with cops."

"I did not," he protested.

I shouted as loud as I could. "You're a liar, Doyle! I was there, so shut your lying gob. I counted at least six cops I know personally and probably another twenty I don't. How do you think I got this black eye? How do you think Murph got to the hospital after he was beaten unconscious? I drove him. Ask O'Malley. I picked up his mother and drove her to San Francisco General. He's her only son, you bastard. Do not lie to me anymore."

It got very quiet all of a sudden.

I took a deep breath. "That's why you didn't jump when I told you Vera had been murdered. You didn't want to believe that your nice little plant had murdered her. You even got the newspapers to squelch the story. How's Murphy?"

"He went home this morning. O'Malley says you saved his life."

"I wouldn't have had to save his life if you hadn't—"

"Okay, say a Pinkerton killed Vera. What about Barnes?"

I shook my head. "Barnes couldn't stomach what his father had done. I've never seen someone so wracked with guilt in my life. Talk to Clarence Stevens. Barnes had a wingding at their house last week. I think he swam out to where he couldn't possibly swim back and killed himself to make sure he died."

"We didn't find his gun at his house, and the housekeeper says he had one, so that makes sense."

"I'm so happy for you."

"Calm down. So this Morgan tries to kill you. Why?"

"I saw a picture of Barnes, Sr., in the write-up on his son's death. And then I saw him drop off McCarthy at the sheet metal shop before the meeting. It took me a couple of days, but then I realized it was Win's father. His son was the spitting image of him."

"He's here to bring his son's body home to New York."

"I figured as much. When I put two and two together, things started clicking. Why would a guy who's supposed to be a dedicated socialist be meeting with someone the likes of Barnes, Sr.? It didn't fit. Unless he was a plant. Did you know he was a hitman, too?

Doyle's face blanched seven different kinds of white.

"Hitman? Pinkerton sent out a hitman? They told me he was a fixer, not a hitman. Why didn't you call me?" he exploded.

"Do you think I knew he was a hitman until an hour ago?" I screamed back. "But you knew he was a plant, and don't tell me different. It's fine and dandy to have him infiltrate the labor unions of honest men trying to make a living, but you turn a blind eye to how he does it. Vera Kowalski didn't float in front of that cab. Barnes played you both. Smiling Tim was so afraid of the threat of strikes before his official campaign began that you two made a deal with the devil and brought in Pinkerton ops, which benefited Barnes in his bid to undermine the union contracts. McCarthy saw me at the meeting before everything went to hell. He might not have killed me today, but he was going to kill me at some point. Everyone came out of that building injured, but he didn't have so much as a scratch on him. I was put in the same spot as Vera. What if I went to the papers with what I saw at the machine shop?"

"You're not thinking of doing that, are you?" He sounded a little panicked. Good.

I was so tired. I leaned my head against the wall.

"No. Not because I have any loyalty to either you or the mayor. Do you think I'm stupid? Smiling Tim is canny enough to turn it to his advantage, and I'd look like a fool and never get another job in this town ever again. I imagine he's going to run on a law-and-order platform, so even if half the cops in this town have black eyes, it was all in the name of eliminating the dangerous communist element in this city."

I didn't know how far Terry Richards could take this. I wanted her to smear the reputation of the mayor and Doyle from here to New York, but I was now cynical enough to know her article wouldn't see the light of day, and at least there were now two of us who knew the truth. I trusted her not to divulge who'd given her the information on the riot.

"I can write your report in five sentences. City Hall and Barnes colluded to stop any union organizing leading up to the election, and Barnes needed to bust the union because Red Cab was going under. Pinkerton knew that McCarthy moonlighted as a hitman in his spare time and, I'm guessing, specifically recommended him as the man who could rile up the crowd and eliminate any loose ends that popped up. Such a talented guy. Barnes played you two like a violin. I called him by his real name. Then he tried to strangle me, so I shot him. I'm done talking. Arrest me if you want. Just leave me alone."

I turned away from him to face the wall.

Chapter Forty-One

Above the murmur of the police, I heard Dickie speaking animatedly into the phone. I think Dickie is physically incapable of screaming, but he was, well, agitated.

"Katherine, I refuse to listen to any more of your nonsense. I'm holding two first-class tickets on the Southern Pacific train that stops in Burlingame in two hours, which will take you and Margaret to San Diego. From there, a hired car will take you and Margaret to the Hotel Del Coronado, where you and your magnificent daughter are booked for two weeks in a luxury suite. I do not want to hear any more arguments. In the time it will take for my driver to reach your house, pack your suitcase, Madam."

Then someone with an elderly voice said to Dickie, "She is all packed. She needs to change."

He must have nodded because she said in the loud voice of the deaf, "Miss Laurent, I am Mrs. Vance. I will not say it is nice to meet you because we both know these are dreadful circumstances, and I am not in the habit of telling falsehoods for courtesy's sake."

The apple didn't fall far from *that* tree.

"Let us get you into some clean clothes. Stand up and follow me," she ordered.

Like a child, I followed her into my apartment, refusing to look in the direction where Tommy's body still lay. I couldn't even tell you what Mrs. Vance looked like. Everything was a blur, like I needed glasses. Except I don't wear glasses. She led me into the bathroom and closed the door. She wiped me down with a warm washcloth, and I let her dress me as if I were a child. She'd filled the bathtub, and I watched as she tossed the blood-stained clothes into the cold water. I'd never wear those clothes again, but it was thoughtful of her.

Once I was dressed, she took me back to the landing. Dickie snapped his fingers, and someone, probably a cop, picked up my suitcase and followed us down the stairs. Dickie led me to a car parked in front of my building. We drove to my mother's house. She was waiting for us at the curb with her suitcase, and we drove to the train station in silence.

I didn't speak for days other than to say, "*Oui, ma mère, non, ma mère.*" I hadn't spoken French to her in years, but I wanted to be a child again and not take any responsibility for anything. No one's life, no one's death. I was numb, absolutely numb. I now appreciated why Nick had pickled himself with alcohol in the aftermath of Eileen Taylor's death. He was searching for the same "numb," where nothing mattered, not even the death of a woman he'd sent to the gallows.

Everyone assumed that McCarthy tried to murder me because I'd tied him to Vera's murder. Not that he would have swung for that, but he'd be deported for sure. There wasn't anyone who could identify him at that street corner, and Barnes, Sr., certainly wasn't going to admit he'd hired McCarthy to kill Vera and Herman. It was a surefire plan. Via Pinkerton, Tommy was already installed as a union organizer to undermine the IWW, hiring him to kill Vera and Herman was only a side job and very convenient. Tommy had no choice but to kill me because I was the only person who could link him with Barnes, Sr.

I didn't regret killing Tommy or Kevin or whoever he was. That might have been an alias as well. With a man like that, who knows? Although my mother and I went to mass every day, I didn't confess I'd killed a man because I honestly didn't see my shooting him as a sin. I also didn't regret wanting him. Oh, I know I'm naïve about this sort of stuff. Can you fake passion like that? Maybe. If you can, I don't want to know. I refused to accept it was all just a job, that I was this inexperienced young woman who'd fall for any lie, any lovesick patter if only someone would pay her attention.

I believed his whispered apologies. I believed he hated killing me. His anger at my exposing him was real, and not because I'd discovered he was a Pinkerton hired to foment violence and undermine the union effort. He was furious at me because, although what he'd felt for me was real, he had no choice but to kill me. Somehow, that made it worse. And even if his passion was nothing more than an act to elicit as much information as he could about Vera and Herman, my passion for him was real. This was my dirty little secret. From what little my mother said, she thought I spent those weeks in San Diego trying to escape the memory of his hands around my neck. It was much worse. It was the feel of him against me, his hands mapping my body, and his mouth against mine that I was trying to forget.

We spent our days on the hotel's terrace. My mother knitted or read books while I watched the waves, wondering if I'd ever feel love, hate, joy, or despair again, any emotion other than this soul-destroying numbness. I suppose it was warm for that time of year, but I couldn't say. I ignored the swimsuit Mrs. Vance had packed for me, indifferent to everything but the hush of the surf.

At some point, I started smoking. Mrs. Vance had found my cigarette case on the dresser and had packed it in my suitcase. Don't ask me when I began smoking, I just did. I didn't enjoy the act of smoking, but the ritual of lighting a cigarette, putting the blunt to my mouth, striking the match, lighting the end, and then inhaling the first burst of tobacco was pleasurable. Every time I lit a cigarette, the pronounced frown on my mother's face told me how much she disapproved, but she didn't say anything. By the time we left San Diego, I wasn't lighting one cigarette off the other, but close.

While I sat there smoking the day away, my mother caught me up on all the family gossip. My cousin Caitlin was having another baby, and Mrs. Dwyer had finally died at the ripe old age of ninety-five. There were two types of Irish: the ones who'd give you the shirt off their backs without a second thought (even if you didn't need a shirt), and the second kind. The mean, greedy ones like Mrs. Dwyer, who'd earned a reputation as the meanest woman in the parish. It was whispered that she fed her family soup by boiling dirty socks. Murphy was recovering, and he'd be back at work after New Year's. Al had proposed to Bridie O'Neill, and they were getting married after he graduated from law school in June. They'd announce their engagement at Thanksgiving. Maureen Dunleavy had decided to become a nun. "You should contact her before she enters the novitiate."

There were always a few girls in our parish who became nuns. Mo Dunleavy didn't seem like the type—too jolly, and my partner in mischief—but she'd always had a bone-deep faith. It said something about my self-imposed isolation. She used to be my best friend, and I hadn't known she was contemplating becoming a nun.

By day ten, I began to "wake up," finally able to mentally separate the man who loved me as Tommy Morgan from the man who tried to kill me as Kevin McCarthy. Even though I knew this was the rationalization to beat all rationalizations, it worked. For now.

By day twelve, I'd decided to return to the office and pick up where I left off. I didn't have another life I wanted to return to. I could move back home, get another secretarial job, and type until I found a fella to marry, but even after all that had happened, I still didn't want that life. I liked being a detective. I liked having the freedom to eat breakfast at my favorite greasy spoon as opposed to the monotony of oatmeal every morning. I liked having my own apartment and deciding when I went to bed and when to get up. I could tail someone into the dark of the night without having to make excuses or lies about where I was going or respond to the inevitable question of why I was wearing men's clothes. I'd moved beyond the confines of just being a daughter, and I couldn't go back. Like Vera, I'd stepped through a door and now it was shut for me, whether I like it or not.

On day thirteen, I turned to my mother and spoke my first complete sentence in days. "Let's go home. We want to be there for Thanksgiving."

"Are you sure?" she prodded me. "Mr. Vance told me we could stay as long as we wanted."

"Yes, it's time. One thing. Do you know why Dickie was at the apartment after I shot…him?"

"Apparently, half the police force is on his payroll. They called him first, the coroner's office second."

I wasn't surprised.

The trip back was as silent as the trip out. Once home, I baked pies, chopped vegetables, and peeled potatoes, all without saying hardly anything. I found I didn't have much to say. On Thanksgiving Day, the house flooded with people, with everyone acting like I hadn't been ostracized for months. They said hello and asked how I was doing, but didn't wait for a reply. After a couple of hours of this, I had to escape. I grabbed a blanket from my bedroom and sat on the back porch, breathing in the cool night air. There wasn't any fog tonight, and it was a full moon. The stars were bright and close. I wanted to grab one and ride it across the sky.

I heard the back door open behind me, and I thought, *Damn, please leave me alone, whoever you are.*

But it was Al, and that was okay.

"Let me have some of your blanket. It's freezing."

We sat side by side in silence for a long while.

I broke the silence by pulling out my cigarette case.

"Want one?"

"Since when did you start smoking?"

I didn't respond to that stupid question. As if a smoking habit were the most important issue facing me. I lit up and sat there savoring the cigarette and the silence.

"How are you doing?" he finally said.

"Okay. Not great."

"Are you going to move home?"

"No. I already told Ma. She's not happy about it, but there it is."

"Why, Maggie, why? Taking pictures of men cheating on their wives. Or shadowing silly women flaunting their cleavage in speakeasies while trying to nab clueless men for husbands. It's all so cheap."

My mother had asked the same question on the train on our way home. My answer to Al was the same.

"Some of it is tawdry, I admit. But there are people like Vera Kowalski and Harold Washington who became pawns in someone's twisted plans. Or Halston Smith, who's so lonely he's willing to marry a grifter who only wants him for his money. I might not do this forever, but I'm doing it for now. I don't want to be someone's secretary ever again. I enjoy using my smarts and wits, and I like living on my own. Do you honestly think I'd make a good housewife?"

He tried to stifle a laugh, but he wasn't very successful.

"Yeah, exactly. Ma won't ever get it or even come close to understanding me. I'm not the daughter she wants, and I have to accept that. All I'm asking for is your respect. I don't think that's too much to ask."

"I don't understand it either." He didn't sound mulish, so much as confused. I can deal with confusion.

"I get that, but you have to trust that I know what I'm doing."

"You were nearly killed," he said in a harsh whisper.

"You forgot about the part where I killed him instead," I reminded him.

He sighed and changed the subject.

"You heard about Mo Dunleavy?"

"Yeah. She had the biggest crush on you when we were in high school. I'm not shifting the blame, but half the time she and I got into trouble, it was because it was her idea. But then she's always been devout, so I do and I don't have a hard time seeing her as a nun. Say, Herman's not going to be able to coach me in boxing until he gets his cast off. Will you teach me? I know the basics, but…" My voice trailed off.

It was a few seconds before he said, "Sure."

I guess he figured if his sister was determined to continue with this detective business, it was better to have her know how to KO the bad guys than not.

"Thanks, Al. One more thing." I lowered my voice. "This isn't a slight on Bridie, she's a nice girl. I like her. But don't marry her. I saw you light up when you'd known Catherine Washington for less than three minutes." I blinked and pushed an image of Tommy's face with that wonderful crooked smile out of my head. "It was like she had a grip on you, and it was mutual. Wait. Let me finish. You don't look at Bridie like that. And you never will. You'll be bored to death with her in two years."

He turned away and stood up.

"Your timing is lousy. We're announcing our engagement tonight. And

Catherine's not here," he said with a belligerence that told me I was right on the money.

"No, she's not, but there's someone else out there who *will* make you glow like that, someone else. It's not Bridie. I wish it were."

I had to believe that for my own sake.

"We need to go in. I came out here to get you. We're making our announcement."

Chapter Forty-Two

A couple of days after Thanksgiving, I returned to my apartment. Although I was desperate to be alone, I wanted nothing more than to be with people. These conflicting desires were somewhat damped down when I turned the key in the lock to my place. Dickie Vance had struck again.

It'd been thoroughly cleaned. The smell of gunpowder, blood, and death was gone, and a new rug had been laid, the pile so deep it felt like walking on wet sand. He'd painted the walls a cheery yellow, removed the sad furniture Nick had left behind, and then raided his mother's enormous cache of Victoriana to outfit the apartment. He'd picked out the most sedate pieces, which were probably languishing in a storeroom somewhere in the bowels of the hotel, not being ornate enough for her tastes. It'd probably been Dickie's furniture at some point. None of it was overly gaudy, and no dolls were staring at me. He'd even hung curtains, real curtains, not Venetian blinds.

It was now the apartment of a well-heeled, respectable young woman with impeccable taste. I was neither wealthy nor even remotely respectable if my relatives had anything to say about it. My taste? I didn't know yet.

The only things he hadn't touched were the photograph of my father, my clothes, shoes, the few bits of cheap jewelry I owned, and my hats, all two of them. He'd filled a large vase with a spray of yellow roses—there must have been at least two dozen—with a sheet of paper folded into thirds with my name on it.

On the train trip home, I considered looking for a new apartment. A place where I wouldn't relive the feel of Tommy's hands on my face, his lips covering mine, and then his hands on my neck, squeezing the life out of me. A room that didn't echo his apologies as he tried to kill me. A sofa that didn't still bear the imprint of our bodies as we struggled against one another until the bang of the gun. I pressed my face against the silk of the curtains that didn't hold any old memories, no familiar smells. I moved over to the vase holding the roses and crushed a couple of flowers in my hand to inhale their aroma as it filled the small room. The bright paint would do its best to defy the gloomiest of fog-saturated days. I decided to stay.

I opened the letter. It had a wax seal I had to break. Dickie's seal didn't use his initials; a quill had been engraved on it.

Dear Margaret:

I will regret to my dying day dragging you into this unholy mess. Even as we both know that Vera Kowalski would have been murdered anyway and Herman probably killed at the hands of that evil man, your death would have been my fault. Had you been killed, I never would have recovered from a permanent dagger to my conscience. I do not want to hear one word about you thanking me or insisting on returning any of this furniture. Mother thought it too dull, and it was ready to be carted off or sold or whatever one does with furniture one doesn't want. Mother's taste tends to be a tad bold, shall we say. If you don't like it, I shall outfit your wee domicile with something different. If you do not like the color of the paint, let me know, and I will have it redone. I think it is rather nice, but then I'm partial to yellow, as my numerous bowties will attest.

Let me know when you're back in town, and we shall have lunch.
Best Regards,
Richard Vance

I wrote him a note thanking him profusely and telling him I was home and would stop by John's Grill soon. I asked that he give my regards to his mother and thank her for all her help. It was a minuscule gesture compared with what he'd done for me, but it was something. In my postscript, I told him I was using some of the money he'd given me for Vera's funeral to pay off my mother's mortgage, and I would pay him back.

The week after I returned to my apartment was about filling time and not thinking too much. I went to mass every day and hit the links after that. I stopped by the house every afternoon and shared a pot of tea with my mother and occasionally Al. Her wedding ring was gone from her finger. I resigned myself to her and Doc Chase getting married. After our pot of tea, I'd drive to Ocean Beach, sit on a bench facing the waves, and say a rosary for Winston Barnes. After a week of this, I was nearly back to my old self with a few exceptions. I couldn't stand anything around my neck, even a sweater with a tight neck caused me to panic, and I'd begun to have nightmares about being unable to breathe. Although the bruises had faded by then, every time I looked at myself in the mirror, I thought I could see the ghost of the thumbprints Tommy had left as he choked me. I stopped looking in the mirror.

One day, as I drove home from Ocean Beach, I saw Christmas tree lots and wreaths on people's front doors and realized it was nearly Christmas. I parked at Union Square and meandered through Normandy Lane, all decked out for the holidays. The smell of cinnamon and chocolate followed me as the bakers churned out apple tarts and yule logs. Today, I replied, *"Oui,"* to the *maitre'd* who asked if I wanted a table in the tearoom. I drank coffee in homage to my father and ate *macarons* in homage to Dickie. I strolled past Podesta Baldocchi, its windows a sea of poinsettias, their pots wrapped in gold foil paper. I bought a tiny one for myself and a larger one for my mother. Next, I walked to The White House. I wished the house dick, Seamus O'Grady, a Merry Christmas. I whispered a "Merry Christmas" to the ghost of Vera Kowalski as I walked past the glove counter and then out the door. The final destination of this pilgrimage was the Sheraton Palace Hotel. I gasped out loud at the gigantic tree anchoring the lobby, with silver and gold ribbons hanging from the branches like icicles. I hummed Christmas carols as I drove home. I'd forgotten how much I loved Christmas. I refused to let Tommy Morgan take that from me.

It took me another week to get up the courage to return to the office, reluctant to face the chaos sure to greet me when I stepped over the threshold. The floor was still covered in paper. I used a broom to sweep a path to my desk. It felt like years since I'd been here. I called the answering service to see if I had any messages. A bank manager was convinced one of his clerks was pocketing small sums of money on the odd occasion, and a woman was convinced her husband was cheating on her and wanted me to tail him. The bank manager had already hired someone else by this time, but the woman with the cheating spouse still needed my services. I told her to come to the office the next day. I needed a day to get the files back in order, or at least get the paper off the floor.

I'd barely made a dent in the chaos before O'Malley and I had our shooting lesson. I'd grab a stack of papers, file them, and then grab another stack. Although tedious, it was strangely satisfying, bringing order to chaos without any consequences other than a stray piece of paper in the wrong file.

Nick didn't bother to knock when he entered the office. His suit fit him again, and his cheeks weren't sunken. He looked good, although older. Not worn out exactly, just older. In the three months since he'd left, his hair was now more gray than blond.

"Nick! Why didn't you tell me you were in town?"

Old Nick was fast on the uptake. New Nick was just as fast. He sidestepped the question and sat on the corner of the desk, surveying the chaos.

"Looks like quite a party. You packing up?"

"No. I haven't had a chance to clean up the mess I told you about over the phone." I spread my hands wide over the paper carpeting my office floor. "Courtesy of the Amazing Victor."

I didn't mention the menacing note in the typewriter. Tommy had picked the locks to my office to type a note to warn me off; I'd swear to it.

"The Amazing Victor? Doesn't ring a bell."

"Eddie Wójcik."

Nick nodded. "The guy who perfected the bigamy tango but moved onto the medium grift?"

"The same. We got into a tiny argument at the Stevens' house. I questioned his ability to speak to the dead. Apparently, he didn't like my tone."

"Imagine that," he said deadpan.

"Hush, you." I swatted his shoulder with a piece of paper. "Anyway, I wasn't buying what he was selling, which irked him a little. So he sent an acolyte to trash the entire file cabinet. Or maybe he did it himself, I don't know. Being a former bank robber, I bet he's aces at picking locks. As far as I can tell, only his file is missing. For a smart guy, he isn't very smart." I knocked on my skull with a closed fist. "He should have taken a bunch of other files to hide who'd done it. I thought Eddie was smarter than that."

"Sounds like your typical grifter. Long on the swindle, short on the brains. I'll send you a copy of our file on him. Is he worth popping?"

"Not yet. He says he's moving his swindle show down to Los Angeles. Bigger pool of suckers down there. You might alert Pinkerton down there. Are you coming back? Please say yes."

"No, sweetheart, just here for a couple of days, and then it's back to Chi-town."

"Look, how about I go back with you? We...we...we...could set up an office in Chicago. Do what we do here. I mean, we're a g-g-g-g-great—" The words were tumbling out of my mouth so fast, that I was stuttering. "T-t-t-t-team. You could teach me the ropes and—"

He leaned over to put a hand on my shoulder.

"I can't, darlin'. Your place is here, with your mother, Al, your church, and your memories of your father. It's all here. And you don't want to be a secretary anymore, do you? Be honest."

"No, I don't. I hate typing."

"Leaving for another city isn't going to wipe your memories clean. Ask me how I know."

I nodded. I understood. I wish I didn't, but I did.

"I had a little pow-wow with Doyle this morning. He gave the Pinkertons the boot, and the boss sent me out here to convince him otherwise. Unsurprisingly, no go. To be honest, I didn't try too hard, and it gave me a good excuse to see how you're doing. On Pinkerton's dime, I might add."

I gave him what was now my standard answer.

"I'm okay. Not great, but I'll get there. How did it go with Doyle?"

"After about twenty minutes of gassing a bunch of moonshine about the American flag, he got down to business. Letting the Pinkertons run roughshod over the city was a bad idea. Smiling Tim doesn't usually make those kinds of mistakes."

"Well, stupid is a universal employer. Initially, I thought that Barnes had brought in the muscle on his lonesome, but now I'm sure that City Hall and Barnes, Sr., colluded on the union-busting. Anything wrong with that scenario?" I asked.

"Nah. Makes a whole lot of sense. With Smiling Tim's eye on the governor's seat, San Francisco must stay law-abiding for the next few months while he runs his campaign. No strikers, no rioters, and no mayhem in the streets."

"Barnes was bleeding money and knew that the son was somewhat ethical. It worked for both of them. The hitman was solely on Barnes' hook." I added. "Maybe."

He eyed me. "You've become a lot more cynical since I left town."

I shrugged.

"How was it? Bad?"

"Yeah. Really bad." I ducked my head to fuss with a file folder or two, but couldn't help but bring up a hand to touch my neck and feel for bruises.

"I don't know if this will help, but McCarthy had an unsavory history. He fled Ireland in 1924 because he tried to play both sides of the fence in that conflict and was eventually found out. He had to board the first ship out of port with only his clothes on his back. After that, he bounced around New York and Boston as a killer for hire until Pinkerton picked him up as an operative in 1928 and fed him into the IWW as a snitch. He'd been acting undercover as an IWW rabble-rouser for the last two years. The hitman thing was a separate gig. How much Pinkerton knew is anyone's guess, but I doubt their hands are clean, let me put it that way."

Hearing it didn't help—and I doubted Nick thought it would—but it gave some context for what happened. Tommy's reticence about his past. Describing himself as a vagabond. Not even the briefest hint that he still had family back in Ireland. The questions about Herman, Vera, and DeSoto. It came across as concern, but he was gathering information about what they knew, what I knew, and trying to determine if he should skip town. And all of his questions about me. It was to determine how much the detective had detected. As I discovered, there's nothing more seductive than someone wanting to know everything about you.

"Is anything going to happen to Barnes?"

Nick gave one of his shrugs. "Doubt it. Pinkerton denies any involvement with McCarthy, and Smiling Tim is looking the other way and has put all his chips down on Waters. Barnes is done for in this town, no matter how much money he has. Waters will let Barnes bleed money for another few months and then bid for Red Cab for pennies on the dollar. If Barnes knows what's good for him, he'll jump at the opportunity. The gossip says Barnes is pretty broken up about his son."

I didn't bother to contain my snort of disgust. "He effectively killed his son, whether he wants to admit it or not, and was complicit in Vera Kowalski's death. I hope he rots in hell."

"Those kinds of men get away with murder, sweetheart."

"I'm finding that out."

"McCarthy wasn't the only mug Pinkerton sent out, but they've been sent packing."

"Yeah, I knew that. They've been roughing up Red Cab employees and vandalizing DeSoto cabs, but I think their involvement ends there. Waters read the mayor the riot act, and Smiling Tim knows which side his bread is buttered, and it's not with an East Coast Brahmin like Barnes. I'm positive McCarthy pushed Vera into traffic so a Red Cab could run her down and took a tire iron to Herman with the intent of beating Herman to death. He had to kill me because I was the only person who could connect him with Barnes, Sr." I said it with no emotion. It was what it was. "If I'd gone to Doyle and revealed his true identity as a Pinkerton plant, thereby exposing City Hall's dirt, I wonder what he would have done? Arrest me as a 'seditious' element or hand Tommy a one-way ticket out of town?"

"I don't know," he admitted.

I snorted. "Probably both. This is just the beginning, isn't it? Men on the streets, people losing their homes. Unions pitted against the Crockers, Stanfords, the Hopkins, and the Huntingtons."

"It will be Montana all over again," he muttered. In a normal voice, he said, "You called it. The cabbies are the weakest link. If they go down, then the docks will be next. The big push will be here in San Francisco, not San Pedro like in '23."

"Terry Richards called the cabbies the 'canary in the coal mine.'"

"Yeah. She's one smart cookie."

"Hey, you used to say that about me," I protested and thumped him on the shoulder.

"There's room in this burg for two smart women. Listen to me, Maggie. I got the gist of what happened from Doyle. He's not a bad egg for a D.A."

I didn't say anything. Doyle had left several messages with the answering service and had called the house four times since I'd returned from San Diego. I hadn't returned his messages and hung up on him every time he'd called. I didn't want to speak to him. Maybe never again.

"A problem there?" asked Nick.

"You could say that."

"Maggie, sweetheart, if he doesn't respect you, then—"

"Oh, he respects me. I don't respect him, nor do I trust him. Not today anyway. Someday I'll tell you about the IWW meeting in the sheet metal shop where everyone was penned in like animals with only one door, and how billy clubs and saps appeared out of nowhere. Doyle can go to hell. He let Barnes walk all over him because the mayor didn't want any fuss while campaigning for the governor's seat. Doyle's hell of smart, but he's too ambitious, which makes him weak. When his uncle says jump, he asks how high."

"If he's as smart as you say he is, he'll soon realize it and become his own man. As you know, I don't like being fair to men like Doyle, but he didn't know McCarthy was a hitman. Pinkerton didn't tell Doyle that McCarthy was also a gun for hire. He was billed as a shill for the IWW."

"Doyle skirted the line during the Washington job, but when push came to shove, he was solid. But this case?" I brought my fingers up to my neck again. "He can still go to hell."

"You'll need to work with him at some point," Nick admonished. "Don't let your Irish temper overwhelm your common sense. Come on. We're having lunch with Dickie. He's picking up the tab. Although he doesn't know it yet."

I stepped away from my desk, grateful for a couple of hours of respite from the file cabinet, Tommy Morgan, and Kevin McCarthy. He stood behind me, reached for my coat on the rack, and held it out. I threaded one arm into my coat sleeve.

"I'm sorry, Maggie. I'm so sorry," he whispered in my ear.

I whipped around to face him.

"It's not your fault. Park that guilt at the door, Mr. Moore. If anyone should feel any guilt over McCarthy trying to kill me, it's Doyle. I'm here because I want to be. I don't want to type for a living. I don't want to get married. I don't want anybody telling me to keep my nose clean or butt out or stop asking questions."

"That's my girl," he said with a touch of his old elan. "By the way, did you shoot him with my gun, the one in the desk drawer?"

"Yes. O'Malley gave me shooting lessons."

His eyebrows hit his hairline.

"We've come to an understanding."

"You say?"

"I do say. Let's go. We don't want to keep Dickie waiting. And you don't want to miss it when they start pouring the 'coffee.'"

He barked that harsh laugh of his as he helped me thread my arm into the other sleeve.

"Am dry these days, Maggie. For how long, I don't know, but for now…"

He buttoned the top button of my coat and kissed me on the forehead.

"I'm still sorry," he whispered. Then he said in his normal laconic drawl. "After you."

We walked down the staircase together like we'd done a thousand times. It didn't feel different, but it was different. He wasn't coming back, and I knew from the dull ache in my chest that I'd been hoping he'd return to San Francisco at some point.

Regardless of what Nick said, this was his town. As we walked to John's Grill, no fewer than ten people tried to stop him and welcome him home. He palmed them off with his usual courtesy and kept walking, but he stopped at the turnaround where the cable cars were parked, waiting to take passengers up Powell Street. His eyes roamed over the cable cars, the stores to the left and right of the tracks, and finally to Powell Street, mapping its slow rise to the top of Nob Hill. He was taking mental snapshots. No, he wouldn't be back.

The grip men who operate the cable cars all have different rings when they pull their bells. If you ride the cable cars enough, you can tell who the operator is just by their ring. A heavy-set man with shoulders as broad as a barn and mutton chops so bushy they probably had an address all of their own yelled to him, "Hey, Mr. Moore. Didn't know you were back in town. How's the Windy City?"

"Great. Getting cold though." Nick fake shivered. "I'm only here for a couple of days. How's the family?"

"Got another baby coming," he replied with false modesty.

Nick laughed and tipped his hat. "How many does that make? Six? Need to go, Jonesy. Give the wife my best."

"Will do, Mr. Moore. This one's for you."

Jonesy started a fast ring, stop, ring, stop, ring before grabbing the grip, hauling it back, and heading off up Powell.

"That was nice of him," I said.

"He's a nice guy."

We didn't say anything else until we reached the front of the restaurant.

"I do miss it here," he said in a low voice.

"But it's not enough," I replied.

"No, not enough, darlin'. Not enough."

He opened the door for me and I went in.

Acknowledgments

As always, thanks to ma soeurs of the Sunday morning critique group, Anna and MK, for so many years of support and expertise. Many thanks to Margaret and Mike for their help with this book. As always, I appreciate your insight on my behalf. Finally, none of my books would be been written without the support of my husband. You're the best.

About the Author

Claire M. Johnson's first novel, *Beat Until Stiff,* was nominated for the 2003 Agatha Award for Best First Novel and was a Booksense pick. Her second book in this series, *Roux Morgue,* received a starred review from *Publishers Weekly. Fog City,* her noir crime novel set in Prohibition-era San Francisco featuring Maggie Laurent, P.I., debuted in July 2024 from Level Best Books. This book, the first in the Fog City Noir series, has been nominated for both a Shamus and a Macavity Award. *City Lights* is the second book in this series, and *Crookedest Street in the World,* the third book in this series, will debut in the summer of 2026. Ms. Johnson was past-President of the Mystery Writers of America's Northern California Chapter.

AUTHOR WEBSITE: https://www.clairemjohnsonwrites.com

SOCIAL MEDIA HANDLES:
  https://www.instagram.com/clairejohnson414/
  https://www.facebook.com/claire.m.johnson.98/
  claire1215.bsky.social

Also by Claire M. Johnson

Beat Until Stiff, Poisoned Pen Press

Roux Morgue, Poisoned Pen Press

Pen and Prejudice, self-published

Resolution, self-published

Swim Town, self-published

Fog City, Level Best Books